CW00739548

THE SHADOWS OF EMPTY MEN

An Adam Park Thriller

A. DAVIES

Crater of the North Publishing

www.addavies.com

ISBN: 978-1535555593

Cover by designed by Perie Wolford

Novel edited by Jayne Wolfe

http://www.wolferossediting.com/

NOVELS BY A. D. DAVIES

Adam Park Thrillers:
The Dead and the Missing
A Desperate Paradise
The Shadows of Empty men
Night at the George Washington Diner
Master the Flame

Alicia Friend Investigations:
His First His Second
In Black In White
With Courage With Fear
A Friend in Spirit

Standalone:
Three Years Dead
Rite to Justice
The Sublime Freedom

Co-Authored:
Project Return Fire – with Joe Dinicola

For those haunted by shadows of the past – stay strong

PROLOGUE

THERE ARE NO GHOSTS.

That's what we're told when our fears burrow too deep. If our friends or children suffer nightmares, we repeat the mantra. *There are no ghosts.* We know it's true because everything has a rational explanation.

Except human nature.

Humans are the most illogical beings, full of terror, hate, and urges the worst of people cannot explain, even when it surfaces within themselves. Like those whose profession is death. They, and we, can only guess at what drives them, what allows them to switch off the part of their brain that for most people refuses to kill another; for them, such an act feels as empty as closing a door.

Kill, get paid.

Close the door, keep the draught out.

Same synapses firing, same degree of guilt.

Then there are those who choose their profession for other reasons.

A man once said to be truly happy, you need to become an expert at something you love, because when you are an expert, better than most of the population at any activity, someone will eventually pay you to do it. Computer games, singing, playing a sport. Find your expertise, utilize those skills for your living, and be happy.

The same holds true for murder.

Do you enjoy inflicting pain and death upon your fellow humans? Then do it a lot. Get good at it. Become *great* at it. And soon, you can earn your living doing what you love.

But if you encounter another who is also adept at killing, yet does not share your pleasure, you *will* be drawn into conflict. You *will* be called to account for your actions, and a person like me will do everything humanly possible to stop you striking ever again.

I have learned over the past year that I am able to kill. I gain no pleasure from it, but I am *willing*. Although I would struggle to justify certain actions to a judge, or even my friends, I sleep fine, and I only regret my mistakes—mistakes primarily concerning not acting quickly enough, allowing bad men to take the lives of innocents around me.

So when a case comes my way, seemingly peaceful, researched-based, I may not be prepared. How can I be? For a job such as this I would not plan on unleashing the bestial side of me. For when a killer of real passion enters my life, I cannot turn away. As ever, when I have no choice, I will act.

There are no ghosts in this world. Except those we make for ourselves.

GREECE

THE ISLAND OF PARAMATRA

CHAPTER ONE

HAVE you ever visited a Greek island in the springtime? The air you breathe is actually sweet. The colors are orange and green, white and red, the sunrises somehow both lazy and fierce. Perhaps that's why I found it so hard to leave.

Varying my routes throughout the hilly island, my morning runs had grown longer of late, starting earlier thanks to sleeping with my curtains open so I rise via natural light. One grain-based bar and a glass of water, and I am out of the door, returning anywhere between an hour and two hours later, depending on my mood.

This morning saw a two-hour jaunt out to the Acara Ruins, an amphitheater pre-dating the birth of Christ and overlooking a swooping crescent of cliff, pulled apart by some long-forgotten earthquake. The dive-boats were out already.

Thanks to my injection of cash to the Archaeological Society of Paramatra (yep, ASP), small teams were currently exploring the local legend of a vast city that once stood out there, grand and proud, before the same shifting of plates five miles wide swallowed it up along with the coastline. The more excitable of their members were talking about Atlantis, but to date we had only recovered a dozen or so pots, which the big museums fobbed off with the notion that, despite being confirmed as genuine antiques, these items can be found all over the Aegean; they did not constitute evidence of a civilization. I joined them three or four times a week, and because of my financing they tolerated my amateurish enthusiasm every time I surfaced flashing a wide smile through my beard and waving what usually turns out to be a tide-smoothed Coke bottle to which a family of barnacles might have grown rather attached.

I mostly tried to keep out of their way and enjoy the scenery; it's springtime in the ocean too.

Yeah, I know. Feeling sorry for me yet?

My return route cut through a village stirring to life, and I arrived home by seven-thirty where I showered, trimmed by beard to keep it tight to my face to fend off the prospect of being mistaken for a hobo, and then sat on my house's second-floor balcony overlooking the rocky bay for a breakfast of bread, meat, yogurt, and fruit. I caught up with the British news via various websites, skipping the more depressing-sounding stories, and briefly checked a couple of US sites in which I held a vague interest. Local news officially confirmed something I already learned from the chief of police: deals between the EU and other countries meant incoming Middle Eastern and African refugees were now processed faster in Turkey with the reduced number of traffickers diverted to islands further west. Paramatra's intake had reduced to a trickle.

I clicked off the news feeds, and nipped out to meet Eric Jones at the indefinitely-delayed airport construction site, where we planned to fire high-caliber handguns at various targets for a while. He was late, which wasn't unusual. It was so not-unusual that I'd taken to bringing a book with me for such occasions. After setting up the tin cans and glass bottles I collected from the beach on the way over, I found my current place in John Connolly's latest, and settled comfortably in the cab of a stalled JCB digger.

Last November, the case that brought me here went on longer than I expected, legal wrangling demanding my continued presence weeks after its conclusion. Instead of returning to the UK, I secured a plush house with a panoramic view, and with my gut still in knots over the actions I took—or didn't take—I spent Christmas alone. New Year's Eve saw me hit it off with a retired British Army officer —the afore-mentioned Eric—and we ended up drinking expensive scotch in a bar right on the beach. I did not go home with Eric. I went home with a German blond woman, twenty-two years-old, making her fifteen years my junior, although she taught me a few things, and I was happy to learn.

Eric showed an hour late, hung-over and red in the face. He'd piled on the pounds since his retirement, but he knew his guns. I didn't *want* to know guns, but there had been too many incidents lately where I could have used a lot more experience.

I had made enough enemies, after all.

"You look like crap," I said.

"We can't all roll outa bed quaffed and groomed like a GQ cover model, oh beautiful one. Here, you need some practice with this."

He presented me with a Sig-Sauer P229, a compact .40 caliber pistol.

"No Glock today?" I asked.

"You want to be good at firing everything. Just in case, right?"

"Right."

"So you tell me just in case of *what*, and I'll tell you what the best gun is for a given scenario."

"I honestly hope I never have to fire one at all, but—"

He pressed the Sig into my hand. "Then if you're not gonna own a firearm, get used to as many different types as possible. This is your bum-gun, the one you got most trouble with."

Using a Glock 16, I could draw and shoot a tight three-grouping at twenty feet in one smooth motion, but the Sig's second and third shots went wild. The shift from its initial double-action to single always threw me.

Eric opened a premium-quality camera bag to reveal four mags and two boxes of bullets. "You owe me three hundred euros for the brass. Now get practicing. I'll be over there in the shade. Shout if you want a hug or something."

What we were doing here wasn't exactly legal, but when Eric first moved out here with his wife, he registered himself a gun collector and sportsman, so for a premium import tax he was able to source bullets for his toys. The chief knew of our practice sessions, though, and after what happened here over the winter, he allowed me some leeway. The real reason Eric kept himself so well armed lay in his past, and no amount of alcohol would pry it from his lips. He attempted the same line of questioning on me, and achieved the same wall of silence.

Eventually, we both stopped trying.

I strapped on my holster, donned the ear-protectors, and spent the next hour accounting for the differential in double and single action. Occasionally, Eric popped over to adjust my shoulders or the angle of my elbow and wrists, and when we ran out of inanimate objects to destroy, he drew faces on flat scraps of wood and mounted them on the wall of rubble serving as our range.

Three hundred rounds later, my hands ached, but I thought I had the action down pat.

"Better," Eric said. "This is almost the same mechanism as the Beretta, so I'll bring one of those tomorrow. Nine-mil makes the recoil a bit different, and the Beretta doesn't have a de-cocking hammer."

"Thanks." I handed over five hundred Euros—for the bullets and his fee for the week. "Coffee?"

"The posh stuff you bring over from South America?"

"Of course," I said.

It made a nice change to have a mentor who appreciated the finer side of life for a change. Eric schooled me in instruments of death, while I educated him in fine beans.

Back at my house, I opened the mailbox—an American-style container at the end of the path—and sifted through the usual assortment of junk. Only a single item looked official.

"Another one?" Eric said.

"Yeah."

I opened it, and read the admonishment from London-based attorneys Dunleavy, Smith, & Clark about how I should not ignore them, and how they were being fair in giving me a chance to respond to their client's demands for compensation. Roger Gorman, my former partner in Park Avenue Investigations, blamed me for the fire that wiped out the profitable core of the business, and demanded restitution to the tune of ten times my actual wealth, even though the police cleared me of any involvement.

To be fair, the police came to an incorrect conclusion, but to be equally fair, Gorman was still a dick head.

"I'll sort it somehow."

Rather than wiping my arse on it and sending it back in a perfumed envelope (which I almost did with the first notification), I folded the papers in half and placed them in my back pocket.

My choices were to stand and fight, or move my money offshore, and migrate to a country with no extradition. It didn't sit well with me. After I turned eighteen, I lived abroad for a long time, always moving around, finding a new perch to lay my proverbial hat, but that was born from my craving for isolation, for freedom, and simple joy; if I fled this, it would be a prison sentence.

Eric followed me inside and immediately ducked into the downstairs loo, while I continued through the open plan ground floor to my kitchen to recycle the junk mail accompanying Gorman's missive: limited-offer timeshares, a mayoral election flyer, the former-resident's pre-approved credit card waiting for her…

"Adam?" It was Eric's voice.

I scanned around, and found him in my lounge holding the Sig-Sauer on an elderly white man and a miserable-looking black guy in his thirties. The older man wore a quality suit, the younger a leather jacket, white T-shirt, and jeans. Eric must have used the facilities and headed straight for the airy living area, expecting me to deliver a steaming espresso of Fair Trade Guatemalan nectar. Which I would have, if not for this little wrinkle in my day.

"One of 'em's packing," Eric said, his shooting stance not wavering an inch. "Wanna guess which?"

I strode across the polished marble toward the two men with their hands behind their heads, slapped open the younger guy's jacket, and relieved him a make of gun I'd never encountered. I located the safety to ensure it was on and tossed it aside. Faced the older guy. He was in his sixties, or a very healthy seventies.

I said, "I'm guessing you're the boss, he's the bodyguard."

"Correct," the elderly man replied with an accent. German, I thought, but not pure. Belgian or Swiss, perhaps. "If I may—"

"What you may do is tell me why you're here. Roger Gorman using scare tactics now?"

"I assure you, I do not know who Roger Gorman is. We are here on an unrelated matter."

"That forces you to break into my home? The door was locked when I got here."

The man indicated the couch where an impression suggested he'd been waiting moments earlier. I nodded and he sat, but I waved a hand at Eric to remain alert.

"Who are you?"

"My name," the man said, "is Herman Prinz. I am a lawyer representing the Kravitz family, and I apologize for giving you a fright." He mopped his brow with a monogrammed handkerchief. "The guard on your gated street would not allow us to knock, and since you are not listed with a phone company we could not call. My colleague, Francis here, facilitated access."

"Your colleague's a burglar?"

"I'm a facilitator," Francis said with a Canadian twang. "May I sit too?"

"No, you may not," Eric answered for me. "You may keep your hands on your head and if you move them, you may have your chest ventilated. Clear?"

I remained standing. Four feet from both men, one sat in front, one stood on my right. I said, "Get where you're going. Why are you here?"

"A case, Mr. Park. I have a case for you."

"I'm not taking cases."

"It is a case for which you are almost singularly suited."

English may not have been his first language, but his vocabulary was almost better than mine.

I said, "Then it's probably crooked, illegal, or at least immoral. Leave now, and I'm keeping the Canuck's gun."

"It is not without rewards—"

"Do I look like I'm struggling for money?"

"Not financial rewards. In fact, it is your current healthy bank balance that means you are the best person for this offer of employment."

I frowned, shuffled to my right, and rubbed my neck. Eric side-stepped for a better angle. *Oops.* I was shielding the older man—Herman—although I doubted he would prove much of a physical threat. Clearly, Eric was a more cautious type. Could be why he was an ex-soldier and I was just a sometimes-private investigator.

I took the hint and held still. "What exactly does my bank balance have to do with this?"

Herman crossed his legs and leaned back into the goose down cushions, hands clasped in his lap. "The previous investigator tasked with examining a certain family tree was the sudden recipient of an anonymous cash gift, and has since started a new life in Belize with a rather fetching young lady many years his junior."

"Genealogy? There are firms who specialize in those matters."

The lawyer smiled, his face forming deep lines from his mouth up to his forehead. "Mr. Park, if someone hires an investigator to assess the accuracy of a family's ancestors, but this investigator is bribed with a life-changing amount of money, what is your immediate conclusion?"

I sat in my reading chair, a wide number with chunky arms and natural light cast from behind. "If he was bribed to stop looking, somebody's trying to hide something."

"And that someone is making life very difficult for a young woman. A girl, actually." Herman creaked forward, elbows on his knees. "Estelle Kravitz is thirteen years old, and is convinced she is *not* the true heir to the Kravitz fortune. And if she is correct, a lot of people stand to lose out."

"And why does she think she isn't the true heir?" I asked.

"Because, Mr. Park, she believes she is possessed. Possessed by a spirit who demands she tell the truth."

CHAPTER TWO

After Francis and Eric patched up their differences and went out for a walk—skipping along the beach hand-in-hand, I hoped—I brewed coffee and invited Herman to the back terrace where the patio doors had been accessed via brute force, and the lock lay in pieces on the ground. Most in this gated community armed their houses with alarms and panic buttons, but my landlord never felt the need, what with a fence, a gate, and a guard on duty 24/7. I'd pass on my notes shortly.

Herman sipped the long espresso and nodded appreciation. I took the chair opposite and he lowered the cup to its saucer.

"A ghost?" I said.

"A spirit."

"Whatever the technical difference is, I'm a detective, not an exorcist."

"It really doesn't matter. Your brief is simply to clarify the family tree, not prove or disprove something scholars have been unable to agree upon for millennia."

"You just told me my client is a possessed teenage girl."

Herman breathed heavily through his nose. "Perhaps if I elaborate on the circumstances?"

I sipped my coffee, not enjoying it as much as I usually do overlooking the long narrow garden under a cloudless blue sky.

"Since her mother's death ten years ago, a great deal of money has sat in trust for Estelle. It will filter through to her in increments, depending how long her father lives. Eventually, she will control over seventy-five percent of the family fortune."

"And who are the Kravitz? Kravitzes? I say that right?"

Herman adjusted his position. For the first time, he really looked his age, as if anticipating the conversation to come would drain him. Perhaps I was the only person in the world for whom "Kravitz" meant nothing more than an awesome musician.

He said, "Judge Gottfried Kravitz works out of the city of Hamburg, but also closely with the European Commission of Human Rights, most recently regarding the case of a ninety-plus-year-old former Nazi administrator detained under a European arrest warrant. You are familiar with the case?"

"Vaguely. Hit some headlines a few months ago. Something to do with his rights being violated if they move him from Italy where his family lives."

"Actually, his family are claiming *their* rights would be violated. *His* rights are inconsequential in this respect, but the matter has no relevance anyway. I know this. When I worked in Berlin I used to prosecute such men myself."

"Private pays better?"

"Chasing old men and women who will be dead soon anyway … it adds little to the world. I merely seek to emphasize Judge Kravitz is an important and respected man."

"I'll take your word for it."

"Good, good." It wasn't clear if he misunderstood my lack of giving a crap. "But he married in to the Caine line, whose wealth was generated largely from the art world, and although he is moderately well-off as a judge, he is not, shall we say, an establishment figure."

"Meaning the majority of his money comes from his late wife."

"From Helena, correct. And he likes his lifestyle as it is. However, my concern is for the well-being of his daughter."

"Estelle."

"Yes. My fees are covered by her mother's estate, so I work for Estelle, not Gottfried."

I'd finished my coffee; the downside of short, strong drinks. "This is the haunted girl?"

Ignoring my sarcasm, he said, "A month ago, Estelle went missing from Kochany Dom."

"Kochany Dom?"

"The family's estate north of Hamburg. It means 'Sweet Home' in Polish. The family is originally from Poland."

"Right."

"She had a dream. She was inconsolable for days after. Her great-grandmother, Katerina, she soothed the girl, helped with the doctor's examination when she would not allow her father near. But after many sleepless nights, Estelle slipped out. The police were called, naturally, and the German press sold a lot of advertising space as a result, but they made no progress in finding her. A sighting in Glinde, a CCTV image in Seevetal, and when they sent experts to dredge a stretch of the Elbe River, well, you should have seen the headlines. Strangely, those days, when they thought her body may be discovered, the news was far louder than when she showed up five days later, alive and unharmed. Of course, the press do not know where she was found."

"Where was that?"

"Kraków," he said.

"Poland. Coincidence she chose the family's country of origin?"

"It is also where Vera and Marco LaPorte live. Vera leads a Romani group, manages a site there. Has done for the past four years, since her husband's death."

"Could his death be related to any of this?"

"Doubtful. He was killed by protesters outside a temporary camp. A Neo-Nazi group wanted to move them on, and things got out of hand."

"Okay, so Estelle found this Vera then?"

"She caught three trains, using only a photo ID, and cash. But we brought her home without the need for fanfare. The newspapers learned nothing of her claims of spiritual possession."

"And the other investigator?" I asked.

"Tony Luca, a German-Italian fellow who came recommended from a friend's law firm. He worked on the assignment for less than a week after Estelle came home, and announced he was ready to make his final report. Then he disappeared. The sudden injection of cash into his account, and its equally-sudden movement to a Caymans bank … add to that his social media account filling up with photos of his new beach home, and we can safely say he was handsomely compensated for burying whatever he found."

"Gottfried?" I said. "Sounds like he'd have the most to lose."

"Indeed. And the family's money has a wide reach."

Eric's voice carried through the border hedges, with Francis's alongside. Not heated, just chatting. Maybe they'd become best buddies after all, patrolling the perimeter of their respective charges' positions between properties. I picked out mention of Iraq, and guessed they were comparing service records. Still…

"Why the muscle?" I asked. "Missing girl, dodgy family background … doesn't add up to your life being in danger."

He clasped his hands together, his old-man discomfort pushed aside, the hawk-like lawyer back in charge. "Mr. Park, you are a man of ill repute. Consorting with gangsters and terrorists. He was here to protect me from *you*."

"Why do I get the feeling if I'd returned home without Eric, our conversation would have taken place down the barrel of a gun?"

The lawyer shrugged innocently.

"So she was fine," I said. "Apart from the sticky-fingered PI, I hear another 'but' in the distance."

"They found her because a phone call was placed by one Vera LaPorte, an elder of the Romani LaPortes."

"Again, you assume I know who they are."

"You know of the Romani?"

"Gypsies," I said. "Or Travelers, whatever the modern term is."

"Different people have different terms. They favor 'Roma' in this case. The LaPortes originated in Poland, driven into hiding by the Nazis in 1938 and '39."

Poland again.

I said, "They have a claim on the fortune."

Herman stood, rubbed his lower back, and stepped forward stiffly. "Forgive me, but I cannot sit in one position for more than ten minutes at a time. Will you walk?"

My garden, for such a nice house, was relatively small, but it rarely bothered me. I was a beach guy and always had been, and far preferred dining, drinking, and reading on the balcony overlooking the sea. A squat palm plant grew in the center of the gravel "lawn", and the flower beds were empty, although I planned on using them as vegetable plots—if I stuck around long enough.

Herman held one of the palm fronds between a thumb and forefinger. "Estelle actively sought them out, the LaPortes. She claims her great-grandfather, Petr Caine, or 'Peter', now occupies a portion of her soul, and asks her to right a terrible wrong."

"And you think the Roma are influencing her?"

"I think my client wants the truth."

"Not sure how much help I can be here, Herman. I find missing people, I review criminal cases—"

He let go of the plant. "You perform background checks, and you know the systems and software, and you have a keen mind, despite your more … unsavory associates."

I wandered slowly to the end of the garden, demarked by a thick tangle of orange trees, the branches knitted so closely together I couldn't push through and fall to my death on the rock-strewn beach, even if I ran at them full-pelt.

"What exactly do you need me to do? Prove she's mentally ill?"

"No," Herman said. "My client wishes to clarify her heritage, and having spent time with Vera LaPorte, she is even more adamant she should not receive the money."

"What if it turns out she's right? What if, daft notions of the supernatural aside … what if the money really *should* go to the Roma?"

Herman shrugged. "Then the truth will out, Mr. Park. I will be paid for my services, and most likely let go. But that is my job."

"And Judge Kravitz?"

"He is confident the claim is nonsense, and that Estelle is just a troubled young woman."

I headed back toward the house, allowing Herman to set

the pace, which was not particularly brisk. "And how much are you paying for this?"

"Expenses only," Herman said with a modest dip of his head. "Despite the company you keep, we understand you are independently wealthy, and only take cases where you feel compelled to help. Remuneration will be pointless in persuading you, but your inability to be bribed makes you valuable."

Confession time: this guy was stoking my ego. I was having a hard time resisting a huge grin because—for once—a facet I could be sort-of proud of had brought someone to my door. It made me suspicious too, though; perhaps he'd done more homework on me than he was willing to reveal.

"So tell me, Mr. Park. Is the notion of helping this girl appealing to your better nature? Or do I leave you to enjoy this pleasant but rather dull life you've chosen?"

Dull?

I'd set up all my small pleasures—coffee, reading, scotch, occasional female company—and continued my training—CV work, a beach gym a half-hour bike ride away, the firearms coaching—but five months of this saw me rejuvenated mentally and physically, and if I was honest with myself, it was a tad *too* idyllic. The road was calling, and I planned to up-sticks and move on anyway. Tourist season was fast approaching, and Fila Town, the capital of Paramatra, became a hedonistic nightmare in summer. My intent was to return to Britain, pack my VW camper, and take off through France, aiming for Italy or someplace farther out, and get to know myself again. Traveling was my passion, my lifeblood, and I was itching to move on, but with no serious impetus to do so, other than the dive I funded, I simply kept putting it off.

So yeah, a little dull.

"I don't speak German," I said.

"They are a family of lawyers, Mr. Park, they all speak English. Even Estelle was taught both German and English from the moment she could talk. We would not be contacting a British investigator if language was to be an issue."

I was running out of excuses.

"If I'm on board," I said, "I'll do what I can. But I'm not attending any séances or daft hocus pocus rituals. Understand?"

"No one is suggesting you should."

"And it's to find out the truth, not provide you with the version of the truth you want."

"That is the job, Mr. Park. Either Estelle Kravitz is heir to her family's hundred-million-euro fortune, or she isn't."

A hundred million...

"This is a bum-on-seat investigation," I said. "I'll meet with the girl, and I'll meet with the family. If anything smells dodgy, I'm gone."

Herman held out his hand and I shook it.

I said, "With no airport here, it's eight hours by ferry to the mainland."

"Oh, I think we can do better than that, Mr. Park. You're not afraid of helicopters, are you?"

GERMANY

HAMBURG

CHAPTER THREE

THE PROMISED HELICOPTER whisked me to the next island, and although Paramatra's neighbor similarly lacked a commercial airport, it did boast a private airfield. Having "donated" his firearm to Eric's collection—an AMT Longslide apparently —Francis arranged for onward travel via the Kravitz family's Cessna, on which I enjoyed a seafood pasta meal prepared by the on-board chef. After a brief snooze, we landed in Hamburg late in the afternoon, where a Land Rover collected me and Herman, while Francis traveled behind in an older model. On the flight from Greece, Herman did not wish to elaborate any further on the case, except for me to read brief one-sheet summaries of the people living at Kochany Dom, which I flipped through again, alongside the jottings in my notebook.

The dossier commenced with Estelle and Gottfried, obviously, while Gottfried's brother, sister-in-law, and nephew occupied a separate wing, but who were out of the country presently, skiing. The estate employed six main staff: a personal assistant to Gottfried, an aide to his brother's family, plus two cooks, a nanny/tutor for Estelle, and an on-site doctor. The doctor was a recent addition following Estelle's jaunt to Romani-Town, as well as the girl's great-grandmother—Katerina—having been diagnosed with several infections of late, thus scaring the family who would surely crumble without her. It was through the ninety-five year-old Katerina that Herman became embroiled in the family's affairs, having demanded they outsource the handling of Estelle's eccentricities to a law firm not connected to the Kravitzes in any way, thus eliminating any conflict of interest.

"Nothing in between?" I asked in the Land Rover. "Seems like it jumps from Katerina, down three generations to Estelle."

"No one in between. A lot of women meeting early ends. Katerina, who survived the German occupation of Poland, had a baby girl in 1946, called Beatrice. She grew up in Kochany Dom, married well, but died due to birthing complications. Helena was born healthy, though, which was 1973, and killed in 2010 in a motorcycle accident. A little wild, that one, and Estelle's arrival did little to calm her."

"So all the men marry in, essentially."

"It would seem that way, at least for the twentieth century."

As we pulled up to a pair of electric gates, far sturdier than those blocking my own street, I reread a handwritten page from my A5 notebook in which I'd tried to arrange the family structure clearly:

- Katerina Caine: Great Grandmother (alive and still running the family)
- Petr Caine: Great Grandfather and sometime-ghost (dead circa 1946).
- Beatrice Shultz: Grandmother to Estelle (died 1973, birthing Helena).

- Hans Shultz: Grandfather who married Beatrice (died 1980).
- Helena Kravitz: mother (died six years ago).

Then Gottfried's side:

- Gottfried Kravitz: father (alive and possibly bribing private investigators to leave his family alone).
- Stephan: Gottfried's brother and Estelle's uncle.
- Angela: sister-in-law and aunt.
- Konrad: nephew/cousin, aged seventeen.

The driveway passed between rows of trees and curled to the left, blocking out the low sun except for blinding glimpses flashing through the trunks. We parked, and stepped out into the shadow of a Georgian-style mansion with two wings on either side of the main house, and pillars rising over the entrance. The staircase had been adapted with a ramp down one side, presumably for Katerina, but other than that I could have been in 1930s England.

At the bottom of the stairs, a clean-shaven Caucasian man slipped a timepiece from the waistcoat of his three-piece suit, checked the time, and appeared to sniff in our direction, then put the watch away. I extended my hand.

"You must be Judge Kravitz," I said.

He shook the hand. "Gottfried. Please. And you are Adam Park." His accent was stronger than Herman's but he did not stumble over any words. "I trust your journey was comfortable."

"Very, thanks." I turned to locate Herman and found him beside Francis, both out of earshot. "They not coming?"

"I wanted to speak with you first. Before you meet Estelle. They will join us shortly."

"Lead the way," I said, forcing a smile.

He waved me through and followed me up the six white stone steps to a door large enough for an elephant. Inside, the elephant would have struggled to march down the hall without dislodging the paintings or smashing the pots and knickknacks lining the way, but it would probably have squeezed through.

"Mr. Prinz, he has told you about my daughter?"

"Herman? Yes, he's filled me in."

Gottfried made a dismissive nasal sound. "It is nonsense, Mr. Park. I hope you will take a more … neutral view than your predecessor."

I left my reply hanging, as if challenging Gottfried to offer me a wad of cash, as Herman suspected he had with Tony Luca. Instead, the judge guided me to the right and up a staircase wide enough for that trespassing elephant again.

"Do you have children, Mr. Park?"

"No, I don't."

"Children have nightmares. My daughter had one, then another, and her grandmother does not help. There is a wonderful word for it in English—potty. The woman is *potty*."

The synonym for "mildly crazy" sounded odd in a German accent, but it fit.

"Katerina?" I said. "I thought she was her great-grandmother?"

"She is, technically. But Katerina practically raised Helena alone, and Helena called Katerina her 'mama'. Here, in this place."

We reached a dogleg on the staircase where an honest-to-God suit of armor stood like a sentry in one corner. It was beginning to resemble a cheesy film set.

"What makes Katerina potty?"

"She indulges Estelle in her hearing of voices," Gottfried said, taking the steps more slowly. "Katerina's husband is *not* inside Estelle and telling her to give away my money."

"*Her* money. Estelle's."

Gottfried paused. "Yes. Forgive me. My English is not always … exact."

"Sounds pretty exact to me."

He lingered on me a second before continuing upward. "This notion that Katerina's husband has returned to give financial advice is ludicrous. You must see it."

"Not my job to see anything."

We reached the summit and the deep carpet almost swallowed my feet as I waited for Gottfried to catch his breath.

I said, "I'm glad you appear more sensible than your lawyer. Perhaps you'll abide by my findings, since they'll be grounded in real life."

Gottfried commenced down a corridor that reminded me of an opulent hotel, with mahogany doors and trim, and lights popping on as we reached them.

"Mr. Park, you will find not everyone here shares your skepticism. Katerina especially. Not only Petr visits her and Estelle, but Katerina's own grandmother too. Have you heard of the Angel of Kraków?"

"Lots of angels during the war."

Gottfried's turn to force a smile. "This angel—Elizabetta—is quite famous. Her exploits even feature in some children's books back in Poland. She was among the first to see the direction Germany was taking under the National Socialists, and moved her family for safety, out of this house—or its predecessor—back to Poland."

"They were Jewish?"

"Yes. A key figure in helping the Nazis' enemies escape the country. The Nazis killed her early in the war."

"The Angel of Kraków," I said. "And Katerina is seeing this ghost alongside her husband?"

"You don't believe it is possible the Angel of Kraków returned to watch over her granddaughter?"

"You know there are no ghosts, Judge Kravitz. You know it and I know it."

He stopped beside a door as Herman approached alone from the other end of the passageway.

"Apologies, I wasn't clear," Gottfried said. "I do not believe Petr Caine is present within my daughter's soul, but Elizabetta, the Angel of Kraków, is very much a part of this building."

"Seriously?" Instantly, I regretted screwing up my face like that. But this guy was a *judge*, presiding over complex criminal and human rights matters. "The only ghosts," I said, "are those we make for ourselves."

He gripped the brass door knob, waiting for Herman to reach us. When he did, Gottfried said, "Mr. Park does not believe in ghosts."

"No," Herman replied. "Perhaps we can change his mind."

I shook my head, again annoyed at myself for displaying my displeasure at otherwise intelligent men acting like rational thought were some sort of oddity.

"Time to meet your client," Gottfried said, and opened the door.

CHAPTER FOUR

ESTELLE KRAVITZ LOUNGED in a leather reclining chair in Incredible Hulk pajamas, shoulder-length blond hair splayed over her shoulders, face trained on a fifty-inch TV, and a game console controller in her hands, guiding a dirt bike through some futuristic death race set in desert canyons full of exploding cars. Her eyes drooped, almost bored in her expert handling of the vehicle. The curtains were closed, sunlight illuminating the material and casting a glow across a bedroom larger than most lounges. Her double bed lay unmade, her desk was littered with novels and an iPad, and two dirty dishes and a mug were stacked on the corner. She did not look up as the three of us entered.

"She likes her games," Gottfried said.

Estelle called in German. I was as proficient in German as I was French, which is to say hardly at all; high school basics only. Herman asked her to switch to English.

"If I must," she said, with an even lighter accent than Herman's. "I reminded him the games keep my great-grandfather's voice quiet."

I looked to Gottfried and pointed her way without a word.

He nodded, and I moved alongside her, pulling up the chair from her desk. Her expression barely changed as she swished the controller and stabbed the buttons so her avatar performed a huge leap across a lava-spitting chasm.

"I'm Adam Park," I said. "I'm an investigator."

"I know who you are." She spoke slowly, but with hardly any trace of an accent. "You want to prove I'm crazy."

Herman wasn't kidding when he said she learned English from an early age. I'm amazed more English-speaking countries don't introduce foreign language lessons sooner. I wish I had tried harder. For all my travelling, for all those years, I only ever grew competent enough to hold the briefest of conversations in the local tongue, and a couple of days after leaving and delving into a new culture, it was all but forgotten.

I said, "I want to prove whether the voice you're hearing is telling you the truth or not. I have no agenda."

"Except getting paid?" She offered a brief smile, still glued to the telly. "You're just like all the others."

"I'm a little different. Why don't you tell me about the person inside you?"

She paused the game, relaxed her arms, and turned her head to me. "My great-grandfather. Petr Caine. He died after coming home from the war. Before, when the Nazis occupied his homeland, he left his wife behind and joined up with the Russians, and returned to her as a savior. A hero."

"How did he die?"

She adjusted her gaze to land directly over my head. "Sadness."

Gottfried mimed with his fingers—a gun at his temple, and his thumb-hammer came down.

I said, "Estelle, you think Petr is instructing you to relinquish your wealth? Pass it on to someone unconnected to the family?"

"There is a connection. A very real one."

Gottfried parted the curtains an inch to peer out, allowing a shaft of light to cut over Estelle. Pale and drawn, she recoiled like a vampire.

"There is no connection," Gottfried said. "None whatsoever. In the nineteenth century, the family converted to Judaism and later, after the First World War, moved from Poland to settle in Germany. The line is clear. Katerina, Beatrice, Helena, Estelle."

"And you, dear daddy," Estelle said. "You benefit too, don't you?"

He closed the curtain and faced her, hands in his pockets. "I do not wish to have this conversation again." To me, he said, "I only want what is best for her."

I made a point of keeping my attention on Estelle. "And these Roma ... the LaPortes, you think there's another line? Something connecting them to ... what? This land? This estate? Something illegitimate?"

"I don't know." Her voice sounded faraway, like some serene blanket had fallen over her. "Petr says I must find them, though, the true family. Marco LaPorte. He's the one."

"But there's been no DNA test?" I asked. "That would clear this up, surely."

"Sadly not," Herman interrupted. "We did try, but it only reveals a family connection. So even though Estelle most certainly shares ancestry with the Roma, even DNA cannot confirm how far back it goes. Certainly not enough for ... Judge Kravitz's satisfaction."

Gottfried stepped away from the window. "If you go back far enough, Mr. Park, you'll find yourself related to your Queen, as shall I. Should the young princes lose the Crown Jewels to you and I?"

He was correct. Dating back this far meant gene pools were too diluted.

"Where did it branch off?" I asked Estelle. "Can Petr tell me?"

She frowned. "I thought you didn't believe."

"I don't. But you do. So there must be some clue that pointed you to Marco LaPorte."

She sighed, and restarted her game. "Kraków." An injection of steel entered her voice, although I was unsure if it was her commitment to the statement or the appearance of a fur-clad marauder with a baseball bat trying to murder her on-screen avatar. "It's Kraków, Mr. Park. Maybe you should ask our angel."

While she laughed at her own joke, I replaced her chair, and signaled to the men I was ready to go. We all reached the door, and in a low voice I said to them, "If I didn't know better I'd say she was high. She's been checked?"

"Indeed," Gottfried said. "Twice. Nothing in her blood."

"Yes," Herman said. "Katerina insisted—once for Gottfried, and once for her. Different labs to guarantee no … contamination."

"Contamination." Gottfried breathed in through his nose and out heavily through his mouth. "Perhaps you should meet Katerina. She might be of more use than my daughter."

I opened the door and stood aside for the two men to exit.

"Goodbye, Estelle," I said, following. "I'll get to the bottom of this. I promise."

"Adam," she called. When I turned, she had paused the game again and stood from the chair. Fingers entwined, she said, "Aren't you afraid you could be wrong? About the ghosts?"

I leaned on the doorframe, considered my response, not

wanting to offend her or upset her in any way. But nor did I want to lie.

"No," I said. "I don't worry."

She looked sad. "The Angel, when she speaks, she says the same thing. Which is odd, because she is a ghost herself. But still, she says, 'There are no ghosts, except those we make for ourselves.'"

CHAPTER FIVE

"SHE HEARD ME THROUGH THE DOOR," I said to Herman's smug half-smile as we walked away from Estelle's room. "Interpreted it as a ghostly message. Or taking the piss."

Both Herman and Gottfried grinned, but did not comment. I asked a little about the drug tests, learning they were carried out in the presence of Katerina, Herman, the family doctor, and Gottfried himself. I confirmed the bloods were examined at separate labs, and Gottfried emphasized it was separate *hospitals*, and both results came back identical: zero contamination.

The pair escorted me toward grounds that swept further than I could see. We stopped, however, at the mouth of the maze, where a lady in her 90s waited. I had expected a wheel-chair, but all I found was a bright eyed woman with grey hair and a walking stick. Her skin sagged from her bones like any ninety-something-year-old, and she was wrapped up warmer than would be necessary for a younger person. Gottfried made the introductions.

"Pleased to meet you," I said, gently shaking Katerina's hand.

"Likewise." She released my hand and shooed the other men away. "This way, I think."

She stooped, so her head reached my chest height, although she had probably been almost as tall as me in her youth. We bypassed the maze entrance and she moved sideways down three steps to a gravel path, surrounded by roses of every color, just starting to bloom. When summer arrived fully the effect would be a carpet of multicolored petals and a fragrance so strong you might think you'd been dipped in perfume.

She said, "I hear from Herman you do not believe my grandmother watches over us."

"If your grandmother wants to introduce herself, I'll gladly start believing."

She chuckled. "You know, most people your age like to humor me. They'll tell me they have an open mind, even when they don't. Your rat-faced predecessor kissed my ass. In fact, he told me he'd seen ghosts on numerous occasions, but I could tell he was lying. He just wanted the job. It paid well."

"Not well enough, apparently."

We left the multiple rose beds and passed through a gap in a hedge into a scruffier space, although the scruffiness appeared intentional. Herbs, ferns, flowerless plants, all growing from beds tended with manure and bark. The path here was paved, and Katerina progressed more steadily as she ran her hands over a flat leaf in a bed raised to hip-level, and gave them a sniff.

"Basil," she said. "Here."

She wafted her wrinkled hand under my nose, and a strong burst of basil hit the back of my throat.

"Mm," I said. "Next time I pop by, I'll have to make you my onion-basil pasta sauce."

"Indeed, I'm sure our Michelin-Star chef would love to

collaborate." She gave a mischievous smile as she dusted off her hands.

I could not help but smile too as we started walking again.

"You wish to ask me some questions," she said.

"Estelle believes the family's lineage got corrupted somewhere around the time your grandmother moved you and your mother to Kraków. What are your recollections of that time?"

"Kraków is a very wide memory. When I moved there it was a happy place, an industrial revolution was taking place, unemployment was low, and the countryside a mere hour away by horse and cart. Less, if you were fortunate enough to own a motor vehicle. Which we did." She paused, staring at a fernlike plant. "Then the Nazis came. And everything changed."

I fingered the plant. "This isn't native to Germany."

"South America," she said.

"I spent some time in South America." I left it there. Didn't think it would be endearing to tell her the degree to which I spent my youth partying. Once, I lost three whole days after taking a handful of loopy mushrooms without checking their potency; I started in Brasilia, and came round in the back of a truck four hundred miles into the Amazon with four other people I apparently met during my trip. We saved some trees, smoked some more dope, and went our separate ways a month later.

"Mimosa hostilis," Katerina said. "An interesting plant. It does very well for itself after forest fires. The whole environment around it can be burnt to the soil, but if a single root continues to live, it can be revived in its entirety."

"Tell me about your husband."

"Petr doesn't mean any harm. I'm sure he truly believes he is telling Estelle the truth."

I tried not to sound too condescending. "I mean before he died."

"Oh."

She started moving again, and although it may have been my imagination, her stoop dipped a little lower. "I married him shortly after I turned eighteen. He lived with me and my mother, and my grandmother, while we saved for a house of our own."

"Your grandmother, that's Elizabetta? The Angel of Kraków?"

"That's what they called her. But I just knew her as Nana. It wasn't until the Nazis started killing Jews and gypsies that she became a guardian angel. By then, my Petr had already joined the resistance. When they found Nana, she refused to give up a single name. Even as they held a gun to the head of her daughter."

"Your mother."

Through the folds of skin, under creases in which I could lose several coins, her face hardened.

"Yes," she said. "I do not know if it was simply a mathematical equation, or if she did not believe those animals would murder my mother, but they shot her, there in the street, along with nine Jews."

She stood beside a bed of herbs, the smell of coriander piercing the air.

"It was not until they threatened me that she broke. And even then, she only gave them routes and maps. The people themselves were long gone. So when the Nazis found out, they kicked her to death."

I said, "I'm sorry, but you understand I have to ask."

"Yes, Mr. Park. I understand." A faint tremor visited her jaw and spread gently to her head. "When people today think of the war, they see heroes and villains, commandants shouting

'*Schnell! Schnell!*' and waving around their arms. They think of concentration camps, of faces, young and old, staring out, almost pleading to us from the past to stop the madness. They rarely consider those everyday folk who suffered the occupation, and the advance of the master race."

It sounded like she'd said this before; a rehearsed speech. Perhaps she'd spoken of it too often throughout her life.

"Because the Nazis were not only a military force, and more than a political party aiming for world domination. They were thugs, privateers, hoarding wealth wherever they went. That facet of their evil is more like today's gangsters than yesterday's soldiers."

I had read of such things, seen documentaries, but rarely had I met anyone who lived through it.

"What happened after the war?" I asked.

"Do you not want to know what happened to me during the occupation of Kraków?"

"Is it relevant to Estelle?"

"You may find some evidence points in that direction. It is not relevant, but you will have questions. Better I answer now."

I nodded to her to continue.

"Kraków was not like most of the cities in Poland. The country surrendered before the worst of the fighting reached us, so the city did not suffer the same massacres, or the same destruction as other places. When the Allies arrived afterwards they were surprised. Some thought it spoke of much collaboration between the occupiers and the occupied. It did not. We merely capitulated. And I believe we were right to do so. You go to Warsaw, and you will see so many new buildings, new roads, new everything. But Kraków is still beautiful."

She lost herself for a moment. I waited for her to fill the silence.

"I was alone in our home now, and a Nazi officer called Friedrich Goetz moved in. 'Barracking' they called it. Sometimes 'quartering.' I was his housekeeper, his cook, his personal assistant. And I did a good job. So good that, once the Nazi occupation was solid, he moved to a farmhouse on the outskirts, and took me with him."

I hated to interrupt, but I saw one possibility here. "Did this Goetz make you … um…"

"No, Mr. Park." She touched my hand and gave me a kind smile, like a grandma comforting an upset child. "And no need to be so coy. We did have sex in the olden days. Lots of it."

We progressed from the herb garden to what I took to be a vegetable plot, with row upon row of fledgling plants: cabbages, broccoli, carrots, and a greenhouse full of tomatoes, amid more exotic legumes.

Katerina continued in a matter-of-fact manner, almost clinical. "In 1945, when the Russians crossed the border, and Nazi columns surrendered en masse, the news reached us. As those in Kraków prepared to pack up and flee, I saw my chance, and killed the officer myself, with a rifle I used to hunt rabbits."

Using her cane, she mimed the action of aiming and firing.

"Three days later, Petr returned to me. I had assumed him dead for six years, so seeing him, holding him, it was the happiest moment of my life. Our old home had been destroyed, so we moved onto the farm. It sounds horrible, I know, but the previous owners perished elsewhere, and left no descendants. Poland needed farms to rebuild, so our ownership was rubber-stamped as legal." She stared at the floor. "But Petr was never the same. We called it 'shellshock' back then, what you call PTSD now."

"Post-traumatic stress disorder."

She touched her stomach. "When Beatrice came along it was easier for him. But did not silence the ghosts."

"He shot himself." I thought it kinder to say it for her.

"I was upstairs sweeping when the gun went off. I rushed down, and found him. The official story is he was cleaning his gun and it went off accidentally. Official suicide verdicts were rare among war heroes."

I nodded to say I understood.

"I sold the farm, and went to stay with family in Paris, I started a job helping return looted artwork to the correct owners. Along the way, I realized some of the Nazi officer's tastes wore off on me, because I instinctively knew what makes a good piece. I was able to assess talent. I used the money from the sale of our farm to open a gallery, and eventually earned enough to return to my roots. In Hamburg."

"You went back, despite the country's history."

"It was my home. Thanks to the hard work of my grandfather, the *Angel's* husband…"

She sounded almost bitter with the word "angel."

"The Nazis had razed it to the ground, having been infected by a Jewish banker and his brood. When I made enough money in Paris, I petitioned for reparations, and was granted them. I received an income from what would have been my grandfather's estate, and full restitution of the land and grounds."

We exited the allotment between a pair of shrubs shaped like swans, bringing us to a view of fields stretching up a hill, and over, out of sight.

"Incredible legacy," I said.

"And now my late husband wishes it bequeathed to a Romani family."

"What do you think of that?"

"I do not see where the family line is corrupted. But let us hope you will."

We watched the grass sway, a wilderness out there, somewhere to ride, presumably, to hike, or simply look out and marvel at one's accomplishments.

"Your great-granddaughter is ill," I said. "Ill, or drugged by something that hasn't shown up on any test."

"What drug could bring such visions and yet not show up on a test?"

"Maybe not a drug. Hypnosis is a possibility."

"If you say so, Mr. Park. If you say so." Katerina patted my arm again. "I hope you keep a more open mind when you travel to Poland."

"How do you know I'm going to Poland?"

"Where else would you go?"

POLAND

Kraków

CHAPTER SIX

KATERINA WAS CORRECT: the obvious place to start was Kraków. Not so much the family tree, and certainly not post-1946, as that line appeared perfectly clear. But if somebody was feeding Estelle information regarding a potentially alternative lineage, it had to originate *before* Katerina gave birth to Beatrice, a legal challenge along alternative avenues. I was no expert in inheritance law, but common sense would dictate if such wealth originated from the sale of land, perhaps those who initially owned that land could stake a claim.

Katerina's mention of selling a Jewish family's farm meant I agreed with the detective who now resided in Belize, because Kraków had been my predecessor's first destination too.

To give me an early start first thing, I turned down Gottfried's offer of accommodation on the estate, preferring to fly to Kraków that evening, where I checked into a Hilton near the airport. I procured a new MacBook Air to sync with my phone, then sampled the local beer until around midnight, before turning in and dreaming about shadows shifting in the periphery of my vision.

I was back in Leeds, walking side-by-side with my old mentor Harry. We chatted, and he told me I was a fool for taking on something man was not meant to understand. I replied it was nonsense, and that man understood perfectly well. Hallucinations, delusions, all common afflictions.

But it was the shadows I remembered most vividly.

They pawed at me as I talked, yet I was unable to move away from them, and they seemed unable to grasp me. And, as Harry's voice grew quieter, a presence around me breathed. It sighed. Like the wind, it spoke: "There are no ghosts, except those we make for ourselves."

I woke slowly, not with a start, not sweating, just tired from a night of tossing and turning. After showering, then dining at the breakfast buffet, I decided it may be worth dropping Harry a line.

It had been nearly a year since he was kidnapped as a means to getting me, and over four months since I laid eyes on him. Last time, he called me an idiot, that I needed to think things through more, instead of reacting with my fists, and I should not ignore the actions of bad people, simply because ignorance suited me. I had promised to give him room.

When we first met, I was an angry man, recently home from Bangkok and bent on revenge for the violence inflicted upon me there. But he helped calm me, taught me a trade. And although since he retired I had grown wealthy through building up our business, he never once felt entitled to a penny more than he took for the initial sale. After our private investigation firm grew into corporate security, which I called Park Avenue Investigations, I thought my violent past was done with. And when I retired from my new firm, I was certain.

But things didn't work out that way, and now I was estranged from the one man alive who really understood me. Psychologists would suggest it was an unhealthy relationship, that Harry was a surrogate father for the one I lost when I was sixteen, but I didn't care what they had to say. I just knew I wanted him and his wife, Jayne, back in my life.

He picked up after two rings. "Adam."

"Hey, Harry. Are you okay to talk?"

"Yeah. Me and Jayne are in Wales fer a week. Doin' a bit of travelin' meself."

"Nice." I was beginning to wonder if he would ever leave the United Kingdom for anything longer than a booze cruise to Calais. "How's the weather?"

"How do you reckon? It's Wales."

So he was soaked through.

"And how is Jayne?"

"Better. We're both enjoyin' retirement. Talked about you the other day. Did you get our Christmas card?"

"Yes, thank you. I didn't send one your way. You said not to contact you until you were ready, but I figured the Christmas card was … maybe I should have called sooner."

There was a pause. Some breathing. Harry said, "What are you up to these days?"

"New case. Either the most interesting or most boring I've ever dealt with." I got comfortable on my bed and recited the interesting parts—Estelle and her supposed possession, the Angel of Kraków, and the Kravitz estate—then the boring part, namely my course of action. "I'm in a hotel in Kraków now. The National Archives are based in the city, so I'm going to trace the previous owners of the farm Katerina sold, and see if there is any connection to the Roma who Estelle visited."

"Sounds sensible," Harry said, and couldn't resist adding, "for once."

He gave a chuckle, which I took to be a good sign.

"So," I said, but didn't know how to continue. If one thing defined mine and Harry's relationship over the past decade, it was an ability to chat inanely about anything. In a weird panic, I blurted out, "What do you know about hypnosis?"

The chuckle became a laugh. Maybe a guffaw. Yes, "guffaw" is better.

He said, "Son, you're actually asking me about some mumbo-jumbo head-shagging conjurer's trick?"

"I don't mean squawk like a chicken, believe you're on the moon. I mean … implanting thoughts. The drug tests were negative. She's shown no sign of mental illness in the past. I thought…"

"Who? Who would have access? The dad?"

"Too much to lose."

"The uncle? Aunt?"

"Same. A lot to lose."

"The great-grandmother."

I thought of Katerina. "No, she adores the girl. Extremely protective. She wouldn't do her any harm."

"The lawyer? He's getting a lot of work out of it."

"True, but he came on board after Estelle visited the Roma." I ran the timing start to finish. "Maybe they got access to her?"

Harry forwent the chuckle. Probably figured it was taken as read. "What? Knock-knock-knock on the huge mansion? *'Hey, wanna buy some heather? By the way, get that little girl to look at this watch a while will ya?'* Look, Adam, concentrate on what you can see and touch. On which note, how're you gonna read the registry records? I'm guessin' you ain't taken up Polish since I saw you."

"I have a translator booked. Meeting at eleven."

"Well, try not to pork her before you solve this thing."

"*He* is sixty-four, Harry."

His chuckle returned. "Ah, Jess booked him."

"Why do you say that?"

"No reason. Listen, when this is put to bed, providin' you don't have to go all cowboy and bring more guns and bombs and whatever else to our lives … Jayne's ready to see you. She … *we* would like you round. Dinner. Somethin' nice."

I swallowed. When you get what you're hoping for, you're never sure how much it will hit you. But winning back Harry's trust, and Jayne's, I was somewhere between punching the air and crying.

"Thanks," I said. "I'll be there."

I spent the next half-hour in the company of Google Translate trying to work out which of the hypnosis centers and experts would be open to a chat before I met the human interpreter who would guide me through the mass of paperwork about to fill my life for the foreseeable future. In the end I flew the white flag and pinged a message to Jess.

I spoke with her yesterday, which went a little more tersely than with Harry. She made a point of telling me about the guy she'd been seeing, then agreed to check the Metropolitan Police database for a suitable translator local to Kraków. Having briefly lost the confidence of the Met last year, thanks to her helping me, she was now firmly back in the fold having reinvented her freelance business as "cyber-forensic specialists" which basically meant snooping through bad guys' computers when the courts allowed it.

She called me on FaceTime. Her light brown skin was smooth as ever, and she was in her pajamas, which was unusual at this time of day—after eight a.m. Another unusual aspect to her was that her hair looked natural.

"Not even highlights?" I said.

"Mike likes it this way," she said, ruffling the frizz hanging loose below her ears.

"Lucky guy. You're relaxing for once?"

She threw a lop-sided grin. "He's waiting in the next room. What do you need now?"

Was it wrong I was picturing a multi-muscled black guy in tiny body-builder briefs? Jess was mixed race Jamaican-British, so her hair had a certain Afro quality but never went all the way, hence her frequent changes of style, trying to find one that was just right. In the years I'd known her, it hadn't stayed the same more than two months in a row.

I said, "I need a shortcut in finding a hypnosis expert, and you're the best shortcut I know."

"Why hypnosis?"

"Because it's one of the few things I can think of that makes sense."

"You're discounting the notion she might really be talking to the dead man?"

"I am."

Jess glanced away for a second, embarrassed. She was not a religious person in the traditional sense, but she had always refused to rule out the prospect of an afterlife. In fact, she actively promoted the notion that "this can't be all there is" many times, without being specific.

She said, "I'm only helping because you're finally taking on a sensible case."

"Don't forget who sent me on the last one."

Her narrow eyes said either "touché" or "go screw yourself." Knowing Jess, "screw" was probably mild.

I told her my hypnosis theory and how I needed an

English-speaking expert. She said she'd check with the Europol database of reference sources, then signed off.

I felt very alone.

I packed a day sack and figured I could spent an hour orientating myself in the city before meeting the translator.

The shuttle from the hotel to the city itself was clean and smooth, and the route in was unremarkable. But as we neared the center, I saw what Katerina meant by the preservation.

By 1945, most places the Nazis invaded were reduced to rubble, partly due to their own efforts, but mostly because that was how the allies drove them out. Kraków, though, still retained its medieval ambience even today: its cobbled Main Square surrounded by cafes and dotted with benches set in circles, all overlooked by St Adalbert's Church with its sunken appearance; Florianska Gate, an ornate yet grand curving arch set in the remaining city walls; the baroque architecture, art nouveau windows, modern fountains dancing alongside scholarly redbrick buildings, and the colonnades of a great many bell-towers and ornate clocks rose proudly from the ground. For long stretches of the journey I was on a weekend city break, absorbing the atmosphere and beauty of a classic European destination conducting its daily life, but when the shuttle halted on the edge of the old town, I pulled myself back to the moment, and to the business at hand.

Almost as soon as my feet touched the tarmac off the bus, a message from Jess pinged through, with the address of a woman who might help me: Lucia Rostov. She owned a practice twenty minutes on foot from my current location. Jess had made an appointment with someone who purported to speak English—not unusual for medical professionals, apparently—and who had consulted with English-speaking law enforcement before, albeit not regarding hypnosis. For an elevated fee, she would make time for me in thirty minutes.

I followed the map on my phone, and arrived in fifteen: a single wood-framed door set in a wall between a garlic-heavy butchers and a vinyl record store. A tiny plaque to the right of the door announced four offices, of which Lucia Rostov's name appeared on one gold badge.

The door was unlocked and opened to nothing but a staircase. I trooped up the damp-smelling passage, and out into a recently-painted waiting room, greeted by several chairs and a smoked-glass window in a varnished frame. Figures moved beyond the glass. No bell. I knocked. Someone sighed, and the glass slid open. A woman in a nurse's tunic sat behind a low desk looking up at me.

"Cześć?"

Thanks to the brief Polish lesson on a mobile app, I knew the word pronounced "chreshed" meant "Hello?" As in "Hello, can I help you?"

I said, "Do you speak English?"

"Nie." The "no" preceded her reaching to shut the glass but my smile and step forward paused it. She said, "Czego chcesz?"

Okay, that's all my Polish exhausted.

I pointed at my chest. "Adam Park." Then I gestured at the waiting room. "Lucia Rostov."

The nurse-come-receptionist checked her list and waved her pen in the direction of one of the doors, so I walked over and knocked. Someone called out, and I entered, greeted by a short woman in an itchy-looking woolen dress. She wore glasses and her hair was shoulder-length and jet black.

"I'm Adam Park," I said. "A colleague booked me in."

"Yes, yes," Lucia said. "You want English speaker. Knows hypnosis. Expert, yes?" She wasn't Polish. Russian, maybe, or Ukrainian. "That is me, okay. Very good at hypnosis. Speak good English."

"I just want to run a scenario past you. See if it's feasible."

She indicated I should have a seat. The room was part-shabby-chic office, part examination room, more shabby than chic. The chair she directed me to was a low one beside a coffee table. She sat opposite and crossed her legs.

"What is your scenario?"

"If I wanted to make someone believe they are … possessed … like, by a spirit … and make them hear what I want them to hear … is that something you could help with?"

She stared, frozen in place. "You should leave."

"What?"

"Is joke, yes? You joke with me." She flung herself onto the table on her hands and knees, and slapped my chest up and down. "You wired, yes? This a prank show. TV? You with *Jackass*? I love that show! Where is your camera?"

I hung my arms out to the side. "I'm not wired. I'm not joking."

Up on her haunches, she tilted her head. "Okay, then no. Is not possible."

"Under no circumstances?"

Lucia Rostov shuffled off the table and remained standing, staring down at me like a schoolmarm. "Hypnosis is making brain do what brain is meant to do. If someone wishes to stop smoking, it can help, but if desire to smoke is greater than desire to stop, treatment only lasts short time. If person does not wish to stop, they don't stop. Simple, right?"

"So you can't put them in a trance and persuade them they hate chocolate?"

"No. Not possible. Maybe for short time. *Maybe*. But is like memory retrieval. Suppressed experience. It is unblocking unnatural blocks, enabling patient to fix what is broken. To force someone to do a thing they do not want to do … would require … magic."

I tended to trust Jess more than most people, so there was no reason to doubt the woman's credentials.

She gasped as if a sudden thought popped into life. "Only if brain is altered already can someone use hypnosis to change real thoughts."

"I'm not sure I understand."

"Of course, of course." She tapped her lip. Pacing, she said, "In America, and Africa, and some other places, some believe being gay is disease, or mental illness. And when prayer does not work, they try other things."

"Like hypnosis."

"Yes. But if a person's brain is wired to be gay, person is gay. Is nature, right?"

"Right."

"So, to change that, you change brain to something else. No sexuality, no urges. Take it away." She slowed her speech rhythm, as if remembering from a text. "Cyproterone acetate is used to treat hyper-activity. When you apply this to gay man, then combine with course of hypnosis, there have been some success."

"In 'curing' homosexuality?"

"In gay men stopping finding men attractive. But yet, they do not find lady attractive either, so we conclude drug is more effective than hypnosis. But hypnosis enhances drug's effects."

"But doesn't turn them straight."

She stopped in her tracks. "No. But is the closest example I think of. Or, the closest *documented* example. There are many, many stories. Which is why, I think, you come here to me. You think you possessed? Have bad thoughts about boys?"

I stood.

"Not for me," I said. "A friend is … troubled. And not gay. She … hears voices. From what you say, hypnosis is probably the wrong way to go about this."

"You are correct, Mr. Park. Will that be all?"

"Can I call you if I have any follow-up?"

"As long as you pay bill." She showed me to the door and held out a hand. "My fee?"

"Sure." I dug out my wallet, glad I changed a wad at the hotel. "How much?"

"One hundred."

"Zloty?"

She laughed exaggeratedly. "Euro, silly man." A shade over four hundred in the local Zloty.

I possessed both euros and Zloty, so paid her in euros, exited the building the way I came in, and set my mapping software to locate the archives office.

I wandered the streets for half an hour, shelving my hypnosis theory for now, and wondering how someone could chemically alter the girl before applying such methods. Refuting the notion were two drugs tests, overseen by both sides of the argument: Gottfried, who wanted Estelle to end this nonsense, and Katerina, who actively encouraged her to explore it.

Pushing that aside for now in favor of prepping for the translator and the slog of paperwork ahead, I arrived ten minutes early at a busy thoroughfare skirting the perimeter of a cobblestone expanse, another square featuring a monument to a pre-war figure. A man in his sixties paced the same segment of pavement by the road, aided by a polished walking stick topped by the silver head of an eagle. He was in corduroy trousers, a white shirt, and a leather jacket, a black fedora atop his head, which sprouted grey hair beneath, and swooshed around into a pointed beard. I approached, reasoning if it wasn't him it would only be a moment of awkwardness.

I smiled and said, "Hi, are you…"

I thumbed through my mobile to review the details Jess sent me.

He said, "I am Jäger."

I frowned. "That wasn't the name I was given."

"No, Mr. Park, my name would not be known to you."

I stepped backward. "You're not my translator."

"No, sadly, I am not. Sadly for *you*, anyway."

I noticed the Bluetooth earpiece and his hand signal seconds too late. A van pulled up beside me; white, with a flower shop decal. I turned to the new arrival and set myself firm.

Wrong move.

I should have run.

But no. Gotta stand and fight. That was the instinct. The primal part of me Harry tried to tame so long ago, the caveman, the *beast* that sought to rampage through Bangkok in search of the men who hurt me. We both thought he succeeded, but over the past year the old me started seeping back. The old me had saved my skin more than once lately, but today … today was different.

The side door crashed open and two men piled out, both in ski masks, while the driver's door swung out to allow a third into the street. The type of thugs I'd faced a dozen times before.

I pulled my day sack straps tight, and planned which to attack first, ready to throw him across the path of the second, before pummeling the third.

What actually happened was a wasp stung me in the shoulder. At least, it felt like a wasp. Then fire erupted through my body, my limbs spasmed, and the pavement rushed up and smacked me in the face, and all went black.

CHAPTER SEVEN

I woke in a dentist's chair, upright, my wrists cable-tied to the arms, ankles secured to the footplate. I couldn't feel my extremities, but I was vaguely aware of my fingers moving when I willed them. Thanks to a spotlight aimed right in my face, my head throbbed. Maybe I'd taken a harder impact than I realized, but I was willing to gamble my unconsciousness was due to a Taser ripping into me. I didn't vomit. I hadn't soiled myself.

I blinked away the spots and made out shapes all around: a table to the left of the white glare. When I turned my head and aimed my view at the floor beneath the table, it dulled the light somewhat and I started to make out objects on top of it.

My day sack was empty, and my phone lay beside it, along with my guidebook to Kraków, my wallet with the money spread out, and a raincoat bundled into a bag. You couldn't accuse me of not being prepared.

One thing was missing, though: my notebook.

It was odd that I still preferred writing things down when it came to figuring stuff out, but I had stuck with it for so long I doubted I would ever change. The problem was if I get mugged, robbed, or tased in the back, whoever attacked me knew everything I knew, which is why I developed a shorthand known only to Harry, Jess, and me.

"Adam." Jäger's voice again. "Are you okay?"

I coughed. "Sure. Peachy."

The spotlight shifted down an inch or so, removing the glare from the tabletop. It held more goodies, including three satellite phones, the Taser, and a video monitor showing my face on a live feed. A second monitor ran the same image in what looked like infra-red. Two figures glided behind the light, while a third stepped in front of the bulb, his walking stick clicking on the tiles.

"Adam, what do you know of the Devouring?"

My standard response here should have been, "I could go for a burger right about now," but this was a professional operation. The diversion, the Taser, the swift snatch from the street. And the tech was impressive too, which led me to wonder what lurked here. Bravado would only prolong whatever they had planned.

"Adam," Jäger said kindly. "Please answer."

"The Devouring," I said. "I don't know what that is."

"You did not study World War II history at school?"

"We learned about the Holocaust, Britain versus Germany, the occupation of France."

Jäger pulled up a plastic folding chair and sat to the side of the spotlight. He rested his elbows on his knees, my notebook in his hands. He leaned over it. I hadn't pinpointed his accent yet. Germanic, if not outright German. A little like Herman the lawyer, but throatier.

He said, "The Devouring was the Gypsies' equivalent of the Holocaust. *O Porajmos*. Hitler, you see, hated them almost as much as the Jews. For different reasons. The Jews, he saw as dangerous, both politically and socially. But Gypsies were simply vermin to him." He leafed through the book. "A shame schoolchildren only learn of one genocide. I am reminded of that period of history whenever I observe Muslims and Africans subjected to the same taunts and accusations today—danger, vermin … 'taking over'. I predict another genocide approaching, if the wrong groups attain power."

I tested my bindings and found no room to move. "You didn't bring me here to test my knowledge of the war."

"If I had, you would have failed quite miserably." He looked up from the notebook. "I am a Jew. Although I have Romani blood."

I lay my head back. "You're with the LaPortes."

"Not at all," he said. "I have Romani *blood*, dating back several generations. I am not Romani now. As I said, I am a Jew. We fled Germany and settled in Israel, but I still hold the Fatherland in my heart. To a degree."

"You're not old enough," I said.

"Thank you. No, not old enough to recall all of those horrors. I was but a boy when my family left, yet I feel true affinity for *all* those who suffered at the hands of evil men." He returned to my book. "The Jewish people saw six million of their brethren slaughtered by the Nazi machine, but the Devouring, as a percentage of population, murdered even more gypsies. Estimates put their losses at five hundred thousand souls. Around half of their entire number in Europe at the time. Some put the total higher, but records are incomplete. Still, half an entire race."

"Again, I'm not here for a history lesson."

"Actually, you are." He snapped the book closed. "At least in part. You need to understand certain things before you can go forward."

That he wanted me to go forward gave me some encouragement.

I said, "Then how about you get to the point?"

"The people who send me on these jaunts have little interest in Roma. They take little interest in such things, unless they cross over with matters pertaining to the Jewish community. And this case of yours, it crosses over."

"I'm not hearing a point here."

Jäger sighed. "For a man tied to a chair, you are making a lot of demands."

"Yeah, I'm standing up a perfectly good translator right now. Pretty sure I've lost my deposit."

Jäger waved my notebook. "We have operatives who can break this code, but I would prefer you to cooperate."

"Sure. What do you need?"

"I want you to tell me everything about this case."

"You know what I'm going to say."

"Does the word 'confidential' enter into things?"

"Spot on … what was your name? Jäger?"

"That is a shame." He beckoned towards the light. "If you won't answer me, perhaps you will talk to my colleagues."

The two figures emerged from behind the spotlight. One was a man in cargo pants, black vest, and what I took to be military boots. The base of his neck was wider than the top of his head, and his shoulders were like boulders, which was in keeping with the rest of his physique. Like him, the woman was deeply tanned, possibly Middle Eastern or Mediterranean. She had long dark hair, and wore a more businesslike suit than either Jäger or Boulder-Shoulder, moving with an easy grace that only came with complete and utter confidence in her surroundings.

I said, "If you know I'm working this case, you already know the salient facts."

"Indeed," Jäger replied. "But there are details. We like details."

"Look, I was approached by a lawyer to dig into a family tree. Nothing more."

"I do not think so, Mr. Park. A man like you is not employed to leaf through dusty archives and write reports."

"Believe what you like. I never intended to get involved with the bastards who built this annoying reputation of mine. I'm not a violent person. I don't seek it out."

"But it finds you," the woman said with a strong lilt to her voice—I assumed Israeli. "And you deal with it oh-so-well."

"If I'm such a dangerous person, why risk antagonizing me?"

Jäger's mouth pulled back in amusement to reveal yellowing teeth. "Because we are far more dangerous than you. As you are about to discover. Unless you explain, in full, exactly what you are doing, and why."

Call it pigheadedness, call it bravado, or simply the ethics of my trade, but I knew right then I could not give up the information without a fight.

"Last chance," Jäger said. "You do not want Clara to start asking these questions."

"I can't break their confidence. If I do, where will it end?"

"A shame." Jäger used his silver-headed walking stick to push upright. "We will prepare."

The three Israelis turned in unison, almost like it had been rehearsed, or they had conducted themselves in such a way many times before, and as they walked back behind the powerful spots, two of the thugs who snatched me earlier came forward and stood watching me, their hands clasped before them like nightclub bouncers.

When some unseen door closed, I said, "So what happens now?"

They gave no reply, so I lay back, and waited to see what Clara would bring to my questioning.

CHAPTER EIGHT

THE RENT-A-THUGS barely looked at one another as they communicated in Polish. If this were a close-knit gang, my suffering would have made them happy—a shuck of the shoulder here, a backslap there—but I saw none of this. They were clearly not military, but nor did they flinch at the threat of violence, marking a level of detachment reserved for the criminal underclasses.

So where did that leave me?

No pity for a victim.

No camaraderie between them.

Thugs rather than professional hit men or soldiers.

They were more than likely *literally* rented. A few hundred euros dropped into the hands of dodgy types hanging on street corners, monitoring working girls or drug deals, hired for their size and their willingness to get physical with innocent people if the price was right.

And the professor looked well dressed, his two shadows too. Satellite comms, HD screens, and 4k video cameras. Obtaining a place this size, in the middle of what I assumed was nowhere, wasn't cheap either, so finance didn't appear to be a problem.

Maybe they were preparing to offer me a bribe? Did they usually strap people to dentists' chairs when about to shower a detective with cash?

Within half an hour, Clara and her boulder-shouldered pet stepped inside and dismissed the rent-a-thugs. Boulder-Shoulder carried two jerry cans, while Clara swung a towel beside her. Which could mean only one thing.

"You can talk now or talk later," Clara said.

"I already told you I can't say anything."

The truth was, British private investigators are not licensed, nor are they committed to a confidentiality pledge. Not in law, anyway. I'd signed some papers before I left the Kravitz estate, but that mostly pertained to legal waivers in the event I suffered an irreparable paper cut during my time in the archives. I owed them nothing, especially now I was bound to a chair preparing for two rather grim looking people to interrogate me in an enhanced manner. I didn't know if Herman or Gottfried or even Katerina were aware of this third-party, but I did know if I gave up all I knew before they had at least probed me physically, I would have nowhere else to go. If I spilled my guts too soon, they would continue until they were certain I was spent.

"Abba," Clara said, "let's start."

As her colleague carried the jerry cans behind me, I said, "Wait. Your real name is Abba?"

Abba did not reply. Instead, Clara said, "Yes, his name is Abba. Yes, like the band. Do not bother with the jokes. We have heard them all before."

"This isn't exactly a joking situation. And there is no point doing whatever it is you're planning. I can't say any more than I have. Unless it's to lay all your love on me."

Abba's meaty hand pressed on the chair's headrest. I tilted back so my feet pointed at the ceiling, blood rushing into my head already.

"Come on," I said. "You don't need to do this."

Clara joined her friend, so I was looking up at her. She said, "Open your hands. I am placing two objects in your palms."

I obeyed.

Two metal tubes touched my skin, and I although I had seen videos of such methods, I dared do nothing except close my fingers around them. They were cold and heavy.

Clara said, "When you are ready to talk, drop them."

She folded the towel in half lengthways, and pulled it tight over my face. I tried to speak again, to plead for them to stop, but the soft material swallowed my words.

Without removing the towel, Clara said, "Anytime you wish to talk, I am ready to listen."

Nothing happened for another five seconds. Five seconds in which I hoped they would reveal they were bluffing, and that I would not have to experience discomfort I only knew of on an academic level. Then a deep thudding sounded in my ears, followed by a massive scream. The pained wail of a guitar solo rang out, and the drumbeat and screaming singer joined up in a death metal anthem, the speakers straining to contain it.

My nose filled with water.

It hit my sinuses hard and I tried to cough, but I could take in no air. My eyes stung. My head overflowed with water, spilling down my throat. I thrashed like a shark caught on a cable and hook. I'd heard waterboarding described as "simulated drowning," but this was no simulation. I *was* drowning. Literally underwater, nowhere to go.

I opened my hands, and the clangs of the tubes hitting the tiles sounded over the death metal.

Instantly, the chair tipped upright, the towel whipped away, and I coughed and spluttered. The music switched off, and when my vision cleared, Jäger sat in front of me in the same chair as before.

"Why?" I managed.

"Because when a family like the Kravitzes engage in matters relating to a period in history that is quickly being forgotten, myself and my friends need to be sure justice is being done. We need to be sure the wrong people do not benefit from the deaths of six million innocent Jews."

I inhaled deeply through my mouth and exhaled through my nose, emitting more snot than water. "Don't forget the half million gypsies."

"Ah, so perhaps you are starting to understand."

"Partly. What I don't understand is why you care this much."

"The human brain can only comprehend up to 150 people in one place at one time. The number six million, or even as you say half a million, cannot truly be absorbed into our consciousness. There is an experiment schoolchildren do, where they line up an arm's length apart, and work out how much space each child takes up. You have thirty children in a line taking up approximately thirty to forty meters. Then, they return to class, and work out, if they were to stand each victim of the Holocaust next to one another, how far would their chain stretch from London. Do you know the answer, Mr. Park?"

"Free my hands and bring me a calculator. And an atlas."

"Delhi, Mr. Park. The chain of dead people would start in London, and end in Delhi. In India."

"As opposed to Delhi in Germany?"

Jäger waved a hand towards Clara, and the chair tipped back again.

"Wait," I said.

But nobody was listening. Clara pinned the damp towel to my face. Jäger said, "Ten more seconds," and the deafening music commenced. I held my breath. And then the water came.

My nose filled, my eyes bulged, my lungs burned. I thrashed and I thrashed, and I felt the skin on my wrists tear, but still I could not surface. I kicked my legs as if that would help me rise into fresh air, and I slapped the chair arms as I would in submission during a sparring session.

The music ended and again the chair wrenched upright, and the towel fell off me. I coughed, snorted, oddly disappointed at the tiny amount of water dripping into my lap.

Jäger had not moved. "Are you ready to talk?"

I was ready to talk three seconds into the first round. But I had to make those glib comments and irritate him.

"Estelle Kravitz," I said. "She thinks the soul of Petr Caine is telling her to give up the family fortune, and divert it to a Romani family."

"The LaPortes," Jäger said.

"See? You do know a lot."

Clara clipped me around the back of the head. "You are the one who brought them up earlier."

Right. I thought Jäger was one of them. "Estelle disappeared from her home a while ago. Turned out she was paying the LaPortes a visit."

"Yes," Jäger said, "that matches with our research. It is not new information. But this ... spirit is interesting. Tell me more."

"The spirit is telling Estelle something happened, something Petr would have had knowledge of, so that's all I'm doing here. Researching the property. If there is some claim going back prior to Katerina and Petr owning the land, maybe there is a genuine claim for the Roma."

Jäger ran his hand over his beard, a frown wrinkling his forehead. "Property? That is the breadth of your imagination?"

"Well, since the Angel of Kraków only talks to Estelle and Katerina, that's all I have to go on."

"The Angel of Kraków. What do you know of this woman?"

"Probably not as much as you, judging by the way your face lit up."

"What of the girl's father?"

I swallowed back a burp containing the odor of vomit. Examined my wrists: deep creases, some grazed skin, but no blood as I'd feared.

I said, "Gottfried is concerned for her welfare. But if the Roma induced her with some drug, or are playing games with her psychologically, or even blackmail, all that matters as far as Gottfried sees it, is the legal implications of what Estelle is saying. Everything else will work itself out."

Jäger pushed himself up on the silver eagle, and dragged his chair closer to me. He sat, patted my leg, and asked, "Why deny the prospect of Petr Caine imparting such wisdom?"

"I do not see how I can possibly prove that one way or another, so I won't bother trying. What I will do is figure out what the hell is going on with her. Whether Gottfried wants me to or not."

Clara faced me. "Even though it is not your job?"

Here's where I started pushing my luck, where the old instinct kicked in. Here's where I would ascertain how serious these people were, and how much of an impact they might have.

I said, "Because of you."

"Me?"

"If you hadn't snatched me, I would currently be buried under a mountain of early twentieth century paperwork. But now I'm curious. Because if there's more to this, more at play that could damage my client, I'm going to find it. And I'm going to end it."

They didn't seem particularly scared.

Jäger said, "Tell me about the rest of the family."

"Tell me about Israel's interest in this."

The professor waved his hand again, but as soon as Abba's fingers gripped the chair, I said, "Okay, okay. Not again."

Abba paused.

Since nobody moved, and I was not subjected to the sensation of drowning, I talked. I told them about the current family, about the skiing in-laws, and about the tragic deaths of Katerina's daughters and sons-in-law along the way. I told them what I knew about Elizabetta—the Angel of Kraków—and I even emphasized hypnosis was an impossible answer to Estelle's supernatural possession.

When I finished, Jäger observed me with the manner of a cat trying to decide if the mouse carcass he was playing with might spring up and punch him on the nose. It was Clara who spoke first, having come to a conclusion ahead of the old man.

"He's done," she said.

"Agreed," Jäger replied. "Take him for recovery, then bring him to me. I will explain to him exactly how he will proceed from here."

"If I don't feel like being used that way?" I asked.

"Then we will have to find a more … permanent solution."

Jäger exited swiftly, his stick clicking and clacking on the tiles, and the two rent-a-thugs elbowed their way in, almost getting stuck together in the doorway. It would've been comical had I not been exhausted and already flashing on images of my drowning. Clara and Abba left me alone with the pair of steroid abusing bouncers, who cut me loose and helped me down to the floor.

The third fella, the driver, came in and crouched at my level. I lifted my head, as heavy as if I'd been drugged, and he said in broken English, "You play nice. You live. You give trouble, you die." To punctuate, he showed me his hand in which was nestled, a small silver hunting knife with a serrated top. "I cut you. I like it."

I nodded my head, and let them take me wherever they wanted, so they wouldn't hurt me anymore.

CHAPTER NINE

THEY HALF DRAGGED me down a windowless corridor, lit by the sort of work lamps hanging from the walls in coal mines. The ceiling was held up with two-by-fours, and appeared well maintained, albeit made of wood. Soil had drifted down from between the slats, meaning we'd been underground all along. We reached a similarly wooden staircase, where the muscles in my legs were sort of working again, and I moved them in a semblance of ascending under my own steam, flanked and supported on both sides. We followed Knife Guy into an office with a desk, a rickety wooden chair, a battered laptop, and several pens, pencils and writing pads. They tossed me onto a cracked leather sofa, and the two stood back while Knife Guy showed me the blade again.

He said, "You rest now. Professor will ask for you. Decide if you go home or not."

I could only nod.

"They do you good," he added. "You drop sticks after seven seconds. Most surrender at five. But then you go back for more."

I didn't have the heart to tell him the second round was a mistake.

"It's all about desire," I said. "If you hold something you really don't want to give up, no amount of torture will pry it loose. But if the information is of little value, then the desire to make the torture end overrides your desire to keep your secrets. So if a parent knows cracking will kill their child, you can drown them, pull their nails out, smash their feet with a hammer, it won't matter."

"You speak fast," the knife guy said. "But I think I understand. If torture not work, why you told them?"

"Because nothing I told them placed anyone in danger. I told them nothing useful, except for them to understand someone else's business."

"Okay. Sure. You a tough guy. You tell yourself all that."

Knife Guy strutted out, leaving me alone with Tweedledum and Tweedledee. Waiting to be summoned by the professor. *To explain to me exactly how we will proceed from here.* My kidnapper, dictating the terms of my release. And if I didn't like those terms, I would have little recourse, little option but to comply.

A more permanent solution.

I asked for water, and they brought me some, along with a portion of bread and cheese I didn't order, and they returned my shoes. Which was nice of them. Although they kept hold of my bag.

It took me half an hour to feel human again, thirty minutes of replaying my interrogation, of sanitizing what they did to me, and playing up my cowardice. What I told Knife Guy was true, but only to an extent. Yes, people will endure real torture, but when you factor in the human need to survive, it was easy to see why even hardened terrorists gave up what they knew. Especially when the intelligence would not impact their families, or their cause at large.

Perhaps if I was braver I would have hung around voluntarily. Pumped the professor for information as he laid out his orders, and learned what I could before pretending to agree to his terms. But at the prospect of remaining here another moment, of risking further torture, risking death, every limb jittered, my thighs heavy and begging to run. It left me no further options.

I requested another glass of water. The slightly smaller of the two acquiesced, taking my glass to the corner where the cooler provided. I coughed as I had in the chair, and held my hand to my gut and doubled over. The remaining thug dashed to my side.

As soon as he put his hand on my shoulder and babbled in Polish—probably meaning "you okay?"—I gripped his wrist, pulled down, and maneuvered his elbow upwards. He pitched forward and face planted the rough floorboard. I jammed my heel into his upper back, twisted his arm, and his shoulder popped out of the joint. He screamed.

The first guy ran at me, proving my guess about his professionalism true, and I used his speed to my advantage. I stepped back, slapped his reaching arm away, and drove my elbow into his face. I barely had to swing. His momentum crushed his nose and blood spattered down his top. I swung my foot at his stomach and slammed my knee through the side of his head, knocking him unconscious.

I dashed to the door, greeted by Knife Guy, whose blade was, thankfully, already in his hand. *Thankfully*, because it made him over-confident. He drove it towards me. I sidestepped and guided his leading hand so the knife impacted the door frame. He still held onto it, but now I controlled his movements. I maneuvered him headfirst into the frame where his knife had been moments earlier, twisted his wrist so his arm turned to jelly, and stabbed his own knife into his chest an inch beneath the collarbone.

He dropped, more out of shock than trauma. The blade would have missed any major organs, including his heart and lungs, but a knife sticking out of one's chest is terrifying, to say the least.

I wasn't about to go back down, mainly because Abba and Clara clearly had access to guns, so I headed upwards. This staircase was steel rather than wood. An old construct, black paint peeling to reveal the grey metal beneath. I took the steps on tiptoes, favoring stealth over speed. At the top, I found a pale blue door ajar.

It opened to the touch.

The hinges creaked.

I poked my head out and pulled it back in immediately. Assessed what I saw.

It wasn't much; certainly no danger.

I pushed the door open fully and stepped into a well-lit room that must once have been a kitchen. Granite work surfaces, a cement floor with linoleum sections still in evidence, and a deep ceramic sink had been wrenched from the wall, to reveal all pipework was missing. Windows lacked glass, and only fragments of the previous fixtures remained.

Conscious of three other potential killers in the vicinity, I hurried through the only exit and into an untamed field of grass and wildflowers. I glanced back to the building: like any old large house fallen into disrepair. Abandoned, and looted by opportunists. At least, that's how it was supposed to look.

The field went on as far as I could see, so I rounded the property, finding trees a hundred yards from the blindside of the house. I paused. Listened.

A light wind.

Birds.

And engines in the distance.

Meaning a road. Or I really was in the middle of nowhere, and what I could hear was a generator. Either way, I had to take a chance.

So I ran. Not quite fast enough to outpace a bullet should they fire on me, and I questioned if this was the wisest course of action. The professor indicated he would let me go, after all. But there were no guarantees. No benefit to me beyond hoping they slipped up an gave me some clue as to who they were or what they really wanted.

Fat chance of that.

Out of breath by the time I reached the tree line, I checked nobody followed. No gunshots rang out, no one yelling at me to stop, which was useful, since I had to lean against a tree thirty seconds after my sprint, nowhere close to having recovered properly.

Again, I listened.

Definitely an engine.

I jogged onwards, careful not to hobble myself via a root or branch. Twenty minutes later, I pushed out onto a Tarmac surface thirty feet wide with a broken white line down the middle. I never thought I would be so happy to see a road.

I checked the sun. Low in the sky, so despite having no timepiece or phone, I guessed it was late afternoon, and even though I knew I must look like utter crap, something of a disheveled loon, I started jogging again, taking a 50-50 chance on the direction, and sticking out my thumb at every passing vehicle until an eighteen-wheeler driver was kind enough to give me a lift back into Kraków.

CHAPTER TEN

I ARRIVED BACK in Kraków's Old Town by sundown, thanked the non-English-speaking Romanian trucker with much nodding and thumbs up, and took a taxi out to my hotel. I was embarrassed I no longer possessed my wallet, but the cab driver waited happily until I sorted out some cash. First, I explained to the receptionist I had lost my key card, then once I gained access to my room I logged on to my Western Union account, and transferred five thousand euros to the hotel's bureau de change, where I collected it in small bills. The transfer would have flagged in a law enforcement server somewhere, but I was now a cash-only guy. The taxi driver charged me an extra twenty euros for the wait.

In my room I checked myself over: dirty, but had looked far worse in the recent past, my face ruddy and glowing, like I'd imbued an excess of local beverages, but my beard hid a lot. Understandably, my hair spread all over the place, and the bags under my eyes sagged so heavily they'd command an excess charge on a shortfall flight. With a chair jammed under the door handle, I showered the grime off me, then set up my

MacBook, which I'd thankfully left in the hotel room, and planned what to say to Jess.

She answered my third attempt to FaceTime her, and sounded rather exasperated down what was clearly her mobile phone. She was walking, dressed nice.

"I'm heading out for cocktails," she said. "You have to do your own research. And what the hell gives you the right to stand up my—"

"I was attacked," I said.

"What are you talking about?"

"Attacked. Guys coming up to me on the street, stuffing me in a van, waterboarding me, before I get to enjoy a cross-country jog, and hitchhike back into Kraków. Clear enough?"

She stopped. In the middle of the street. Fellow commuters swept by her, some grumbling. There is little Londoners enjoy more than somebody stopping dead on a busy thoroughfare.

Jess said, "Can't you go anywhere without winding people up?"

"That's nice. Blame the victim."

"Since I don't see any scars or bruises, and the fact you're back in the same hotel room as this morning, I'd suggest you came out okay. Now why are you calling? Because I'm not getting involved in anything heavy. I'm meeting Mike at seven."

I wasn't sure if she was playing with me, or if she thought I was exaggerating what happened. This wasn't like her. Usually, she would bend over backwards to help me, so I hated laying on the guilt.

"The same people who took me learned everything about Estelle and her family."

"How?" she asked.

"Because I told them."

"Why did you do that?"

"Did you miss the bit when I mentioned waterboarding? Because it wasn't nice."

"And I'm blaming the victim again?"

"Yeah, you should stop doing that. It's demeaning."

Jess shifted into the doorway of a store locking up for the night. A shoe shop by the looks of it. "Are you serious? All this happened today?"

"Yes. I'm not kidding. I got kidnapped, waterboarded, and I escaped."

Whispering, she said, "Did you kill anyone?"

"Left one guy unconscious, but I didn't stick around to assess the damage. Another guy took a blade, but I missed all the serious organs, so unless infection sets in, he'll recover. Mostly."

"What do you want from me?"

"I don't know how serious they were," I said. "I don't even know why they wanted the info. But they were well equipped, and dedicated. Israelis, maybe Mossad, no way to tell. So considering the worst case scenario, I want to go scorched earth. I need protection for the family. Especially Estelle."

"You think they'll go after the kid?"

"They asked a lot of questions about Estelle. The old guy in particular, Professor Jäger, he played up the supernatural mumbo-jumbo Katerina Caine seems to believe in. He also talked about the 'wrong people' benefiting financially from the war. If they think Estelle is giving money away to the unde-serving, earned fairly by an oppressed Jew, that may not go down well."

Jess sighed but I couldn't see it because she dropped her hand in exasperation, so my screen filled with a dimly lit upside-down shelf full of overpriced shoes.

She raised the phone, her face filling the screen. "Come

home, Adam. I'll call Harry, and he'll meet you at the airport—"

"Why are you even trying? You know what my answer will be."

Again, the screen travelled away from her face, in this case ending on a damp pavement. When she came back, she said, "You're asking me to get hold of your old friends, aren't you?"

"They're not my friends," I said. My fists balled either side of the MacBook. "I don't *want* them involved. But at short notice, they're our best option."

I thought our connection had frozen. Turned out she was just thinking about it. "I'll tell Mike we'll do it another time. I'll be home in fifteen minutes. You take care of yourself until then."

She hung up.

I spent the next quarter of an hour on the computer, cancelling my cards, checking if the Find My Phone app was working, disappointed to see it wasn't, which meant either there was no Wi-Fi or phone coverage wherever the professor was hiding, or the phone had been comprehensively destroyed.

FaceTime trilled with an unfamiliar number. I worried it was the professor trying to trace me, but I reminded myself of Jess's efficiency, and clicked the green "answer" icon.

Hugo Hunter's face loomed, and his broad Scottish tone hummed out of the speakers. "Oh ho-ho, how the hell are ya?"

As if we were old buddies catching up.

I said, "I have a job for you that doesn't involve killing anyone."

"It must involve killing *someone*, otherwise you wouldn't be callin' us."

His wife, Emiliana, appeared at his shoulder. "Oh wow, you weren't joking. It's really him."

Their apartment looked like that of any middle-aged

cosmopolitan couple, except within almost every fixture, in every room, I imaged a false panel containing a gun, ready to shoot their way out should an enemy track them down. I met the pair in Greece before Christmas, and although they helped bring my case to a conclusion, the price I paid thanks to their sociopathic methods was still a high one.

"I'll pay your regular fees," I said. "But this is a protection job. Any killing is an absolute last resort."

Hugo saluted. "Oh, absolutely, I get you." He winked twice. "No killing."

I rubbed my head, suddenly dog tired.

"I think he's serious," Emiliana said.

"I am serious," I said. "I could go the legal route, but I'm not sure how well-connected the threat is. Are you taking the job or not?"

Hugo rubbed his chin faux-thoughtfully. "I dunno. I mean, you did get Emmy shot last time."

"You said they wouldn't hit a cow's arse with a banjo at that range. And you're the experts, so don't blame it on me."

Emiliana shoved him aside. "He's messing with you. We already checked with Fanuco if it's okay to contract out."

"You're freelancers."

"It's a sorta retainer. He's our main guy, but as long as we're not working for his competition, he's alright with it. Especially since it's you."

I still didn't understand Vila Fanuco's fascination with me. He believed I was of his breed, but I was not. He was a well-connected, ruthless criminal, with his fingers in so many businesses, he'd probably lost count himself. A seasoned fighter, remorseless killer, and highly intelligent businessman; I didn't want to be around him. I certainly didn't want to be like him. And the only reason I was in touch with this pair was out of desperation.

Hugo said, "By the way, Fanuco asked us tae pass on a message. An offer. Says if you need him tae sort out that Roger Gorman prick, just say the word."

"Fanuco knows I want nothing to do with him," I replied. "All I need is your expertise. This is a business transaction, not a holiday."

The pair grinned.

Emiliana said, "I'm guessin' it'll be more of a holiday than the last time we got together."

"So you're on board?"

"Well let's think fer a second," Hugo said. "Big house, servants on tap, good beer."

"Great. Send your account numbers through, and get on the first plane to Hamburg."

I hung up.

Yeah, it was a terse closing, but I wanted to keep this as formal as possible. Now, with the Israeli group in possession of my credit cards, and judging by their resources, they would track me to this place, if they hadn't already.

As tired as I was, it took me less than five minutes to pack, and then I was out the door, and into the night.

CHAPTER ELEVEN

LEAVING ONLY a fake driver's license acquired last year and a generous wad of cash, I hired a ten-year-old Renault Clio near the airport and, using a freshly-purchased iPhone as a satnav, moved on from my airport location. Around nine p.m., I booked into a hotel whose name translated as "The Firebrand", in a part of town not covered on my new guidebook. Yes, Professor Jäger even kept my Lonely Planet. I hoped he found it useful, but if I were writing an entry on my latest accommodation, the words "earthy," "urban," and "by the hour," would feature heavily.

Although my notebook was also missing, I still held the information emailed by Herman, which detailed the locations of various contacts, so the sensible thing was to investigate the other interested parties. Since Professor Jäger and his friends seemed rather shy in terms of sharing intel, my next move was to pick up where Estelle left off.

The Roma camp where she absconded to several weeks earlier was located five miles outside the city. It served as a stopping off point for travelers passing through the country, or for reconnecting with family members who worked on the site. One of only a handful of permanent settlements across the continent, Kraków residents knew the location of these perennially under suspicion people at any point, and were fairly confident they would not rock up on their land on their way to somewhere else.

I knew little about gypsies. Or "Roma" or even—in the UK—"the Traveler community." I heard many negative things, such as how dirty they are, how crime spikes when a new group gathers in a residential area, and how they were fiercely protective of their heritage and lifestyle. So with my limited knowledge, when I arrived at ten p.m. in what amounted to a wide concrete parking lot, I had no idea what to expect.

It serviced a campsite-like set of caravans, mobile homes, and—disappointingly—only one ostentatiously decorated horse-drawn home.

I sometimes lived out of a VW camper, and other times out of a canal barge. I love my camper van. It was my home for many years, but I could never see it as a permanent arrangement. Until last summer, I'd been making a circuit of the UK's coastline, surfing, rock climbing, just bumming around, sheltering from Roger Gorman and the others who were seeking to drag my company into the murky realms of bad corporate ethics. Yet, every so often, I would simply *have* to indulge myself in a hotel to iron out the kinks and indulge in a proper shower.

Okay, fine, a bubble bath.

I parked in the first space I found, climbed out, and really wished I'd brought a translator with me. The first chap I came across, when I asked if he spoke English, shook his head and laughed, then shrugged his shoulders and walked away.

Herman said the elders, and the more well-travelled-members of the LaPortes would probably speak some English, along with French, Spanish, and German, such was their need to communicate wherever they went, so I remained hopeful of being able to hold a conversation.

I played a hunch, and walked by the others milling around the parking area, and headed straight for the homes. Specifically, the ornately-decorated wooden caravan that would require the absent horse to move it. The other caravans were modern and those closest to the wooden one even sported flowerbeds around half their perimeters. People sat on their stoops, light jackets and shawls against the chill of a spring evening, smoking, drinking beer or hot beverages, all watching me in silence. A handful of children in vests and shorts paused in their late-night soccer match to watch as I ascended the three steps and knocked on the door.

The children gasped. The tallest picked up the ball, and led the others to a different area of the camp.

One tall thirty-something chap with hands the size of shovels stood in the doorway of his home, while his neighbor —a younger woman in a headscarf—stubbed out her cigarette, and her hands disappeared beneath her dark blue shawl.

Perhaps it was past the occupants' bedtime.

Rummaging sounded from within, and the door opened. A woman of around sixty, wearing a yellow headscarf stretched her head out like a turtle.

"Speak English?" I asked, immediately annoyed at my pidgin-English tone.

"You from Hamburg?" Her voice was strained, as if her neck might have cracked at any moment.

"Yes, sort of." I glanced at the observers, who hadn't moved. Back to the woman. "I am working on behalf of Estelle Kravitz, and I'm looking for Vera LaPorte."

"Why you want her for?"

"I have no agenda. I'm taking no sides. My job is to establish the truth, and nothing else." It was a line I had repeated far too often already—to Jess, to Harry, to my torturers. "If you could let me know where I can find her, and possibly…" I referred to my new notebook in which I had jotted points to remember. "Marco. I'd love to speak with him as well."

The woman stepped out. Her outfit could have leapt straight from a fancy dress shop with the label "Gypsy Princess" emblazoned on the package: chunky jewelry, loose white blouse, breezy skirt with gold trim and sequins.

"I am Vera." She raised her chin to Shovel-Hands, whose legs reached the floor in one go, and within half a dozen strides he was almost upon us. "This is Marco."

I held out my hand and said, "Hi. Adam Park."

Marco's hand engulfed mine and with one huge yank I was on the floor.

Vera called, "Marco, nie!"

He glared down at me, ignorant of the fact I was less than a second from kicking out his kneecap had Vera not ordered him to control himself. His fingers slackened, allowing me to pull free. I stood, dusted myself off and affected a brief laugh.

"Phew," I said. "Glad the misunderstanding is over. So."

Marco's head tilted to the side. "So … what?"

I pointed and winked. "Down, big guy." He was a head taller than me, making him close to six-foot-five, maybe six-seven. "Okay, so, I just need to ask a few questions. Once we're all satisfied, we can take it back to Hamburg and start working on your claim."

I had suddenly transformed into a social worker, using placating language to get them to chat; "we" can take it back, "your" claim. Smile. Eye contact. Open body language. Refusing to allow my second physical assault of the day to get my blood up.

"Marco, make some tea," Vera said. "We will join you."

Marco mooched away, bypassing his own abode, while the surrounding residents' attention lingered on me.

Vera said, "Wait. Then we walk."

The old woman ducked inside, returning wrapped in a bulky Saltrock ski jacket, white with orange trim. She descended the stairs smoothly and strode past me, which I assumed meant I was to follow. I kept up, aware of the audience as we progressed, a cross between a campsite and a residential street, the neighbors nosing out as a cop accompanied a much-respected resident to their gate in handcuffs.

"You are honest man?" Vera asked.

"As honest as any, I suppose."

"What that mean?"

"It means if I told you I had never lied to anyone, it would be a lie."

She emitted a noise in her throat, which may have been an expression of humor, but was closer to scoffing at my pat response. "Honest men do not work for lawyers. Honest men do not knock on my door this late and ask questions. I am a tired old woman."

"You don't move like a tired old woman," I said.

She was keeping step at my regular walking pace.

"No flattery," she said. "Will not work on me."

We rounded a static caravan with no lights on, and found Marco at the end tending a fire in a trashcan. On top, a grill held a kettle, and to the side a small table with three folding chairs waited, with three large white cups on saucers.

"Expecting company?" I said.

Her eyes narrowed to slits. "Always."

I passed the end of the caravan, Vera a step or two behind, and two further Romani men eased away from the aluminum wall, both beefcake types with non-designer-stubble and too-tight tee shirts. They folded their arms but made no move on me.

"They speak no English," Marco said. "Do not try to bribe. Or threaten."

"Wouldn't dream of it." I sat on a chair and Marco gestured for me to stand.

I obeyed.

Vera swanned by and lowered herself to the chair I vacated, and inspected the kettle. It was cast iron with a wooden handle. She removed the lid and stirred with a long-handled spoon, then replaced the covering. Her hands slapped her thighs, and Marco pressed on my shoulder. I sat next to Vera and Marco took the chair on my other side.

The Beefcake twins remained in place. The soccer match played out of sight, voices interspersed with the *thwack* of a foot striking the ball. Beyond the trashcan fire, two more rows of caravans lined up, some with lights, others in darkness, a darkness spanning to where fields spread out for a quarter-mile, ending at the permanent homes of a small town called Hoj.

If anything went bad, I would shove past the old lady, kick over the fire in Marco's direction, and sprint directly ahead, hoping the house-owners would help a kindly fellow in need.

Vera said, "In answer to your question, Adam Park, cousin Estelle called to inform of your arrival. I expect you sooner."

"I had a prior appointment," I said. "Professor Jäger. You know him?"

Vera's expression did not change, but Marco shifted. An eye from Vera silenced whatever he was about to say, and Vera asked me, "What can we tell you?"

"Why do you really think you have a claim on the Kravitz money?"

She smiled. "Because Estelle Kravitz say so."

"But you're preparing a legal challenge. You must have more than the word of a young girl."

"Young *woman*," Marco said. "Old for 'girl' I think."

"Semantics." I shrugged. "What makes you think you can win a case like that? DNA already showed a distant family connection, but couldn't prove the heir."

"Marco is the heir," she said. "And he will share with his family. All his family." She spread her arms to indicate the camp.

"So explain it to me."

The flames flickered orange through the grill and the holes at the trashcan's base. The kettle bubbled. Vera wrapped a cloth around one hand and lifted the lid again, stirring, inhaling the vapors.

She said, "Is not the business of outsiders to question how we conduct our affairs."

"Yet you were ready with this little setup for me. The traditional dress, the tea session that's at least partly ceremonial—I noticed you have electricity here—all supposed to take advantage of my preconceptions about you."

She jammed the lid back in place. "This morning. We think you come this morning. Or this afternoon. Marco."

Marco jumped to attention and poured three cups from the kettle. Nobody spoke while Vera handed one cup and saucer to me, then one to Marco. I sipped the tea. Like regular tea, but a tad sweeter.

When Vera replaced her cup on the saucer, she said, "We do not wish to be rude, or threaten. I know how people look at us, at *Romanipen*."

"Romanipen?" I said.

"The Romani way. How we live."

"I don't care about any of that. I only want—"

"The truth, yes. We hear this before. But we have no use of *their* truths."

The fire danced in her eyes. Someone moved behind, sending a shadow into a jerking stretch over her shoulder. Then another shifted, and I dodged aside, expecting a blow from one of the Beefcakes. But neither had moved an inch.

I said, "I assure you, no matter what I learn, it will be disclosed to all parties."

"Even if your master forbids it?" Marco said.

"I don't have a master."

Vera leaned forward, gesturing with the cup, her lip curled up. "Everyone answers to someone."

Again, I sensed a presence reach for me, *past* me, the air cooling on my neck. A breeze, I guessed, narrowed by the valley of aluminum caravans.

I said, "If I do, it isn't Gottfried Kravitz. Or Herman Prinz."

She held my eye as she raised the cup and sipped. Replaced it with a clink, and set the saucer down. Then she stared at the fire. Whether a trick of the light or my sheer exhaustion, the night around her seemed to shimmer.

"We know the game Katerina is playing," she said. "And we can prove it."

"Tell me," I said, unable to imagine what possible subterfuge that frail woman could enact.

"No," Marco said. "You will bury her."

I had no standing, no track-record of this sort of thing, and I didn't think another promise would carry much weight.

I said, "If you tell me, I will hold it in the strictest confidence. Does it concern the sale of her farm? The soldier—her husband?"

Vera reclined in her chair, an air of disappointment hanging over her. "I cannot say. Like you, we have sources.

Locate our source, and that person, I think, will help you. Katerina, Adam Park. She is who you look at. Who you find … that is where you see your precious truth."

She stood and shifted her chair back. When I tried to stand too, Marco said, "uh-uh," and so I waited. I watched as Vera returned the way we came without so much as a goodbye, and then I waited as Marco followed her. The Beefcakes had vanished, and suddenly I was alone in a near silent camp, with only the crackle of flames for company.

Who you find … that is where you see your precious truth…

CHAPTER TWELVE

I HATED STATIC INVESTIGATIONS, but by the time I returned to my hotel, it was one a.m., which was way past my scotch time. However, I stick to the rule that when I've been kidnapped, tortured, thoroughly interrogated, creeped-out, and confused, a clear head is my most vital piece of equipment. That, and a wedge under the door, granted me a short night's sleep.

Last year, after the unwanted experience of killing a fellow human being for the first time, I expected nightmares; I experienced precisely zero. In the wake of others who died at my hands, I have felt little in the way of remorse. And even the innocents who should never have died, those who lost their lives thanks to my mistakes, their blood is on the hands of men who since paid the price for their actions.

Yet, the *absence* of bad dreams has troubled me far more than nightly terrors would have done. For if I suffered more, perhaps I would not worry about becoming the people I detest.

Tonight was different.

Tonight, the shadows came.

The faces of Jess and Harry morphed out of the black, and further behind them, Jayne screamed. I ran from them, laboring uphill, like slogging through mud. It was odd none of those who visited me were dead; only those I feared losing. And I lost them again tonight, as those shadows erupted in flame.

In the morning, it was as if I hadn't slept. There was no breakfast buffet in this place, just coffee and pastries in a room that reminded me of a school cafeteria, so I slipped out at seven a.m. and breakfasted at a cart in the street, serving sausages in bread rolls, smeared in a pickle high in vinegar content and onions. I endured three mouthfuls. It made The Firebrand's strong coffee upon my return taste even worse than I expected. After half a cup, I gave up.

I could either seek out a worldwide corporate coffee chain, or return to bed straight after calling Jess. I needed her to either persuade the translator to give me another chance, or find me a new one. There was digging to do.

She did not answer, the call dropping to voicemail. Maybe she forgot I had a new number, thanks to the professor keeping my phone. I left a message mentioning how I hoped I wasn't interrupting her and Mike, and explained briefly I needed those records even more than before.

I used the time to catch up on my usual news sites, drank a little orange juice (bitter, from concentrate), and ate what purported to be a croissant but had the flavor and consistency of a flaky sock. Ten minutes later, I texted Jess to ask if she received my message.

It might sound overly-persistent, but I had never known Jess to allow her phone or some method of communication out of her grasp for more time than it took to use the bathroom.

I finished reading the news, and—like an obsessive stalker

—considered using the track-my-phone option that Jess and I shared, and maybe asking her business partner if anything might be keeping her from answering at this time.

"I dumped him," Jess said behind me.

I spun in the cheap metal-framed chair to see Jessica Denvers in the flesh. Leggings, long blouse, cardigan, and suitcase on wheels the size of a wardrobe. Plus her carry-on, which was essentially a bulky laptop bag.

I stood, opened my arms automatically to greet her. "How did you find me?"

She made no move to sweep into them for a big ol' hug. "Well, I didn't actually forget you have a new number, and since our online profiles are synced, it's easy to track your hardware. Easy for me, anyway. Surprised?"

"What are you doing here?"

"I'm helping, Adam. I can work more efficiently if I'm local, and since you seem to alienate every person I put you in touch with, I figured I'd keep an eye on you personally."

"That wasn't my fault. I was—"

"Kidnapped, yes, I know. So who did you piss off to the point they'd do that to you? And why the hell are you still interested in land registry?"

She stashed her case in my room and insisted we head out somewhere "better than this litter tray" to eat and drink, at which point she would permit me to fill her in. We chose one of the world-spanning coffee shop corporations I had successfully avoided thus far, and I indulged in a ham and cheese toastie to go with my generic coffee beans, while Jess opted for a skinny muffin. I regaled her with tales, expanding on details I skirted over the previous day, and added the information—such as it was—from Vera LaPorte.

"So they're targeting the old lady," Jess said.

"Not targeting. Just … I don't know. What are you *doing* here?"

She dabbed at crumbs from the remaining half a muffin. "You're always alone, Adam. Always over-reaching. You use me as a sounding board and an eye-in-the-sky, but if you need another brain here and there, you can use me."

"You got a taste for being in the field, didn't you?"

"I didn't enjoy it, and I'm not like you. I'm no thrill-seeker. But if you're running around all over town, I'll be backing you up." She patted her case. "I'm meeting our translator at ten. You're going to file a report with the local police about your kidnapping—"

"What good will that do?"

"It's how it's done *properly*." Her fist hovered, about to bang the table, but she lowered it and ripped another chunk of muffin. "Surprisingly, there really *is* a Professor Jäger."

"He used his real name?"

"Possibly. If it's him, he spent a little money here in Kraków." She showed me a photo on her phone.

"That's him," I said. "Meaning he was either never planning to let me go, or was so confident I can't hurt him, he didn't bother to conceal his identity. How'd you find that?"

"I've almost reconfigured DDS, and I located only one prof called Jäger active in the city. He bought a hat."

So the fedora was a new addition. I assumed it had been part of his "look." But the fact Jess had DDS—our Deep Detect System—back up and running was a major boon. Roger Gorman moved it offshore so if my activities brought the authorities calling they would not locate a program that spun itself into most major banks and financial institutions, allowing real-time access to accounts, credit cards, and also mobile phone accounts (not calls, just billing and, sometimes,

GPS tracking) and driving association data. Passport monitoring was harder, although Jess being tight with the Metropolitan Police helped on that front.

"Who is he?" I asked.

"Not sure. Seems to be an academic who splits his teaching between Jerusalem and Salzburg. Has homes in both places, although he skips out on Salzburg during the winter months. He's a visiting fellow at Oxford, and had stints at the Centre for Military Ethics in London, Harvard, and the Center for Irregular Warfare in the States."

"That's a lot to remember."

"Not when you break it down. Homes in Jerusalem and Salzburg. Additional part-time jobs in Britain and the States." She tabbed to a different app, scraped her chair round to me so we were shoulder-to-shoulder, and a YouTube clip geared up. "This is from three years ago."

The same man who watched as Abba and Clara duped my brain into believing I was drowning stood at a podium before a hall of around five hundred people, the shaky cellphone footage annoying but clearly showed a good chunk of audience made up of military personnel. American, mostly.

"And because we must never forgive their crimes," he said, "their age, infirm state, or recollection of events, must never be an excuse. Do not look upon these men of evil and say there is no point in punishing them. Because *they* did not look upon the elderly, the infirm, or the soft of mind, and grant *them* mercy. We must continue to hunt them. And when they are too old to be hunted, when there are no more who contributed directly left alive, we look to their offspring, and the next generation. Those who profited down the line, and said nothing. Who got rich, while the relatives of survivors suffered, attempted to rebuild their lives without the advantages their forefathers hoped for them."

Jess cut the video short. "It goes on a bit."

"I want to hear it."

"I've emailed you the link. Watch it later. But you get the gist, yeah?"

"He's talking about Nazis again. An educated guess makes his team Mossad or similar, and we can probably infer he's an investigator. The man's obsessed."

She elbowed my shoulder. "Remind you of anyone?"

I stuffed the final piece of sandwich in my mouth and washed it down. The generic bean they used was like a liquid rainbow compared to The Firebrand's swill.

"I am not obsessed," I said.

She smiled. "I checked out the city on my way over—a three a.m. flight, by the way, thanks for asking. I can get to the records office in half an hour, then mooch through the paperwork. Once you've filed the complaint, let me know, and I'll send you to the next place, if I find a clue."

"A clue?"

"I might need you to go somewhere physically."

I was about to take another big gulp but stopped with the cup an inch from my lip. "Hang on, who's in charge here now?"

Her head tilted. Eyebrows raised. "It's a research gig. No matter how many fights you get into, I'm better qualified."

"I haven't actually agreed to you coming on board."

She pouted and batted her eyelashes. "Oh, pul-*ease*, my master. Let me join the quest!"

"Shut up." I sipped.

The tight curls of her hair bobbed gently as she laughed. "You know, I dumped a perfectly good stud muffin to come out here."

"You didn't need to do that."

"Sure I did. He gave me an ultimatum. You or him."

Our shoulders still touched.

I said, "And you chose me."

"I chose *me*." Her coffee-breath was hot on my face. "Nobody tells me what to do. And any guy who says I can't be friends with someone who does a lot of good … despite being, sometimes, a dick … he isn't worth having around. Okay?"

"For you."

"Right."

Our faces were close. Her hand rested on my knee. I placed my own over it. Licked my lips.

Then I pulled away.

Jess took a deep breath and fingered her hair behind her ears. "Right, then. Let's get moving."

"Jess," I said.

"It's fine. Nothing going on here." She fumbled on her cardigan. "Two tired people, that's all. About to go on a grand adventure."

"We'll talk when…" I couldn't raise my eyes from the table. "When I'm not as confused about things."

"Okay." She frowned. "What things?"

"Yesterday. When I was in that place … when they were doing the water thing. It was frightening, like I was going to die. Then, when the three guys took me away … I knew I would live. *Knew* it. I could have killed them if I had to." I turned my near-empty mug on its spot. "I wasn't scared around *them*."

She stood close, my eye-line at her belt. Her finger pressed under my chin so I looked up. "The fact you worry about it means you haven't fallen all the way. You'll figure it out."

"You believe that?"

"If I didn't," she said, removing her finger, "I wouldn't be looking forward to our next 'talk' so much."

As she left the coffee shop, I couldn't resist watching her go.

It took me a few minutes to realize two things: one, I was grinning like a schoolboy with a hot supply teacher, and two, I had no course of action to take until she reported back from the records office. Which left me only one option I could think of. And it didn't involve reporting an elderly Nazi-hunter to the local cops.

CHAPTER THIRTEEN

Rather than wasting the morning fannying around with Google Translate, I ordered a calorific mocha with all the trimmings, then called Herman Prinz to clarify Katerina's history. Hesitant, he conceded to chat only under the condition he would not breach his client's confidentiality, and when I reminded him Estelle was his client, not Katerina, he stalled again.

"I work for Katerina, too," he said.

I didn't hold out much hope of any juicy secrets spilling forth in a waterfall of detail, but one trick I learned long ago when someone tried hiding things was to hone in on what they *didn't* say. So he summarized mostly what I already knew about her:

When the Nazis rose to power, Roma-raised Elizabetta moved the family to her ancestral country of Poland—Kraków, to be exact—while her husband promised both men would join them later. They never did, murdered by a Hitler-supporting mob during a riot instigated by the Brown Shirts. Their property was seized and eventually razed to the ground by more patriotic supporters of Herr Hitler.

In Kraków, Elizabetta—grieving and angry—sought vengeance the way she saw would piss off the Fuhrer the most: she greeted Jews and Roma fleeing Germany on their way east, facilitating their escape with help from a complex underground—one linked through whispers, back-handers to rail and freight officials, and an enforcement squad as brutal as any SS unit unleashed upon those whose lips parted too easily. No one could place an actual figure on the number of people she helped, although it most certainly reached the hundreds, probably the thousands. Experts estimate between five and fifteen hundred, placing her firmly in Oskar Schindler territory.

The other details emerged like a list:

- Katerina married Petr Caine aged eighteen.
- After the Nazis invaded, Petr joined the resistance, presumed killed.
- Never a practicing Jewish family, they were able to hide, and no one suspected the religion into which more than one of the female line married.
- Katerina's grandmother—Elizabetta—when questioned publicly in a newly formed ghetto, was beaten to death, cementing her sacrifice into both Jewish and Romani folklore as "the Angel of Kraków."
- After the war, Petr returned a hero, and moved onto a farm with Katerina.
- They had a baby less than a year later, called Beatrice.
- Shortly after, Petr died, officially whilst "cleaning his gun" but we all know what that means.

"What happened during the war?" I asked of the glaring six-year omission in his summary. "Katerina mentioned she was some sort of domestic servant to a Nazi officer. Friedrich Goetz?"

"I believe Katerina has already explained this to you."

"Briefly. I need to know more, though. Details. It might all be in the detail. If you know more than the bare bones, please, give it to me."

The lawyer paused, nose-breathing for several seconds. "Captain Goetz moved in after Katerina was left alone … and I do not wish to call anyone cowards, Mr. Park. I do not like to accuse people of being conspirators…"

"Especially not your employer. It's okay. I understand. The Jews were ghettoized, and later brutally imprisoned and murdered. But people survived. They did what they had to. Disclaimer over. Please continue."

Herman sighed with either relief or indignation. "When the captain decided he would like to live on a farm, he moved himself and Katerina out to a formerly-Jewish smallholding. He held her prisoner there for three years. Rarely allowed even into town. She says Goetz did not harm her, though. She suspected him of being a closet … you know … it would not sit well. She thought, maybe, he took her out there to deflect rumors, so he could point any accusers at her and say 'look, I am with this woman.' Of course…" Herman chuckled. "If they found out he lived with the offspring of a Jew, there would be much worse consequences."

"Katerina said she killed him with a rifle. How did she manage that?"

"As the Nazis were packing up to leave, Katerina waited until the officer was asleep, obtained a gun, and shot him in the head. Then she cut him up and left him for the pigs. When Petr came home, they attempted to find the family who owned the property, but they were … lost. All of them."

Which is what I, and my predecessor on the case, were thinking about now: the original owners' ancestors.

"Do you know Professor Jäger?" I asked.

Silence. Then, "Why do you ask about him?"

"Has he been in touch?"

"When Mr. Luca commenced his studies, a Professor Jäger phoned several times, wanting to speak with Katerina first, then Gottfried."

"Did he get through?"

Silence again. Then, "I am not sure I should reveal what may be privileged information, Mr. Park."

"I just want to know who he spoke to. It might be important."

"How can that be?"

Those who profited down the line, and said nothing. Who got rich...

I said, "After her husband died, Katerina wanted to get out of Kraków, right? She sold the farm. The farm originally owned by a Jew."

"Correct."

"So if she used it as seed money to set up in Paris ... anyone who inadvertently profited benefited from the Holocaust." I ran a dozen scenarios through my head, but only came out with one. "Herman, have my ... colleagues arrived from Scotland?"

"We sent a car to collect them."

"Good," I said. "Because I don't think the Roma are the only ones interested in the fortune."

"Mr. Park?"

"I think Professor Jäger wants to claim it for his own cause."

With no contact from Jess, and a caffeine buzz lighting up my brain, I had to keep moving, even if it was inconsequential.

The headstone marking Petr Caine's final resting place protruded from the middle of the western side of a Jewish military graveyard sprawling over ten acres, easily found on an English-language site run by a Rabbi in Leeds, my hometown. I knew of the synagogue in which he served his God, a thirty-minute bus ride from the dilapidated estate on which I grew up.

Significantly different areas.

While mine saw homes infested by damp, and neighbors for whom mattress burning was a valid hobby, the synagogue occupied a stretch of real estate surrounded by houses, the smallest at least four times the size of mine; tennis courts were accessible for free, woodland too, and soccer pitches open to all. We had a soccer pitch near my house, but it was festooned with as many needles as blades of grass.

If someone had taken a depressed, twelve year-old Adam Park, pointed him at that district, and told him the Jews had taken all the wealth that should have lifted him from the poverty in which he was raised, would he have supported a figurehead who promised to rid the world of them?

I hope I would have seen through it.

I see through attempts to paint teachers, nurses, and single mothers as scroungers, and the notion all Eastern European migrants are benefits cheats hell-bent on stealing my tax money. So perhaps, in 1939, I would have been on the side of the angels.

Again, I can only hope.

I crouched at the grave, overgrown, as most of them were, with some notable exceptions gleaming with pride in the noon sun. I picked at weeds and tossed them aside, careful not to contaminate another grave. The grass was harder to tidy up, but I cleared enough of it with my bare hands to read the pale stone inscription:

Petr Caine. Mąż. Ojciec. Bohater.
Husband. Father. Hero.

"A hero," said a male voice.

I angled my chin that way, gazing up at a teenager in a suit.

I said, "Yes," and stood.

The kid was ashen in his face, like someone coming down with the flu, or who had suffered a recent loss, still reeling at their passing. He focused on Petr's headstone.

"A shame, dying whilst cleaning one's gun." His voice rattled deep in his chest, with no trace of an accent.

"Doing what?" I said. "I'm not great with Polish, but I'm pretty sure that detail isn't on the headstone."

"He would not be permitted a burial in a Jewish cemetery if it were suicide. A tragic accident."

"You travelled here for a funeral?"

"Of sorts."

"Where from?"

He shifted his line of sight to me. "Where do you think I am from?"

Now virtually face-to-face, I gauged him to be a couple of inches shorter than me, and older than the "kid" status I assigned him. Actually, I could not tell if he was in his twenties, thirties, or forties. His hair was greying, his smooth, ashen skin a natural hue rather than a temporary state of mental instability, and his suit fit better than I first thought. The jacket was one size too big, which usually meant a concealed weapon.

I said, "Why are you here?"

"For you," he said.

I shrugged. "Since you didn't shoot me in the back of the head, I'm guessing this is another kidnapping?" I planted my feet firmly. "Shall we get on with it?"

"This is not a kidnapping," the man said. "The professor wishes to send a message to anyone following in your wake. Shooting you is a little … simple." He reached inside his jacket.

I lunged forward, putting all my weight behind a kick toward his wrist. He pivoted and guided my foot with his free hand, sending me flying. I landed on my back. Rolled. Sprung up and went at him with more caution.

I feigned a punch, which drew no reaction. His hand rested within his jacket; I aimed a heel at his knee, which he evaded with a tiny movement. I feigned another punch and followed in with a combo.

One-handed, he threw me aside like I was nothing. Weightless for a second; the next, slapping the ground. Again, I rolled and sprung up.

"Krav Maga," the man said. "How very crude."

His insult stung somewhat. I was good enough to handle the average bloke in the pub or even hardened street thugs, and held my own against most trained fighters. But those more experienced than me insisted I could be so much better. Vila Fanuco, that Eastern-European gangster—SAS-trained, ex-special-forces, and God-knows-what-else—recommended a form of kung fu known as Wing Chun, and that I progress to a discipline devised by the late Bruce Lee called Jeet Kun Do.

The classics were classics for a reason.

I stuck with Krav Maga, the form used by Mossad and the Israeli military, so if this person represented Professor Jäger, he'd be familiar with my methods.

He slid his hand out, which now contained a blade, nine inches long, gleaming in the sunlight.

"This is not a kidnapping," he said. "But I need to ensure your death lasts long enough that the message is clear."

Fine, I thought, and ran as fast as I could.

CHAPTER FOURTEEN

THE ASSASSIN, whoever he was, moved as quickly as me, his formal attire no hindrance. The headstones and boxes and statues raced by in a blur, my legs pumping, thankful for not abandoning my fitness regimen the way Eric had back on Paramatra. As the cemetery pitched at an angle and my sprint continued upward, though, I wished I'd cut the booze out entirely. It might have given me the edge I needed to outrun this man with the knife.

Why was the cemetery so damn empty?

He kept pace, square on, perpendicular to me, keeping the graves as a barrier, but at the first opportunity he arrowed across so he sprinted behind. His face did not alter. Mouth closed, lids hooded, arms pumping mechanically. It was as if he were walking at the same speed I ran.

And I would never reach my car before he closed in.

I slowed in increments, saving my strength while he gained on me. Waiting until I spotted what I needed, then intentionally "tripped." I rolled with the movement and scrambled to find my feet, hoping the ruse worked.

It seemed to.

The ashen-faced man calmly slowed and his knees folded so he crouched close. I swung the metal urn from a grave overgrown with grass, clanging it off the side of his head. He frowned. Blinked. And I slammed the urn into his knife, dislodging it from his grip, which flung it into the undergrowth. He looked from his hand to the grass, then wrapped his fingers around my neck.

I hit him again and again with the metal pot, his ribs, his back, his arm; but it was like striking wood. My vision blurred. Through the spots and swirling colors, his facial muscles twitched for the first time. Only slightly, but it was definitely there.

He was smiling.

I dropped the urn, and with both hands I dug my fingers into the dirt, came out with globs of dry soil, and flung them towards his face. He reared back, grunted, but held onto me.

It weakened him, though. Changed his grip.

I pulled my legs up to my chest and thrust them with as much force as I could muster. An explosion of strength concentrated through my heels burst into the man's sternum, and he let go.

He rolled to the side, and onto his feet.

I was up too. Ready now. Knew how dangerous he was. I wouldn't get cocky again.

He watched me for a long moment, his blank expression daring me to come at him.

The way he was throwing me like I weighed nothing didn't make sense. It was impossible. No one was that strong, and last I checked I was heavier than the average toddler. There was more to his ability, something I had never faced before.

"Not my place to start things," I said. "Come on, if you want me."

He walked forward and his open hand shot out. I

managed to block it, but stumbled with the force, and the heel of his other hand hit my gut, blowing the air out of me. He gripped the scruff of my neck, and whipped me around, jerked me back, and I spun upside-down. A hard object cracked into my hip as I crashed to the floor.

Ignoring the pain, I sprung up and took a chance.

Stepping back before I knew where he was, my vision cleared and found his arm at the apex of its reach. I moved into him, grappled his wrist in a reverse-hold to apply pressure to his elbow, and pulled down. Most people buckle to one knee.

This guy said, "Hmm," and leapt into the hold. An elbow to my sternum sent me reeling. He took my arm and somehow flung me six feet onto a flatbed tomb.

Winded, my whole body aching, I groaned as I dragged myself off the other side. He stopped opposite the chest-high grave. Now we were in a playground stalemate, where I couldn't escape one way because he'd cut me off, and he couldn't attack because I'd escape the other. Ditto if he leapt over.

We held position. I had more to lose by blinking first, though, so it wouldn't be me who gave in.

"Walk away," I said. "I'll talk to the professor."

"Come. We should finish this."

"Why not shoot me? Can't be as simple as making me suffer."

"Sometimes things are as they appear."

"Why no Taser?"

"First, I do not own one, and second…" He breathed through his nose, constantly scanning the landscape. "Second … I did not anticipate I would need it."

If I wasn't about to die, I would have been happy at that

subtle compliment. He was an experienced killer, one who clearly gleaned pleasure in his craft, and I—lowly Adam Park —had surprised him.

His eyes darted again.

I couldn't be sure if it was a trick or not. Look away, and he attacks. But a second would be okay, right? Less than a second.

I flicked my head to the right and back again. The man had not moved, but I had seen his concern: two male soldiers, both in their eighties, accompanied by women I took to be their spouses. All carried small wreaths.

"Worried about witnesses?" I said.

"I do not fear people seeing what I do."

My turn to watch him. So much going on behind his mask of grey skin and immobile features.

"You're a man who wants to inflict pain," I said. "But you're working for Jäger ... and Jäger is an idealist. Warped, yes, but strong of principle. It makes sense he would need a person to perform the tasks he can't. And the government can't be a part of it."

If this creature before me followed Jäger's orders, perhaps I had a way out after all.

I said, "Let's see how far Jäger is willing to let you off the leash."

I turned and sprinted toward the gathering. Didn't shout, didn't cry out. I ran. Downhill. I didn't need control; I needed distance. And that's what I achieved.

A swift glance behind found my attacker paused opposite the barrier I used, having started to give chase, but must have figured it wasn't worth it after all.

For my part, I kept on running. Even as the soldiers and their wives called in Polish, asking—I assumed—if I was okay.

I ignored them, and circled back to the road, checking my hire car every which way to ensure the ghoul was not hiding inside, before starting it up and pulling out, speeding toward the main highway, gaining distance again, fighting the pain, wondering what the hell had tracked me down.

And, perhaps more importantly, *how* it found me.

CHAPTER FIFTEEN

I RETURNED THE CAR, but before handing back the keys, I checked the underside and found the kind of magnetic tracker I had used countless times before. They had discovered my whereabouts, possibly while I slept, and located the vehicle. I'd used cash and a fake license, though. Perhaps they had a Trojan horse similar to DDS, one more sophisticated, able to examine photo IDs rather than just data. Logically, though, since they intercepted me as I headed to meet the translator, they knew a lot about me, so probably had someone on the original hotel from the moment I landed, and simply followed me to The Firebrand.

The easiest explanations are usually correct.

My next expenditure was a taxi to Dr. Rostov's office rather than a hospital, where I waited for an unscheduled appointment, giving me time to call Jess and warn her to go nowhere near The Firebrand. Instead, I instructed her to head directly to the airport and wait somewhere busy and public, and to not talk to strangers.

When Dr. Rostov was free, despite not being an ER doctor, she examined me to ensure I had not suffered a concussion, and agreed to supply painkillers to take the edge off my aching bones and muscles. After paying her handsomely, I chanced swinging by The Firebrand in a taxi. I ran in, snatched up my computer and other gear, and then whizzed off via a dilapidated fire escape to meet Jess.

Jess, who had texted me the most sarcastic message imaginable; my "don't talk to strangers" joke hadn't gone down well. The private jet made up for it.

One of my calls whilst waiting for Dr. Rostov was to Herman Prinz, where I explained we found all the records we needed (my faith in Jess's research ability being greater than in my own), and that I was in more danger than we realized, so on the promise I would issue a full report once back in Hamburg, Katerina afforded me another ride on the Cessna.

Not that it mattered much, but I expected to be zigzagging back and forth a couple of times before this was over—the Romani family still resided near Kraków after all—and if the people pursuing me experienced confusion over my physical whereabouts, all the better. The other advantage was in keeping Jess out of the Israelis' sights.

I wouldn't tell her that outright, though.

Once in the air, we faced each other in cream leather swivel chairs across a walnut table. A smiling German woman in a designer stewardess outfit with her hair in a tight bun offered us champagne. I said no, but Jess said yes, so I reluctantly went along. When comfortably equipped with bubbly, Jess perked up and presented a folder full of papers.

"Sixty-three euros," she said. "Photocopying, printouts, the works."

"Bargain. How about you give me the bullet point version?"

"Fine." She sipped her champers and placed it down, pinky extended. "The farm belonged to Harold and Maude—I shit you not; that's for real—Griffin. They were fourth gen farmers. In their sixties, so preparing their kids to take over running the place. Crops, cattle, chickens. Being Jews, and supplying largely Jewish businesses, they kept no pigs, and adhered to Kosher requirements."

"That's a lot of detail."

"It's a combination of official records, trading agreements, and personal accounts. There are a lot of local history books in there—"

I held up a hand. "Apologies for interrupting. Please, continue."

And she did.

The Griffins' farm saw three generations living on the property: Harold and Maude; their son, Victor, and his wife, Maria, and their three kids, Alfons (14), Gerik (10), and Stefa (4); finally, their daughter, Narja—recently widowed, doubt cast upon her capacity to reproduce, hence why some referred to her as a "spinster."

When the Nazis plowed their war machine into Poland, their "September Campaign"—or the "1939 Defensive War" as the Poles preferred—had already laid waste to the major cities, entering Poland on September 1st, with Britain and France impotently declaring war two days later. But Poland's supposed protectors were not prepared, and could offer no practical support, so once the Soviets also invaded on the 17th, it took only ten more days of this onslaught for Poland to officially surrender. The country was divided between the Soviets in the east and Germany in the west, where the Nazis ruled their colony from the most intact major city—Kraków —presided over by Hans Frank.

The Nazis barracked their officers with enlisted men or

commuted from nearby Vienna, but while the cleanup of the city began many soon quartered themselves in larger homes. Jews were rounded up and herded into ghettos, with architects, doctors, businessmen, all forced to perform the manual labor required to keep Kraków running.

Then they came for the outliers.

The underground—of which Elizabetta was a key member—helped many outliers' children to flee. But the Nazis treated the Griffins well at first, and some in the community even thought of them as conspirators. To maintain their business, their only concessions were to cease the practice of Kosher slaughter, and to rear pigs; Germans have always been fond of their sausage.

But in 1941, Hitler turned on the Soviet Union, taking the War to a whole new level, and as the ghettos grew too expensive and—frankly—tiresome to maintain, and with senior figures' rabid hatred of Jews growing to unheard-of depths, the residents were shipped out to "camps" where no one at the time could have imagined what awaited them. Such was the scale of the policy, no Jew could be allowed to remain in polite society, lapsed or not.

Records show that, on March 13th, 1943, as the liquidation of the Kraków Ghettos commenced, a truck pulled onto the Griffin property, and all eight residents, young and old, were loaded on, and transported to their new home—*Konzentrationslager Plaszow.*

Or the *Plaszow Concentration Camp.*

Meticulous record-keepers, the SS reported the deaths of Harold and Maude in October 1943, and when Gerik (by then twelve), and Stefa (now six), froze to death in January 1944, the remaining family—Alfons (who turned sixteen that summer), his two parents, and aunt Narja, were all "terminated."

Captain Friedrich Goetz, a farmer in his native Bavaria before enlisting in the Army, put forward a case for him taking over the "administration" of the Griffins' land, which was granted, and he moved out there with Katerina, who had managed to conceal her Judaism far better than the Griffins.

Two and a half years later, liberation came, Goetz died, and Katerina's husband, thought long dead, returned. The town treated him and dozens of other former-sons like heroes, marveling at their rebirth. The home in which Katerina and Petr originally lived had been turned over to another family, one who held some standing both before and after the war, and were widely regarded as having made life more tolerable under the Nazi occupation thanks to their ability to negotiate skills exchanges and such, but by more militant groups as conspirators. As the Nazis evacuated Kraków, the couple were dragged into the street by less well-informed types, and hanged from lampposts along with, according to one newspaper clipping, other "more deserving traitors and cowards." And their house was burned.

Katerina did not warrant a mention in any news articles relating to that period, at least none that survived to be included in modern files, and the only two accounts of her time on the farm came from her witness statement to the Allied inquiry, and her petition to the council, both of which read virtually identically. The captain was a hard man, she said, psychologically controlling in that he never let her out of his sight, never let her leave, but not violent with her. He taught her how to tend the land, to treat the animals, and manage the books, making her able and competent to run the property. Combined with there being no other claim on ownership, the relevant people agreed to sign over the land and all animals and crops to her, and the locals who were forced by Goetz to work for nothing more than sustenance were offered paid positions, all of whom turned them down.

But she and Petr slowly built the business back to its former heights, and with such supplies hard to come by, prices shot up, and so did their income. Articles of the day praised them for their entrepreneurship, and wished them well, briefly outlining Katerina's "captivity," a hint that perhaps she suffered more than she let on.

The bottom line was, despite the horrors of those six years of Nazi rule, the murder of the adults and children of the Griffin clan, and the "accident-whilst-cleaning-his-gun" that stole Petr's life, it seemed fairly concrete no one who could claim title to the farm had survived the war.

"So none of the Roma I met could be descended from the Griffins," I said.

Jess stacked up the maps, old photos, and photocopied newspaper clippings she'd been using as props, and returned them to their labeled folders. "Seems that way. Unless the records from Plaszow were doctored or wrong."

"Not likely." My ears filled with pressure. We were on our descent. "The line from Beatrice and onward is clear. So either the Romani have no claim, or they see another legal reason that we don't."

"What other reason? Katerina sold the farm years later, used the money to set up an art gallery in Paris. The untimely death of one of her principal artists sent his value rocketing, and when the business ballooned, she returned to Hamburg. Which is where she reclaimed her grandfather's home. Each generation grew richer off the back of that foundation."

"Maybe it's simpler than we thought."

"How?"

"What about Katerina's grandfather? We know her grandmother went on to become the Angel of Kraków, but we never looked at the Angel's husband. If he fathered someone prior to Katerina's mother, would that warrant casting doubt on Estelle?"

Light turbulence juddered the aircraft as we dropped further. I swallowed, held my nose and mouth, and blew so my ears popped. Jess strapped herself in.

"I assume I'm going to meet the family," she said. "Maybe I could ask them."

"Sure." I buckled my own belt. "But first, I'll prove Estelle isn't possessed by a ghost."

GERMANY

HAMBURG

CHAPTER SIXTEEN

By the time we landed and Herman's bodyguard drove us back to Kochany Dom, it was ten p.m. and too late to rouse Estelle. After dinner, she had suffered a prolonged episode of screaming and hitting herself in the head, yelling at her great-grandfather to go away. She was doing the right thing, she told him, and asked why he wouldn't leave her alone. After consulting with Gottfried, and when even Katerina's presence failed to calm the girl, her doctor prescribed a mild sedative. Likewise, Katerina was in bed, although that was more to do with age than medication.

Gottfried had someone prepare a second room—having initially mistaken us for a couple and only prepared one—and told us to "make ourselves at home" as he, too, was retiring for the evening. He would be on a six a.m. flight to Brussels.

"Commercial," he told us with no little degree of scorn. "Thanks to your use of our Cessna."

I'd told Herman I might need to return to Krakow at short notice, or maybe another city, depending how information panned out, so Katerina grounded the jet for our exclusive use.

I thought about telling Gottfried it wasn't my fault he was only rich enough to afford one solitary jet, but worried he might rescind his instruction to make ourselves at home.

With his invitation still in place, I found a reception room and guessed correctly he kept good scotch. I poured two generous measures and carried them out into the night, where Jess leaned on a stone barrier surrounding the fifty-foot patio. A fountain bubbled in the terrace's center, twenty feet across and four deep, in which koi swam and occasionally broke the surface. I handed her a tumbler and we both gazed over the grounds, floodlit in a five hundred yard perimeter.

"How does any one person afford all this?" Jess asked.

"A small increment at first, then iterating the business over and over, until one day you have more money than you can spend."

She sipped her scotch. Swallowed, and made a "mmm" sound. "I know you have enough money to never work again. But I also know how much it is. And it isn't anywhere near this level."

"If I'd sold up to Roger Gorman when he first offered, I wouldn't be far away."

"The money you made from him eventually, you distributed most to the people who lost their jobs at Park Avenue Investigations. A heckuva generous redundancy package."

"They needed it more than me, and it was mostly my fault anyway."

"You *burned* the offices. But no one can prove it was you. Plenty of suspicion, though."

That beast of mine stirred. I felt no shame in what I did. It wasn't pride, as such, but if cornered, I would do the same again.

"Jess, I'm a millionaire, not a billionaire. I can't fight a six-month legal battle with someone like Gorman. I don't have the money for a settlement, and he knows it. This is him destroying me the way I destroyed our company."

The voice of a Scottish man interrupted us. "If he's after revenge, how's about we get down tae his level?"

We turned to see Hugo Hunter exiting the French doors and rounding the fishpond: blue suit, white shirt, open collar, and his hair was brushed and set as if he had concluded a rather long board meeting. It would take someone with experience to notice he was packing a high caliber pistol under his left arm.

"I thought you'd be with Estelle," I said. "Was going to catch up with you first thing."

"Emmy's with her. My turn tae sleep for four hours. But I heard voices, so thought I'd do my job, and see if anyone needed a bullet or three."

"I don't think we've met," Jess said. It was the sort of thing you say with an open hand, ready to shake and make a new acquaintance. Not here. Jess knew what Hugo did for a living. "If you boys want some privacy…"

"No," I said. "Hugo needs some shut eye."

"Aye," he said. "Beauty sleep ain't just fer the girls."

He looked Jess up and down, threw me a wink, and returned inside. My shoulders went slack, and I turned back to the view, but Jess kept focused firmly on the doors.

"I know what you think of these people," I said. "But they're very good."

"You can afford a legitimate close protection service. And the Kravitz family sure as hell can. Why them? Why invite Fanuco's fingerprints back into your life?"

"I can't explain it, but these two are more trustworthy than any private firm. Professor Jäger is well connected. Politically, militarily, and personally. There's no telling how many people he has on his payroll, or what he'll do to achieve his goals. Vila Fanuco, as corrupt and evil as he may be, seems to have my best interests at heart."

"Then why not let him take care of Roger Gorman, if he's offering?"

I finished my drink with a big gulp. It burned, then settled smoothly in my gut. "Partly because I don't want to take that first baby step toward proving him right about me. But mainly, no matter how much I detest Roger Gorman, he doesn't deserve the punishment Fanuco would deliver."

"And Jäger does?"

"Only if he comes for a mentally ill thirteen-year-old girl." I pushed away from the wall and faced the house.

"Mentally ill?" Jess said.

"I'm sorry, I understand you want to believe in … more. But I can't work that way."

"Turning in already?"

"I need a clear head for the morning. I'll see you then."

Unbeknownst to Jess, I poured another three fingers of smoky single malt and adjourned to my room, a cavern the size of the whole of my downstairs house back in Greece, with a bed large enough for a game of rugby, where I caught up with three episodes of The Daily Show via iTunes. It took my mind off things, and when I finished the scotch I wanted another, but dragged myself to bed.

I woke with a thickness to my head and dryness to my tongue that didn't quite qualify as a hangover, but was a long way from "clear."

I ate breakfast with Jess on the same terrace as we drank

the whisky. Katerina and Herman joined us to hear my confirmation the farm did not appear to be the source of the Romani claim. Katerina seemed almost disappointed. Perhaps she wanted the money to funnel elsewhere, having been a burden for so long. If she wanted Estelle to lead a "normal" life, it could do her good to get her out of this insulated existence. Or maybe it was simpler. Maybe Katerina missed her husband.

Estelle was bright this morning, with Hugo and Emiliana at her side. She had got dressed today, and looked like any other teenager on a summer morning, with smart shorts, and a T-shirt depicting Superman, Batman, and Wonder Woman. Hugo stepped out onto the balcony, while Emiliana patrolled the hall. I introduced Jess to Estelle, and Katerina nodded her approval. Herman stood in the background, while I knuckled down to business.

"How did Petr die?" I asked.

Katerina was about to answer, but my raised finger shushed her as I stared at Estelle.

"Why ask that?" Estelle replied.

"Because I would like his take on things."

She stared at the floor.

"If he's with you, surely you can ask him."

She tensed, concentrating.

I said, "What's his answer?"

"It doesn't work like that."

"Who was his commanding officer in the Russian Army? Or a single one of his comrades?"

Jess placed a hand on my arm. "Adam…"

I acknowledged her with a brief nod, and adopted a softer tone. "Can you tell me how old Petr was when Beatrice was born?"

Estelle looked around as if searching for the specter of the man himself. It did not manifest, and a tear rolled down her cheek. "He won't say."

It was enough for me. She could not communicate with the dead, nor the dead with her. If any of this was true, the spirit would not have obscured the information we needed, much like those phony mediums who earn their trade by preying on the bereaved. Estelle did not seem to be a con artist as such, but her brain had to be making things up as she went along, filling in gaps, causing her distress if there were no ready answers.

I patted her hand, and said, "Don't worry. This isn't your fault. I'm sure your father will help you through it. But whatever the truth about this inheritance, we will work out how to get the voices to stop."

Estelle nodded. Sniffed. Wiped the tears with the heels of her hands.

I stood and turned away, smiled at Katerina and Herman, and gestured for Jess to accompany me to the exit. A wave to Hugo drew him back in from the balcony.

"We're done for now," I said. "I just have to work out where we go from here."

I had taken three steps, when Estelle said, "Wait."

I paused, and gave her my attention again.

She said, "Petr wants you to know, you should 'fear the pale one'. It means nothing to me. You?"

I frowned. Glanced at Jess, and then for some reason offered Hugo a longer look. He, too, frowned.

"The 'pale one'?" he said.

"Yeah," I said. "Someone Jäger sent after me. Pretty much all grey—suit, tie, even his skin."

"Not a youngster?"

"Couldn't tell." I stayed on Estelle. "Could have been twenty, could have been forty."

"The Pale Boy," Hugo said.

"You've heard of him?"

"We've all heard of him. And if Jäger is aiming him your way, Park, yer a dead man."

CHAPTER SEVENTEEN

THE PALE BOY was something of a bogeyman in hit man circles. Hugo spoke as if he were a bedtime story come to life, the embodiment of a literary character taken form. Some said the Pale Boy did not exist as a person. That he slept between jobs, between murders. It was well accepted that he worked for Israel, or at least *out of* Israel, but nobody had laid eyes on him, except in fleeting moments, where the witness did not qualify as a target. The pallor of his skin was due to dwelling out of daylight until called upon by masters no one had ever seen, or knew how to get hold of, should they wish to hire a man of true brutality.

Because, Hugo said, no matter what I thought of Vila Fanuco, the Pale Boy was worse.

Other rumors said this man, this creature, savored each kill, not simply because it "sent a message" but because it made best use of his sickness. There's a saying along the lines of, "murder is never acceptable, unless it is committed on a great scale and to the sound of trumpets," which is also true of assassinations under the guise of national security, or greatly deserved vengeance. And who deserves vengeance more than the Jewish people upon whom was inflicted one of the worst genocides of the twentieth century?

Critics of the Holocaust memorials often cite other genocides that go unremarked upon, and ask why we should continue to remember this one, and not others. It is these attitudes, the lack of understanding of how a government can slaughter on an industrial scale, that sets in place the necessity for people like Professor Jäger, and—evidently—the ghoulish bloodhound known as the Pale Boy.

He does not age. He does not stop. And he never fails.

But he does not cross paths with others, not in the way Hugo and Emiliana had done in the past. Even in a line of work involving murder for money, professional courtesy exists, so unless their interests conflict, it is unusual for one hit man to go up against another. The best in the business are usually well-known in those circles.

Yet nobody knows the Pale Boy.

"That's why," Hugo speculated, "there are so many stories about him. Nobody can pin him down. But the bodies in his wake, carved, beaten, disemboweled … they tell us he enjoys his work way more than any professional should."

"He is a golem," Katerina said.

We all turned to her, and found her standing, using her walking stick as support, one hand clasped over the other. Herman loomed behind her like a sentry.

She said, "The golem is an empty man. Legend says he is made of clay, and rises to do the bidding of his master. It means 'shapeless mass' or ' body without a soul'. The academics used to discuss this, even during the war. Some said Hitler's army was made entirely of golems, for surely so many people could not be willing to rise up to erase another race, could not hate in such high numbers, as to march under the swastika, and believe they were doing good. So perhaps the academics were correct. Perhaps my grandmother had it wrong."

"What did she get wrong?" Jess asked.

"She thought good lay in everyone, even as her fate was sealed and she saw her death coming. That very morning, when someone told her of the soldiers' plans, she told me and my mother to have faith. Nobody is an empty vessel, the golem isn't real, and the worst of men can be redeemed."

Everyone here knew the woman who was beaten to death in front of her neighbors by these men.

"I have heard of the Pale Boy," Katerina said, "but I never thought it was real."

"Tell me the truth, Katerina," I said. "Do you know Professor Jäger?"

"Years ago, I heard the name. He hunted those who tried to kill my people and millions of others, like the Roma. Yes, the Devouring was more crippling to the Roma than the Holocaust to us, but our numbers were far greater. If six million died back then, imagine how many would die now, given the same level of hatred, and given how few good men stood up to them." Katerina hobbled over to Estelle, and stroked her hair. "My Petr was one of those who stood up. And just because he does not reveal the name of his commanding officer, it does not mean he cannot warn you about a threat. Golem or not, the Pale Boy is not of this world."

That weightless sensation returned to me, the Pale Boy tossing me against one hard object after another, how he seemed to move so slowly, so intricately, but placed no emphasis on speed or strength. It was as if I were nothing to him.

Katerina said, "He may not be molded from clay, but he most certainly has a master, and he does not venture out unless he is ordered to. If he is looking for you, the golem will not stop until his master is satisfied."

Again, Katerina and I walked the land. Jess adjourned to her room to tend to matters of her business back in London. Her partner, Phyllis, had left a message asking her to "stop dicking around with Adam, and sort out this database," meaning something they had been working on for the Met was now reaching a head. Arrests called, and Jess needed to do some work.

We trod the same path as before, but reversed the route, starting at the cabbages and broccoli, winding our way to the herb garden. She talked more about her time kept on the farm, again emphasizing the Nazi captain never subjected her to anything humiliating or dehumanizing. Friedrich Goetz simply feared she may run and leave him without an assistant. I could have argued that level of control was as dehumanizing as physical abuse, but compared to the horror she witnessed on a day-to-day basis, perhaps it seemed a preferable option than returning to the ghetto.

Among the herbs, she said, "When I killed him, I took a huge risk. It felt bad. Like I imagine a prisoner being set free after twenty years. I did not know what life would be like afterward. I did not know Petr was still alive when I fed the man's remains to our pigs."

After all I have done in this past year, there I was talking to a ninety-five-year-old woman whose tales of violence trumped my own several times over. I had killed, yes, but I had never killed someone who kept me prisoner for five years, then disposed of his body through a pig's intestine.

I said, "It must have been terrifying."

A stiff movement in her shoulders suggested a shrug. "At times of war, you learn to make do."

"Why did you stay?"

"Why did I stay in a place where I was essentially a prisoner? A place stolen from a family murdered by … empty men?"

"That's one way of putting it."

"I suppose I was honoring their memory. And we needed farms. You would not guess today, but farming is the backbone of society. And I had become good at it. Although not my choice at first, I grew to love it. Do you understand?"

"I think I do."

"He used forced labor. Not only to tend crops and animals, we did much work ourselves, but Captain Goetz grew paranoid. He built lookouts and mounds to use as gun turrets. The workers dug out rooms beneath the house, but I did not know the reason. Presumably to hide in. I was never allowed to see them. I made dresses, and clothing at night. It kept the boredom away. And I handed clothes to our workers, and the new clothes made them feel human for a short while. Until the labor recommenced."

We passed through the next border, to the more exotic garden, which held the ferns I remembered were called Mimosa hostilis, and where someone had planted a new flower, a pink, bulb-like head with black dots.

"What about your … 'golem'?"

"To bring the golem to life," Katerina said, "the master molds the man in clay, then the word 'emeth' is inscribed on its forehead. 'Emeth' in Hebrew means 'truth'. Magic then gives it life. To kill it, some in the early twentieth century rein-

terpreted the Kabbalah to suggest it could be killed by innocence, and there was even a film made showing a female golem
put to death by a young girl offering it an apple. But the original way, according to the Talmud, is to erase the first 'E' of
the inscription, leaving 'meth' in its place."

I admired the pink flower growing above the ferns of the
Mimosa hostilis, how it drooped like a sad mammal mourning
the loss of its mother.

I said, "I didn't see any inscription on the Pale Boy's forehead. And he certainly wasn't made of clay."

"The word 'meth' has power. In Hebrew, 'meth' means 'he
is dead'. When you erase the 'E', when truth is gone, all you
have left is death."

"Then I had better hope this thing is human after all."

"Why is that?"

"Because as soon as I'm done here, I'm heading back to
Kraków. Today."

I did not say goodbye to Jess, because she would have stopped
me. Instead, I told my plan, such as it was, to Hugo, and he in
turn asked Emiliana to join us.

"I'm gettin' the feelin' this is a bit sexist," Emiliana said as
we walked the perimeter of the house, crunching over its
gravel path.

Ostensibly, we were checking the security, the access
points, while Estelle blew up alien cities in the guise of a
cyborg, with Herman and Katerina for company. The doctor
was elsewhere, but on call. I still hadn't met Gottfried's brother
or his extended family, their holiday keeping them out of the
country another few days, but Hugo and Emiliana had inter-
viewed and vetted the staff on duty. Nothing untoward in
their finances, their mobile phones showed no unusual activ-

ity, and the Hunters' sheer gut instinct threw up no red flags. They hammered shut a number of decrepit windows leading to the basement, arranged for the addition of razor wire to what was nothing more than an enclosure for garbage, and positioned a dozen stick-on motion-activated CCTV cameras that fed into both a high-def monitor in the room next to Estelle's, where Hugo and Emiliana were based, and directly into their phones. As we passed each one, both Hugo's and Emiliana's phones pinged, and Hugo showed me the three of us wandering past.

"It's not sexist," Hugo insisted. "It's common bloody sense."

"Yeah, right," Emiliana replied. "*I'm* the woman, *I* get to house sit, *I* look after the girl."

"Four months ago, you were shot. The surgery was twelve hours, and every frickin' night you complain yer shoulder's stiff." He looked at me and gestured to his wife. "Seriously, I spend more time microwavin' that bloody hot pack, and drapin' it over her precious wound, than I do cookin', cleanin', and generally keepin' the house goin', since her disability means *she* clearly can't." He placed his hands on his hips and cocked his head towards Emiliana. "So there's yer choice, love. You wanna come chase down some ghost assassin, fine, but soon as we get back tae Scotland, yer on washin'-up duty fer a month."

She rubbed the spot south of her collarbone where a lucky bullet penetrated. "I suppose hanging 'round in a mansion with a gun and waiters on tap will be my contribution to our fee."

"Yer lucky we're married, 'cause there's no way I'd be takin' fifty-fifty on this if you was some hairy psycho brought in fer the muscle."

"If I was some hairy psycho brought in for the muscle, who'd you think Adam'd be picking for a trip on the Cessna?"

Hugo looked at me, his hand on his heart. "Adam? Really? Say it ain't so, pal."

I looked between the two of them. When I originally met Emiliana she could probably have taken me one-on-one in a fist fight, such was her experience, but now she was physically weaker and somewhat slower. From what Hugo told me earlier, it pained her more than she let on; until recently, some days she'd literally lay in bed gobbling painkillers. Despite all that, Emiliana was far from helpless. I'd already seen her disassemble, clean, and reassemble a Beretta 9 mm that morning, and when she held it there was no shake, and no doubt in her eyes.

I said, "I'm confident Emiliana has the ability to defend Estelle from whatever comes to this house. With help from Francis, if need-be." I smiled at her annoyance. "Anything not touched by the supernatural, that is."

The pair chuckled awkwardly, the awkwardness either from the poor quality of my joke, or if they, on some level, believed the way Katerina and Gottfried did that a force or presence roamed Kochany Dom from a world beyond our own.

We completed our tour, then departed in a Range Rover driven again by Francis. Hugo took the front seat, and babbled away to Francis about the best guns used in close protection, concluding the Glock 17 was a good all-rounder, although the debate included Sig-Sauers and one or two odd sounding brands I'd never heard of.

The first call from Harry came as we made our way

through the private airfield's check-in, which essentially consisted of a quick flash of photo ID and ticking our names off the manifest Herman forwarded. I ignored the call, knowing full well Jess had probably called when I disappeared with Hugo. Disappearing with Hugo only meant one thing to her, and she was correct.

Jess, however, waited on the tarmac, leaning against the stairs-on-wheels leading to the Cessna's cabin. The wind tousled her hair and flapped her trench coat. Hugo giggled as we reached her, but she didn't even make eye contact as he ascended the steps.

"What the actual *fuck* are you doing?" she said.

I checked up and down the runway. No car, no motorbike. I had no idea how she made it here ahead of us.

I said, "The actual fuck is ending the danger to both me and the Kravitz family. If Jäger is prepared to send that … thing, whatever it is, after me, there are secrets I'm close to uncovering. We need to go on the offensive. How did you know?"

"Because I tapped the phones of the assassins you're so keen to partner with."

The simplest explanations…

"He's arranged through your BFF Vila Fanuco to buy a 'standard infiltration package' once you touch down, and I'm buggered if I know what that is, but it sounds kind of shooty-bangy-killing-people."

"Fine, you caught me, but you're not coming."

It wasn't quite a smash-cut in a movie, but suffice it to say, she climbed on board with the intention of talking me out of getting my hands dirty, strapped herself in, and her pleasant features dared me to remove her physically. Hugo offered, but I told him it wasn't necessary. We all buckled in while I assured Jess the plan was nothing but surveillance, and how the firearms purchase was just-in-case, a condition both Hugo and Emiliana insisted upon if they were to split up. Hugo backed me up on the lie as earnestly as I'd ever seen him.

The second call from Harry came as the engines were winding up, and even though there was no requirement for me to switch off my phone on a private jet, I did so anyway.

Once in the air, Jess moved to a seat with a higher table and opened her laptop, while I ran through my intentions with Hugo, and he strategized about our next move. He was still annoyed that I refused to invite Vila Fanuco to send more backup.

"You are one dumb fuckin' amateur," he said.

"I am not getting into more debt with him."

"It's not your debt. It's theirs. The Kravitz … Kravitzes … how do say their name when there's more than one?"

The same attendant who brought Jess and me champagne yesterday offered the same today, but we all declined, instead requesting coffee. She bowed slightly and retreated in the back.

Hugo said, "They can afford it, and it isn't on you."

"That's not how he'll see it. You know that. I made it clear to him, I am not joining his band of merry men, even as a part-time freelancer."

"Yeah you're the epitome of good. Remind me how many men we have to kill today?"

I wished the prospect of killing instilled fear in me, but it did not.

I said, "None, if we can help it."

"But you're willing."

"Then their deaths will be on me. I'm not bringing any more people into this than I have to."

"I take it you have a plan. You know where we're going?"

"I didn't want to say anything earlier because I wanted to process it a little longer. But from everything I've heard, Jess's research and what Katerina told me today, I'm pretty sure I know where they were holding me. And if confronting them there is the only way to call off the Pale Boy, then I'll have to spill some blood."

POLAND

Kraków

CHAPTER EIGHTEEN

WE LANDED, hired a car with Hugo's fake license, and drove to the outskirts of the city, while Jess checked in to the same Hilton near the airport I originally stayed in, but paid cash. She would wait for us to conduct our surveillance and then provide additional info as needed. It was a task she could have performed from the safety of Kochany Dom, but stubbornness was one of her more endearing qualities.

In a run-down neighborhood, which mimicked poor neighborhoods the world over—decrepit cars, overgrown gardens, abandoned buildings, youths milling around in great numbers—Hugo drove straight to an address on his phone, told me to watch the car, and jogged up the path to a tenement. He returned less than two minutes later, chucked a heavy clanking sports bag into my lap, and jumped in. As he drove away, I opened the bag to find two Sig-Sauer handguns, an MP5K submachine-gun, a dozen spare magazines, and three boxes of bullets.

"Five grand," Hugo said.

"Submit your expenses to the usual place."

Hugo laughed, and I punched in the coordinates to Katerina's old farm, obtained via the records Jess dug through. This was the place I was convinced they tortured me, and from which I barely escaped with my life.

When I first escaped that hole, I didn't know which way was up, unable to tell the direction I was running. I took little notice of my surroundings except to ensure nobody was following. But then, when Katerina talked about the additional works at the farm, and the tunnels in which to flee should the resistance come calling, it started the cogs whirring and firing together connections I was unsure should be there. It took some time to process the idea. Although I could not remember my exact route back to Kraków with the lorry driver, the journey time approximately married up with the distance on a map. Add that the professor would be familiar with the location and structure of the place, that it was abandoned and set in the middle of nowhere, a giant leap of imagination became an educated guess.

As we drew closer to Katerina's former home, I spotted landmarks, the roads, the pitch of the land, even some road signs I couldn't hope to read. It must have been located at a high elevation, as fog descended the longer we drove. We pulled up a mile away down a narrow lane, and parked the vehicle behind a hedgerow.

Hugo checked the guns, and handed me a Sig, plus two spare magazines now filled with bullets. "Want a quick demo before we go in?"

The gun was older than the one I trained with, but it worked the same. I racked the slide to check a bullet was chambered, then decocked it using the lever mechanism.

"Someone's been doin' his homework," Hugo said.

"Reluctantly." I snapped on the safety, and held the weapon as Eric had shown me, with my finger outside the trigger guard.

"Nice. Textbook. Just be sure you can pull the trigger when it counts."

"Let's hope."

"*Hope*? Well that's a confidence booster."

We jogged through overgrown grass and skirted the edge of the road until we drew parallel with the former farm. Once I recognized the woodland through which I escaped, we ran. Hugo kept one Sig in his shoulder holster, and carried the MP5K raised to shoulder height, aimed along his eye line like a SWAT commander preparing for breach.

When we reached the open land bordering the main house, Hugo crouched, hidden under a thick evergreen bush, its lower branches high enough off the ground for him to scramble out at pace if required. I took a breath, prepared myself, and sprinted into the open, aiming both my gun and my route at the front door.

The large wooden abode rose out of the mist, and sported peeling white paint, pointed corners on the roof, surprisingly well maintained gutters, showing the lie that this house was abandoned. It struck me too late that, if they kept the house in such good nick, they must have been here longer than a week.

A gunshot sounded. I didn't see where, didn't feel the whiz of hot lead anywhere near me, so I kept on going, arrowing forward. The second shot landed closer, kicking up dirt a couple of feet from me. I raised the Sig, flicked off the safety, and let off two rounds.

Without ear defenders, my hearing took a kick, but my

continued practice meant it didn't shock me as much as my first experience with gunfire.

My shots went wild, not aimed anywhere in particular, but to draw them out, reveal their locations. And it worked. One of the thugs I beat up leaned out of an upstairs window as he tried to get an angle on me. The large handgun boomed twice, but he was clearly even less experienced than me. Still, he was close enough to hit me if I stopped.

A crack sounded and the thug's head caved in, spraying crimson and gray on the house.

Thanks, Hugo.

I made it around the corner, so Hugo was now blind to me, but as soon as I sighted on an access point, namely the front door, the rattle of automatic gunfire thudded rounds into the dirt where I was about to run. I dived for a pile of logs. More bullets kicked up in front of me, wood splintering and showering down upon me. Then three heavy slugs battered the ground to my left.

They had flanked me, not yet fully exposed.

I raised my hands above the logs, the Sig held by my thumb and forefinger.

Nothing happened for ten seconds. That doesn't sound like a lot, but ten seconds of silence in the aftermath of exchanging shots with trained killers, it seemed long enough to write a mental will.

The two remaining rent-a-thugs showed themselves. One out of the front door, the other stepping carefully from the side of the house.

"What you doing, Englishman?" the first asked. He only had one free hand to carry his pistol, the other in a sling. To tend to his knife wound, no doubt.

"I need to talk to the professor," I said. "I know he wants

me dead, but I have something to exchange. Information he needs."

"Give us information. We ask professor if we kill you anyway."

I tuned in to the birdsong in the woods, the crisp breeze, and scent of wet grass. I didn't want those things present; I wanted to hear Hugo storming to the rescue.

I said, "That's probably a really dumb idea, if you don't mind me saying. I think I'll wait for the prof himself."

"You think you can attack like this and live?" the speaker said. "Come out. Maybe you do live, maybe not. Gamble, yes?"

I stood, at their mercy, but they had come at me from poor angles, almost facing one another. If they both fired at once, they would perforate me but take each other out too. That single fact snagged on a thread in the back of my head, but before I could tug on it, the guy speaking crumpled in a heap as his chest spat blood and two gunshots rang out. Instead of ducking for cover, the other snapped his head back and forth, looking for the assailant. He never saw Hugo, though, as I righted the Sig in my hand, drew down on him, and fired once into his head.

Hugo joined me as I stood over the body, his skull having ruptured, spilling red and grey mush onto the ground.

"Shit," Hugo said. "Vila might be right about you after all."

"I'm not like you," I said. "I'm not like any of you."

Although, feeling nothing but relief as the man's brains leaked out, I wasn't so sure how true that was.

"You ever breached a house like this?" Hugo asked.

"When would I have ever breached a house?"

He shrugged. "Stay close, cover our six."

"Six?"

"Our *backs*, arsehole. Make sure no one sneaks up behind."

"Fine," I said. "Our six is covered."

Hugo adopted his SWAT-commander stance again, and we set ourselves by the door, ready to confront whatever awaited us inside.

CHAPTER NINETEEN

HUGO RUSHED through the empty kitchen to a hallway where a door most likely once hung. He stalked through, beckoning with turning his head. I followed, gun aimed, more mimicking Hugo than actually understanding the skill. In reality, I was half-hoping Vila Fanuco was right about me, that my instincts and nature made me a good fit for this work.

Half-hoping.

Fully-hoping it would keep me alive.

Hugo called, "Clear," each time he swept a room, and there were three down here, plus a shelved space I assumed to be a larder or pantry. To check upstairs, we would have to traverse a smashed flight of stairs with no banister. It looked too aged to be a ruse, which left the cellar door in the kitchen.

"Ladies first," Hugo said.

"What happened to me being under your protection?"

"You? *Estelle's* our principle now. You're a middleman along for the ride. You do know, if you die here, we still get paid, right?" He lowered his weapon to speak close to my face. "And let's get another thing straight. There's no instruction from Fanuco tae keep you alive. This is you an' me. A partnership.

We're here tae kill everyone, then go get drunk on the rich pricks' dime. Understand?"

I opened the door a crack and peeked through. "So I'm 'breaching' first?"

"Yeah, breach away." Hugo returned the stock to his shoulder and aimed at the cellar. Nodded.

I pulled it open and sprang through, pinning myself to the far wall, gun pointed down the stone staircase. Hugo's barrel poked in, followed by the man himself. Lights glowed all the way, but darkness loomed beyond the last step.

Hugo went first after all, his feet silent on the surface. At the halfway point, he flicked on a wide-beamed pen torch attached to the MP5K. Dust danced in the harsh light, but no one came for us. No gunshots.

At a bend in the structure, Hugo stopped, using the angle as cover. I sidled up to him, stepped in front , but he pushed me to the side. Jabbed his finger at the other wall. As with Eric and his line of sight on Herman in my house, I'd blocked the guy covering me.

Amateur.

That's what I had to remember here. Sure, taking the life of someone who would take mine was far easier than I was comfortable with, and while I bullseyed tin cans and outlines almost to competition standard, tactics were equally important here. And I had zero experience in clearing premises like this.

I took the outside lane, so to speak, inching along until I observed the dimly-lit corridor ending at the staircase leading down to the office.

I couldn't remember if it was this dim during my last stint here or if my sight adjusted before fleeing, but the spacing of bulbs reminded me of emergency lighting rather than a functioning grid.

I chopped my hand in the air as I'd seen on the movies and

Hugo seemed to know what I meant, as he glided past me and on to the next turn. I descended the stairs, lit the same as above, and waited by the office in which the deceased thugs held me. Hugo darted in, whispered, "Clear," and returned to my position, before continuing onward. There were more rooms to check, but we eventually came to the torture chamber.

My turn to clear.

My feet rose and fell in a deliberately wide pattern, assessing the space with new eyes: the chair remained, as did the table and monitors, while they left only one laptop on a desk in the corner, teed up beside a modern office chair. No cameras, no mics, nothing but the echo of my pitiful attempts to walk silently.

I lowered the gun. "They're not here. Must've been in the process of clearing out when we showed."

In a stage whisper, Hugo said, "No assuming. Go 'round assumin' shit in places like this, you make an ass a' you and a dead man o' me."

"Be my guest. I'm going to take a look at this computer."

"Fuckin' amateur," he said.

When he was gone, I unfolded the laptop and checked it had power before turning it on. It ran through the BIOS and the Windows 10 welcome, then demanded a password. I tried "password" in a number of ways, including starting with a capital letter, adding "01" after it, and substituting numbers in place of common letters, like "pa55w0rd."

Unsurprisingly, Professor Jäger wasn't quite that stupid.

I sat in the chair and hit the shutdown command. As soon as the screen darkened, a sudden movement reflected in the black rectangle. I shoved the chair back and dropped to the floor.

The chair slammed into the male Israeli, Abba. His gun-arm tipped wide, a small blocky auto gripped there. He foolishly concentrated on his weapon, forcing his arm towards me, giving me time to move inside his range of motion. My forearm swung out, directing the gun upwards, while my other hand jabbed at his eye. He deflected with his free hand, exposing my back. I dropped to my knee, balanced myself on one hand, and my foot swung up and caught him under the jaw. It stunned him long enough for me to shift his gun back inside, and over-rotate his hand, which released the weapon.

His Krav Maga was up to date, though, hence why he broke free so quickly, and returned with an elbow to my chin. He attacked too fast for me to use the gun, so I tossed it and blocked another jab.

But this wasn't like the Pale Boy's attack. It was one-on-one; strength, speed, and skill, with a side-helping of sheer, bloody belligerence. I had his measure now, could gauge his technique: pure military, regimented, and therefore somewhat predictable.

In a flurry of close-in strikes, my heel thumped into his groin, and from then on in, he was done. That same heel crashed through the side of his jaw, flaring into the pressure point that rendered him unconscious.

I searched around for the guns, but then Clara was suddenly in the room.

Had she been here all along? Or did Abba get in some firmer shots to my head than I noticed?

She glanced at the fallen weapons and shook her head. Empty-handed. Nothing in the holster at her hip.

"No gun?" I said.

"I have one," she replied. "But you looked so smug when you dropped Abba, I decided to manage without it. You alone?"

"You think you can stop me from picking up one of those guns and shooting you?"

"I think you will not. If I was trying to kill you, sure, you might kill me first, if you are fast enough. But I'm unarmed. My gun is right over there."

I looked where she twitched her head to find an identical gun to Abba's next to the laptop. A split-second later, when I came back at her, her knee hurtled toward my eye.

There was no impact. Instead, she grappled me with her legs, and jerked into a spin to pull me down. I over-emphasized the momentum and tucked under so I didn't face-plant, then twisted and pushed so she released me. On our feet, I attacked with a feint jab, followed by a real stomach-punch. She sidestepped and a tap from her sent me into the dentist's chair. I pushed back, and used my foot to lead, but she grabbed my wrist and gave me a tug.

I was airborne.

I spun in mid-air, and she flung me back the way I came. I landed hard, dizzy. She followed up with another knee, but I managed to lower my jaw to avoid a knockout. My head merely slammed sideways. I rolled onto my feet, but a kick to my ankle sent me off-balance, an open hand to my neck took my breath away, and when she yanked me towards her, I flew easily onto the table with the dead monitors.

It was like fighting the Pale Boy again.

But I had a hypothesis. And it was nothing to do with super-strength or mystical powers.

I rolled off the table and picked up a flat screen. As I threw it, my hypothesis became a theory.

It was instinctive on her part. The shifting of her body-weight, the lightning calculation of where the threat of force lay—in this case in the object's momentum—and the redistribution of strength, as she swatted it into the wall behind her.

And just like that, I knew why I was struggling.

My newfound knowledge didn't mean I could defend against it. Her Krav Maga, when she used it, was superior to Abba's, and her inferior strength was all that stopped me from succumbing immediately. I wouldn't last much longer, though.

I yelled, "*Hugo! Where are you?*"

Laughter burst through the room as Hugo stepped forward with his gun raised. "Alright, sister, my gut's about tae burst holdin' this fuckin' laughter in. Better call it a day, eh?"

Clara dropped her stance and placed her hands on her head.

Breathing hard, I said, "You were watching?"

"Yeah, I was watching. Really fuckin' funny. Wait'll I tell Emmy you got beat up by a girl. How'd you manage that?"

"Let's get these two secure," I said, "then I'll explain. About her, *and* the Pale Boy."

CHAPTER TWENTY

CLARA GLARED from the same chair in which she'd interrogated me, likewise secured with cable ties to her wrists and ankles. Abba was still unconscious but hog-tied and lashed to a sturdy-looking pipe. Hugo confirmed the rest of the basement was empty—"no old man, no grey-lookin' wankers"—then asked about why a girl could take me out like that.

"Aikido," I said. "What they teach in the west is usually a watered down version. Jess learns back in England, and from what I've seen she's okay. But the Pale Boy, and this Clara here, they're on another level. You ever see old videos of Steven Seagal in his prime?"

"Can't say I have," Hugo said.

"They look as if his opponents aren't even trying. But Aikido isn't like Krav Maga or Wing Chun, or any of those direct combat techniques. It concentrates on using the attacker's strength against him."

"Like Ju Jitsu."

"To a degree. Look." I positioned him so his fist pushed against my chin, and shaped his legs into a solid stance. "Comfy?"

He twisted his back foot. "So now I'm directin' my strength through my leg intae the punch."

"Right, and you're planted well, yes?"

"Sure."

I looked to Clara and asked, "So how does he end up flying through the air, almost weightless?"

She turned her head to check on Abba. He was clearly breathing so she returned her attention to me. "Keep the power of his punch moving upward, the direction it was always traveling. Alter the angle of his arm so he leans forward, then pull down and to the side. All his power that should be shattering your nose pulls him off-balance."

I said, "In any advanced self-defense class, they teach you to do that, but it tips them over, and you run, or lock the arm. But not you guys."

"No. You keep going down. Their body reacts automatically—you don't notice it yourself—but it's you who pushes off the ground."

"To cope with the pain."

"Correct." She sighed, frowning with disdain. "Once you are in the air, I move the arm in the opposite direction, which flips you."

"And because my center of gravity is in mid-air, spinning…"

Hugo clapped his hands together once. "Ha! You're effectively weightless. Totally cool. Man, I studied Krav Maga, Wing Chun, and that Brazilian Ju Jitsu stuff, but I am totally signin' up for Aikido when I get home."

"Doubt it'll do you much good," I said.

"Why?"

"Because," Clara said amid another sigh, "to reach my level you have to study from a young age, under a true master."

I said, "I lived in Japan for a while, before I worked as a

detective full time. I saw those demonstrations, where old men destroy six strapping young students at a time, and it's almost supernatural. Like the Pale Boy."

Hugo didn't seem too put off as he took up position by the door. "So how come you didn't spot it before?"

"It's different being on the receiving end. And if I already have the notion of ghosts in my head…"

"So this junior golem ain't some super-powered clay man after all? Shame."

I retrieved the laptop and flipped up the lid. Turned it on. Faced Clara.

"Password, please."

She snorted in reply.

It made a change from sighing, I suppose.

I placed the machine down and moved to her side. "Last time we were here, you did some pretty nasty things to me. And I'm guessing you follow Jäger and the Pale Boy because of some idealism."

She spat. "The Pale Boy is not my choice. He was sent because of you."

"Me?"

"A man who wages war on his enemies, who allows innocents to die, using their deaths to achieve your wins. Yes, Mr. Park, we know about the town of Bafam, and what you did. And you consort with terrorists."

The gossip between spies must be worse than a tea party of bored pensioners. Bafam was a mistake, not a mercenary act, and the so-called "terrorists" … well, it depended how you looked at it.

"The professor is a great man," she said. "He sniffs out the remnants of the Third Reich like a bloodhound. Not just the people who helped murder so many, but—"

"The undeserving who still benefit to this day. I know, I

heard the speeches. You arrest Nazis or kill them, and loot the vaults of anyone with a connection. What did you mean when you said this sick killer is out there because of me?"

"You are allied with people of interest. We take no chances."

"So what's your problem with Estelle Kravitz?"

She did not reply.

"Explain it to me," I said. "Why are Nazi killers so interested in whether Estelle signs over her fortune to the Romani guys? If it's the Caines' money they can do what they want. If it should be with the Roma, then hooray. Their people suffered too."

Her eyes adopted a hooded poise, mouth pinched into silence.

"She's not going to talk," I said to Hugo.

"I coulda' told you that five minutes ago," Hugo replied. "Want me to cut off her toes or you got the stones yourself?"

I wasn't sure if he was joking or not, so I made sure he understood. "I am not torturing her."

I tapped the laptop.

"Password," I said.

Abba stirred and Clara checked on him, back to me.

"You get nothing," she said.

I fiddled with the machine, searched for its leads, and found nowhere to plug in an Ethernet cable. No Wi-Fi signal either. The computer was dead. I should have taken it to Jess at the hotel, but I couldn't leave the pair and risk them escaping. I wasn't willing to execute any more than torture.

"Stay alert," I told Hugo, and wandered out to find a floor with a mobile phone signal. When I snagged one, I called the one person I could think of to help. "I've been bad, Jess. But I need you. Do you have enough euros to catch a cab to Katerina's old farm?"

CHAPTER TWENTY-ONE

"I can make her talk," Hugo said as I returned. "None of that water bollocks, though."

"I told you, no torture."

"You're such a pussy."

Once, I broke a man's fingers one by one until he revealed information I needed. That act of violence still hurts me more than any life I've ever taken, but it saved someone close to me, so it would be untrue to say I regretted it entirely.

"Fifty euros," I said. "She talks without me resorting to violence."

He held out a hand to shake, but pulled it back quickly. "You're not gonna bring in someone else tae do it, are ya? 'Cause I noticed you said *you* wouldn't lay a hand on her."

"No torture of any kind."

"Okay." He shook my hand.

Jess's ETA approached, so I armed myself and headed up top to meet her. And to move the bodies of the rent-a-thugs into the long grass.

She arrived five minutes later in a battered minicab, bumping its way up the untended drive from the main road—

an access point I had avoided for obvious reasons. She paid the driver a handsome tip and, once he was on his way, she slapped me hard across the face.

"Another one for the collection," she said. Tears welled but did not spill.

I wanted to hold her and promise her I would never lie to her again, but I simply couldn't know what the future held.

I said, "I'm sorry. I didn't want to worry you."

"I'm here for Estelle. I'd do it for any kid in danger." She stomped toward the house, pausing to emphasize, "I mean it. I'm not here because *you* asked me. Once I'm certain everyone is safe, I'm heading home."

"Thank you," I said.

But she was already gone.

In the office halfway to where Hugo kept watch over Clara and Abba, Jess worked her magic with the laptop. She started in BIOS and worked her way into what I recognized as a DOS screen, and spent half an hour breaking the encryption. Once in, we ploughed through it together, but she demanded I stop looking over her shoulder and leave her to figure it out.

The office was internet-ready, but slow, yet Jess was able to install some interpreter software a little more advanced than Google Translate, but still not perfect. She took notes as the relevant documents popped up, and I soon grew restless.

I relieved Hugo for a bathroom break, and he complained he was hungry, so went hunting for supplies. He must have located a supply stash, as he returned munching on a military ration pack. He tossed one to me along with a plastic spoon.

He said, "I gave yer girlfriend one but she said she wasn't hungry."

"She's not my girlfriend," I said, "and she's tasted them before."

They are not nice.

I said, "Give this pair some water if you think it's safe."

When I rejoined Jess, she was sitting on the couch, staring at a stain on the floor that could only be blood. The rent-a-thug I stabbed.

"You have something?" I asked.

"Who's down there?" She nodded to the door.

"The pair who waterboarded me."

"Are they dead?"

"No. And I won't hurt them unless they come after me. They're neutralized, so it's all good for now. What do you have?"

"We already know they're Nazi hunters. Assassins where necessary. They've targeted the chap Judge Kravitz is dealing with, the human rights case in Italy, but declined to move on him due to the publicity. Their superiors worry about their gang being exposed, because it might bite them."

"Israel?"

"Unclear. If it's Mossad, it's a deep, dark operational part. Probably deeper than the government can dig."

"Nothing mind blowing there."

"No. Although you'll get a kick out of their name."

"They have a name?"

"The Fist of God."

"Sounds like specialized porn."

She giggled, then cut off the humor as she clocked my smile. "They're after a betrayer. They took the work done by Tony Luca, *bought* it off him judging by the payment, and Professor Jäger and his higher-ups concluded it was worth pursuing. Their beef goes all the way back to Elizabetta."

I realized I was pacing. "So they get the research, dive into some more history, but then a new detective shows up, and they don't want to share what they know. They don't want any other players muddying the waters."

"Right. They reported all this to their high command and were awaiting orders here."

"Those orders come through?"

"Decrypting the message now." She pointed at the computer, at a series of symbols and hashes and numbers unscrambling. Each segment of released material was then seized upon by Jess's digital translator and threw out results in a random order. "Apparently they have more intel from German records accumulated over the years, intelligence from Nazis interrogated before they were killed or handed over for trial."

"Does it mention a specific person?" I asked.

"It seems to be referring to a 'target' but no names."

Data streamed. Jess worked the trackpad, rearranging everything into a logical order. She was frowning within minutes. "This can't be right."

I tried to see around her. "There's a name?"

She shielded the screen, hoarding the bounty for herself. "Let me check I'm reading this right before you go off half-cocked."

After my deception today and her subsequent fury, I allowed discretion to overcome my curiosity, and returned to pacing the room. This usually annoys the crap out of her, but she seemed to concentrate perfectly well. Eventually, she closed the laptop, and stared at it.

I ceased pacing. "What is it?"

"I still can*not* see how they came to that conclusion."

"What? Come on, don't play games."

Her eyes bored into mine. "No game, Adam. But it has to be a mistake." She stood, laptop dangling. "Professor Jäger's target is someone they see as a betrayer, someone who profited from it, and who betrayed one of the bravest women in Jewish folklore. Not to mention a man who left his family to fight the resistance."

I wanted to snatch the laptop from her. "Like you said, it has to be a mistake."

"The person they're investigating," she said, "the person they think is a collaborator, a traitor, is Katerina Caine."

Jess was correct in that I would go off half-cocked. But perhaps not in the way she thought. I moved up a flight of stairs to grab a signal, and called Emiliana to see if anything had happened since we last spoke.

"Such as?" she said.

"We don't think Estelle is the target. It's not necessarily about the money, either, but I'm damn sure they want a chunk. They want Katerina."

"Ah."

"What does 'ah' mean? Don't tell me 'ah' without following it up."

"I mean 'ah' as in 'ah, that explains why she ain't around anymore.' Is that better?"

"Not around? She's gone?"

"She said goodbye to Estelle this morning, plenty emotional. I gave them space, don't like to eavesdrop."

"So what did they say?"

"Katerina said she had to go away for a while, but she'd protect Estelle from what was coming. Told Estelle to be strong, that everything would work out. Then blah, blah, blah, goodbye."

So, Katerina was now missing, and clearly hiding far more than we had realized.

CHAPTER TWENTY-TWO

WITH JESS IN ATTENDANCE, I confronted Clara. I told her what we now knew, and asked her if she truly believed a woman in her nineties could possibly warrant the wrath of the Fist of God. Clara and Abba, now conscious, exchanged looks, Abba granting her a brief nod.

She said, "There is nothing I can tell you that will make a difference. You know it all now."

"Try me," I replied. "I'm a good listener. And I like details too."

"Let me out of here, and I will tell you whatever you want."

We allowed the two agents to go partly free. Their hands remained cable tied at the wrists, but Hugo conceded to switch them to the front, and their feet also retained a set of ties, several looped together so they shuffled like prisoners on a chain gang; hand-to-hand combat was impossible, as was fleeing into the woods. The pair smoked outside on the stoop, a platform of rotting wood and long-gone paint, the surface bleached by the sun, and attacked by the elements, while I stood before them with my arms folded. Hugo maintained his lookout role. Jess observed from behind the pair.

"The local council do not know what to do with this place," Clara said. "The bank repossessed it from the most recent owners, but failed to find a buyer. They are short of land for building houses, so used a law to make them sell … emirate?"

"Eminent domain," I suggested.

"Yes, this. Eminent domain law came into effect. Forced the sale. But again, nobody wanted it. Not enough value for foreign investment, and locals have too many stories. Captain Goetz, Petr Caine, the Angel of Kraków. Take your pick who haunts this place. I have not yet seen anyone, but we are definitely not alone here. And nobody wishes to take the chance."

The fog had all but cleared, only faint wisps swaying between the trees.

I said, "The Angel of Kraków is renting space in Kochany Dom full-time, and Petr Caine is squatting inside Estelle. So I guess that leaves the Nazi."

"Which brings us to why Katerina may be one of the Jewish people's greatest betrayers."

I held up my hand to Hugo and clicked my fingers. He placed fifty euros in my palm, I scrunched up the money, and stuffed it in my pocket.

Clara tutted. "We are not one hundred percent sure about her, but she has disappeared. Is that not an admission of guilt to you?"

"She believes in ghosts and spiritual possession. So it's not a great leap for her to think your Pale Boy might be a golem who won't stop until she's dead."

"I told you, the Pale Boy is not with us. We did not call him in. Our commanders in Jerusalem did not trust us, and so sent him to tidy up what they saw as our mess. But the professor is a strategist, and he is patient."

Jess had kept her distance, yet remained within the group. "What about your government?"

"We live in a country surrounded by savages who wish us dead. Our government has no time for shadows of the past anymore."

"If you're not sure about Katerina, why put the detectives off?"

She gave Jess a withering look. "I know nothing of Tony Luca and his new life. I thought that was Gottfried, but those who control the Pale Boy may have bought his silence." Back to me. "Katerina's account of her fortune does not sit well. She *says* she and her husband grew wealthy because of business and farming, which pushed up the value of this property. But their wealth did not commence growing until *after* he died."

I said, "Could be the investments didn't start paying off until later."

"Possible, but why immediately after his death? Once the mourning period was over, she moved to Austria with their child, and returned far wealthier."

"I thought she relocated to Paris."

"First to Austria. Straight after making the farm for sale. Six months. She came home to complete the transaction, draped in fine furs, and jewelry."

"I found none of that," Jess said.

Abba puffed away on a pungent cigarette, interjecting for the first time. He spoke gingerly, barely moving the left side of his mouth, a lump the size of half a tennis ball having swollen where I hit him. "You look in wrong place, sweetheart."

"For someone who doesn't speak much English, you've got the sexism down pat."

He raised his eyebrows and blew a column of smoke towards her.

I said, "Jess is right. Where did you get this information?"

"We do not always know," Clara said. "The Fist of God is not the only group who operates. But all of them do so only as long as Jerusalem allows it." Meaning Mossad. "We do not work for them, but to stay free, we must send all our intelligence to them. They will review it, and decide if it is relevant to anyone else's mission."

"So what's the theory? Stolen money? It's only since the big financial squabble was made semi-public that your group took an interest. How come?"

She dropped her cigarette butt and squashed it out. "Because the Roma asked us to."

I checked the gun, more to allow a pause that wasn't entirely empty than worried it would not work. I eased the safety off, then back on again, before realizing Jess and Hugo were both staring. Clara and Abba held themselves as still as rodents in the presence of a circling hawk.

I slipped the weapon into the back of my trousers. "What if the story Estelle told the Roma is true? That there is another line? Might Katerina have a brother or sister?"

"This is not something we care about." Clara's shoulders visibly relaxed. "We care about what is right, about what is wrong, and about the wronged people seeing justice. It does not matter if the Roma have some claim to this land, and I think they do not. But the most simple explanation, if they do, is that Katerina was not truthful about her time here with Friedrich Goetz. There is no one but Katerina who hints he could have been gay, so maybe things were more intimate. And what happens, Mr. Detective, when things are intimate?"

We knew from Jess's research that no one—not a single person from the town—saw her during that time. Even the laborers, offered paid work after the war, supposedly rejected it, yet none of their names were recorded, and so could not be tracked down for their account.

I said, "You really believe Katerina could have had a baby whilst secluded at the farm?"

Jess was on the same page. "If so, the family tree took a diversion *before* the current line. Before Beatrice."

"No one can confirm it," Clara said. "Too much history has gone. Is just a theory, based on many rumors."

"Hearsay and guesswork," I said. "Katerina *might* have had a secret baby. It *might* have been sent away, and it *might* be the ancestor of Marco LaPorte. Katerina *might* have learned of Captain Goetz's stash of stolen Jewish money, and she *might* have travelled to access the stash once her husband was dead. And she might—*might*—have used that as seed money to move to Paris, and build an art brokerage, that grew into a multimillion-euro business."

"Hey," Hugo said, "when you put it like that, it does sound kinda flimsy."

Clara fidgeted. Accessed the cigarette box, and took out another. I lit it for her, and she watched me all the way. I noted how wide her eyes were, their deep brown shade, and chided myself doing so.

She said, "It is enough for suspicion."

"So you're primarily an investigation unit?" I said. "And you have the ability to act if your conclusions warrant it."

"Before we had a chance to match records with statements from people who lived through 1943, '44, and '45, Katerina's lawyer sent a detective to investigate her great-granddaughter's possession. When he vanished, we were free to continue, but then your presence forced us to act. Again."

I scratched my head. "Why couldn't you just let me get on

with it? We never would have crossed paths, until you confronted Katerina, if you ever got round to it."

"You are well-known, thanks to your association with Fanuco, and willingness to aid terrorists. Nobody was willing to risk you might interfere. Violently."

I don't know where it came from, but a fire burned inside my chest, and I kicked the balustrade, shattering the hundred-year-old wood. Everyone jumped back.

I said, "I am sick of justifying that to people. I *stopped* them."

"You escape with great skill," Abba said. "Act like professional agent. Report from the old man alerted those higher up chain. They need you take out of play."

"Now we're back with the Pale Boy. Who is he? Really. No golem talk."

Clara sucked hard on the cigarette, and the paper sizzled as the tobacco burned. She exhaled a long grey column. "He has operated since the 1950s, but nobody knows his actual name. And you see him, you think he is a child. His eternal youth leads many to believe he is not of this world, not clay perhaps, but possessed of true power."

Jess shifted uncomfortably, a movement only I registered.

Clara said, "It is more likely our leaders choose someone who is damaged, a young person who is physically impressive, and mentally able to learn, but who enjoys what we do far too much."

"They identify serial killers," I said.

Clara shrugged. "But that is only another rumor. More hearsay. That he is something ... *other* ... is a more common belief."

"Sounds about right, though," Hugo said. "Get a sick fucker, train him up in as many martial arts as possible, as many weapons as he can handle, keep the brainwashin' goin', make him see he's a noble soldier, but keep him indoors 'til he's needed. Can't be bribed, can't be reasoned with, and he loves what he does."

"Nothing supernatural then," I said. "Just a psychopath on a leash, lacking in vitamin D." I pulled out the Sig, cocked it, and pointed it at Clara's head. She pulled away as I said, "So if they think I'm equally bad, a criminal, a terrorist sympathizer, an expert special agent, or whatever, maybe I'll play it up a little. Call your superiors, and recall the Pale Boy."

"We cannot," Abba said.

"Try."

"Adam..." Jess said.

I ached to tell her I was bluffing, but the Israelis had to believe I was serious. Providing I could later persuade Jess I would never have pulled the trigger, I'd consider that a success. But if she genuinely believed I could murder someone in cold blood, then she was lost to me forever.

"Once the Pale Boy is in play," Clara said, her head still angled away from me, her hair covering her face, "nothing can stop him. His orders cannot be countermanded. It comes from a higher power than my father—"

She cut herself off, clearly realizing a mistake in revealing her relationship with Jäger. Deflated, she continued.

"It comes from a higher power than a group of Nazi hunters, and that higher power is convinced of Katerina's crimes. They care not for lies or ghosts, and they do not even care whether Katerina had a baby, or if that baby spawned descendants legally entitled to money."

I lowered the gun. "If Katerina did have a baby, then got rich from Captain Goetz and his share of whatever was taken from the ghettos ... that makes it even worse."

"How is that worse?" Jess asked.

I wanted to leave right now. To take Jess by the hand,

speed to the airport, and catch the next plane home to England, and maybe test how close we had grown, or how far we had been torn apart. I needed to know. That's all I needed to know right in that moment.

But I knew more than that. I knew people who wielded the power and the means to create a creature such as the Pale Boy were now locked upon a goal that would not end well for anyone involved.

I said, "The family tree is irrelevant. Either Katerina is bequeathing Jewish wealth looted by the Nazis on Estelle, or it gets diverted to Marco LaPorte. The only way it goes to Marco is if he's related to the bastard offspring of Katerina and Captain Goetz. In which case…"

She twigged, and seemed as taken aback as me. "They can't allow the descendent of a Nazi to get his hands on the fruits of Nazi crimes."

"They want it all for themselves," I said. "And if they can't recall the Pale Boy, even with these two as hostages, there's nothing we can do. I'm a dead man. And Katerina won't be far behind."

CHAPTER TWENTY-THREE

IF THE PALE Boy truly was a sadist whose mind worked like that of a serial killer, then his actual goal could be to wipe out all trace of dissent in terms of the hundred million euros in cash, not to mention the physical assets, of the Kravitz Empire, all to which his masters saw themselves as entitled. How he would transfer the cash, I couldn't be sure. But it didn't take a rational mind for him to go out and slaughter those he deemed his enemy.

Naturally, Hugo wanted to execute Clara and Abba, but I never entertained the idea. Hugo returned the guns, arranged for a cleanup crew to erase all trace of us from the farm, and flew back to Hamburg on the Cessna. Although I wanted Jess to accompany him, she insisted on staying.

With their tongues loosened, I believed them when they said they did not know the whereabouts of Professor Jäger, that he had evacuated as soon as his masters' prize assassin showed up, returning—Clara suspected—to Israel to protest and request more time to continue in a more subtle manner. At least that was the plan. Professor Jäger never landed in Jerusalem, so they were as much in the dark as me. In the end, we left them bound in their current state, unable to move quickly in the short-term, but they would free themselves once we were gone.

Hugo, before departing, again tried to talk me into asking Fanuco to assist, or at least look into the matter. He surely had the resources and contacts, and probably knew more about the Pale Boy than the rest of us, but my answer remained the same.

"I will not accept his help. Not for this, not for Gorman. I hired you, but that's a cash transaction. Bringing him into this, he will demand more than money in return."

I instructed Hugo to treat Estelle as his priority but he warned me Fanuco would learn of the situation, and if harm were to befall me, Fanuco would blame Hugo, despite his earlier assertion that I was on my own in this. That sounded stupid, but Vila Fanuco's obsession with somehow converting me to the dark side like a sleazy, earthbound Darth Vader tempting his son with the promise of order, did not have to be logical, any more than a ninety-five-year-old woman paying in blood for perceived crimes from seventy years ago.

So Hugo returned to the mansion alone, and later explained how he relayed my orders to Emiliana. While she distracted Francis—the one true threat to their mission—Hugo sedated Estelle and smuggled her from the building, then transported her to a safe house twenty miles outside the city known only to four people: him, Emiliana, a German ex-special forces sergeant turned trafficker, and the landlady who greeted them and granted access via a back passageway.

When Gottfried called, he shouted, threatened to call the police, and told me he hoped Katerina was dead for bringing this all down upon them. I persuaded him it was for the best, that we knew what we were doing, and he should ensure Francis could protect both him and Herman, or to find somewhere else to wait until it was all over. Because, I assured him, it would be over soon.

One way or another.

Although I could only guess how they traced me to The Firebrand Hotel , it wasn't Jäger who stalked me in the graveyard; it was the Pale Boy himself. And it was *me* they were after, meaning Jess and I booked into separate hotels for now, and I gave her no choice in the matter.

I could fight the killer with help, perhaps other mercenaries that Hugo or Emiliana might've put me in touch with, or perhaps even break a vow to Jess that I would not cave with Fanuco.

Yet, I couldn't avoid the notion my most powerful weapon right now was truth. It was the promise I made to both myself and Herman, and to Estelle and Katerina, that the truth will out. If I were to have any chance of closing this satisfactorily, I needed the truth in all its dirty glory, because if all parties agreed, and all transactions concluded in a legal and public manner, I doubted the Pale Boy's handlers would chance exposing themselves to the world.

The only person who knew for certain was Katerina, and I could not ask her. So I had to talk to the other interested party instead.

I kept hold of Hugo's car, retraced my route to the Romani camp, and reached it before nightfall. They made me slightly less welcome than my previous visit, with no tea on offer this time. In fact, as I hammered on Vera LaPorte's door, and called for her to come out, Marco and his Beefcake friends jogged over with their mouths and noses twisted into snarls more in keeping with pit bulls. I was deciding which order I would try to take them out, when Vera appeared out of her door. She wore jeans and an oversized pullover, showing her traditional garb the other night was definitely for my benefit.

She said, "It is only fair that I give you a chance to walk away. We tell you everything we will tell you."

The trio of heroes paused yards from me.

"Thanks," I said. "But before you start trying to remove me from here, I have one question. Would you rather answer to me, or the Pale Boy?"

The color visibly drained from Vera's face, as if morphing into the golem himself, and her hand touched her heart. "Why do you ask of him? Why would he come here?"

"If you've heard of him, then you know what I'm talking about. He and the people who control him, they don't want anyone else to inherit the money. They think it was looted from the Jewish people, but you know that already, don't you? You spoke to the professor, you knew his group would get involved here. You just didn't count on the other guy showing up. The golem."

Vera sat on her steps, looking down upon me. I sensed the two Beefcakes step away, but focused on the old lady. She twitched her head, and the footsteps receded, although Marco remained and joined his grandmother.

"It was not stolen from Jews," she said. "It was proceeds of *O Porajmos*. Of the Devouring."

"You think that will stop them coming for you? For Marco?"

She struggled to speak for a moment, her mouth opening and closing as she formed a response. "We are no threat to them."

"Nor am I, not really."

They could have walked away when I escaped, and just worked through the historical record to make their case. But they didn't. They needed every trace of a challenge wiped out, which is why I suspected they might target the LaPortes too. Vera clearly shared my unease. Whether they really were in danger was not my concern, but now I'd planted the seed it was time to apply some pressure.

"We think we know most of it," I said. "But not all. If we can convince the right people that they're wrong, maybe we can also convince them to leave you alone. To leave us *all* alone."

"You brought them here," Marco said. "You need to make them go away."

"No," Vera said. "If the Pale Boy is coming, the time of the secrets is over." She focused on me. "This is what the spirit of Petr Caine told Estelle, and what Estelle told us. It is the truth, and it will be proven."

CHAPTER TWENTY-FOUR

As we were all familiar by now, Vera's story commenced with a girl called Katerina. A fine girl, who married a fine man called Petr Caine, in the town of Kraków. But when the Nazis invaded their country, Petr fought back and was presumed dead.

None of this is disputed.

Nor are the murders of Katerina's mother and grand-mother, the latter to become known as the Angel of Kraków, and her order to Katerina to survive the war any way she could is accepted as truth.

But some accounts differ from here. Stories diverge. Rather than facing her enemies covertly and bravely, after losing the two women whose strength kept her going, some say Katerina gave up. And when one of the less vile officers who ran their town was quartered in her home, she chose not to spy on him, or to hinder his work.

She did a wonderful job, so much so that when Captain Goetz found a new property, more in keeping with a man making this country his home, he insisted she accompany him, and work the farm the way its undesirable former owners had done. Except, this time, they would do more than grow crops and slaughter livestock.

Because what nobody knew—not Goetz's commanders, nor the neighbors, and certainly not those who revered the Angel taken from them—was that Katerina also shared a bed with Friedrich Goetz.

How willingly is not known. But accounts survive. Accounts that remained hidden from official eyes, but have more recently come to light.

For when Friedrich moved in, according to one such recollection, Katerina hated him, and when he instructed her in the ways of his business, she hated him more. But as he showed compassion, where he could have been merciless, she saw in him things no Nazi had ever demonstrated in her life. He did not blindly march, blindly hate, or blindly kill. He was thoughtful, he had plans, aspirations beyond the war, and stretched far into the future.

This Friedrich Goetz was no empty man.

And, whilst barracked in their original home in the city, on an evening when she risked showing him true hospitality, with wine and a sweet pudding of her grandmother's recipe, and talked of things a man and wife may do, he took his role much further, and forced himself upon her.

It was a release for the man, who had long-coveted his assistant, and although he initially regretted his actions, when he sensed the fear radiating from Katerina, he chose to strengthen his hold over her, and made her his concubine. A role she performed as admirably as her secretarial duties.

On the surface, Goetz's move to the farm was an exercise in Nazi profiteering, moving into the shoes of the three generations of Griffins slain in a death camp; but behind the curtain he hid the burgeoning new life within Katerina, for such a child would never be accepted by her brethren, nor Goetz's.

Much of the labor building defenses and tunnels on the Griffin farm—now the Goetz farm—was shipped in from the local camp, known as Płaszów. Among them were Roma, as well as Jews.

In time, news of the Soviet advance reached the Goetz farm, and the wider command at Kraków, where a retreat was ordered. In the west, though, the Allies were bludgeoning Germany to her knees. So where would a Nazi officer hide with his mistress and bastard son?

Perhaps he convinced himself Katerina's heart had truly melted for him, and the act of sexual violence that preceded her acquiescence to further exploitation was now forgotten. He suggested she run with him. They could go to Africa and marry or, as rumor had it, follow other senior officers to South America, where sympathetic governments would shelter them for all time.

Naturally, Katerina gushed about how much she yearned for such a life, free of war and the military, where it could be just the three of them, or—possibly—four or five.

By this time, the laborers were living on-site, in the tunnels they dug beneath the property, and on the eve of the owners' planned flight, one of the prisoners ventured up to investigate the sound of a gunshot, and found the man dead, and Katerina trembling as the rifle slipped from her hands. She wept in the man's skeletal arms and insisted she was sorry for the conditions in which they were kept. She convinced them she was like them, a prisoner, albeit well fed, and cared for. But she had garnered the courage to break free, and she needed their help.

Under her instruction, they disposed of Friedrich's corpse, all the time lacking the knowledge Katerina possessed, that liberation beckoned mere days away. Even then, she did not know Petr was leading the charge with the Soviet infantry. All she knew was that as a woman with a baby to a Nazi, she would be tried as a collaborator, and executed like any common administrator who catalogued those on their way to their deaths, and redistributing their remaining wealth.

And dying like that would be a betrayal of the promise she made to the Angel of Kraków.

She pleaded with the newly-freed laborers to take her son and keep him safe. An act of mercy it seemed, but in reality, without Friedrich around, she was disposing of evidence without the guilt of murdering an infant, because although she did not love him as a mother should love a son, she could not bear his blood on her hands.

When Petr finally turned up, her delight, her sheer joy, truly overflowed. Thanks to whispers among the occupiers, all the locals knew of her imprisonment, and her story of killing the officer, so her omission of the existence of a child meant Petr resumed his life in the aftermath of the worst conflict in recent human history.

But he knew.

He knew his wife's body. Through the blood-soaked battlefields, the freezing winters, the memory of Katerina kept him going. He saw births, he saw infants die, and mothers perish in childbirth. He knew mothers who survived, and because six years is a long time to be away, not knowing if his wife died or survived, he found much comfort in the arms of widows, and so he recognized the marks of a mother.

When confronted, she confessed all, recounting her time as Friedrich Goetz's slave, and how she did not recognize the boy as her child. After much soul-searching, Petr accepted her explanation, and set about siring his own heir. And they called their daughter Beatrice.

It was not enough.

The pain of knowing his wife bore another child, it

combined with the nightmares of the war, and eventually he could stand it no longer. At the sound of the gunshot, she dashed down the stairs to find her dear husband, now truly dead, and would not be resurrected a second time.

After, Katerina had little choice but to sell up, and care for Beatrice alone. She would find a career more suited to a single woman in the 1940s, a widow, and the granddaughter of the now-famous Angel of Kraków.

CHAPTER TWENTY-FIVE

"THE GRANDFATHER, Petr, his spirit confirms this," Vera said. "Through the girl. His soul is as restless now as it was when he took his own life."

The stars were out, a crescent moon in a cloudless sky, and while the Roma donned coats and sweaters, I pretended the cold did not bother me. We sat where we had the night before, and Marco had only just nursed the fire properly to life when Vera ended the story.

I said, "Where is the proof?"

"The Nazis were excellent record keepers. And this was not different for their doctors. We have located his records, exactly where Estelle tell us where to find—locked away in doctor's safe, hidden in his old house in Vienna. When she visit us, Petr knew. He told her to reveal its whereabouts, this journal."

"And you plucked this out of some wall?" I said.

"Marco persuaded the current owners to let him examine the study, found safe behind a wall built up many years ago. The doctor was caught and tried in 1956, and died in his prison cell. But his attempts to hide evidence of his crimes remain."

"Why not burn it?"

"True Nazis believe a Fourth Reich would rise from the ashes of Third, and strike back at the Allied forces. Perhaps he wished to boast of his achievements in future. Or maybe he blackmailed others with what he knew."

As if rehearsed, Marco produced a journal from inside his jacket. It fit in the palm of his hand, the leather binding warped, but as he flicked through the pages, the paper was aged but intact, and the ink had not run. I couldn't hope to translate its contents, but if they were supplying it as legal evidence, its authenticity would be examined.

"So you see," Vera said, "this is proof Katerina had another child before Beatrice, and we can trace Marco's parentage line to Katerina and Friedrich, and the adoption in Austria."

"How did a gang of starving concentration camp survivors reach Austria with a two-year-old?"

"That is mystery. But not relevant. What *is* relevant, is Katerina also travelled to Austria, so she knew of her child's location, yet abandoned him to adopted parents. Her money, earned through thousands of murdered Roma, is owed … to *us*."

The fire crackled higher. Sparks danced. Virtually no heat emanated from the trash can.

"But how do you *know*?" I said. "How would she have obtained all that wealth?"

"Because those tunnels were not only for hiding from Russians." Vera shuffled closer to me on her folding chair. Pressed her bony finger to my head. It was warm. "They store valuable items—art, jewelry, cash. It was transported to Austria as soon as they heard of the Soviets' successes. And was Katerina's first stop after Petr died."

"I don't understand. She kills her tormentor, then has the child smuggled out so nobody can accuse her of collaboration, or worse. Then she welcomes her husband back, has another baby, and then when her husband dies, she heads off to the place where the unwanted child was adopted. It doesn't make any sense."

"The story we tell you," Vera said, "is all we can prove with journals, official records, and the guidance from Petr, through Estelle."

So they were still using a ghost to make their case.

I said, "There's a 'but' coming, isn't there?"

"Yes," Marco said. "But we have guesses to make."

"Guesses," Vera added. "We guess that after Petr took his life, Katerina made promise to the Angel extremely seriously, and chased happiness only way she know how. To change, to compromise. She knew how to find Friedrich's money, and how her child was sent to the same place, because is where she instructed her workers to send him. They would be rewarded at other end, but they did not know what reward would be. She wanted to reunite with him, even though she had that money. Whether she planned to take it all, we cannot be sure. We know, though, when she was not allowed near the boy, she did take it all, and set about starting over. After a stroke of fortune as one of her artists died, she made a bigger fortune. Now her mistake has returned."

"But she is the one pushing for Estelle to come clean," I said. "She hired a lawyer to get hold of Estelle's facts, and prove them. She must have known if there is evidence out here we would find it. And since all of this nonsense about spirits possessing young girls cannot possibly be true, who is putting these ideas into her head?"

"Maybe you find journal, she pay you to destroy it." Marco threw another log on the fire. "But is foolish to say there is not more working here than man can comprehend."

I had thought about this a lot, whether I could entertain

the theory of a long dead, troubled soul, returning. If Jess considered it possible, perhaps I should do the same. Should it be proven real, it was understandable Katerina might wish to follow through. And if that spirit provided the proof, she could be impacted by her true love's desire to see justice done.

I said, "I don't have much experience with inheritance law, but I can't see them simply raining money down on you guys. In fact, I'm pretty sure, at best, you would get a 50-50 split, possibly less if the Kravitzes were to fight it."

Vera opened her mouth and it widened in an "ah" gesture, revealing a healthy set of teeth, yellowed by age. "But the judge, Gottfried, he sit over cases of Nazi criminals, and makes decisions of their fate, both in Germany and in Brussels. Could he survive the shame of fighting the case if the woman in his house is a Nazi collaborator who birthed a bastard and covered it up? If she used even one franc of stolen good to create a fortune that Gottfried enjoys … he is a politician … he have to give it up."

"But with Pale Boy hunting," Marco said, "it might be simple."

I saw what he meant. "If Estelle were to die, that makes the lineage much clearer."

"Marco does not mean Estelle alone," Vera said.

Just as I was starting to warm up, as the fire grew strong enough to radiate a circle of heat, a new coolness swept through me.

I said, "The line that comes down with the first child … it's tainted. If Estelle is the final link in the chain on Petr's side, if she is killed, it clarifies things on Friedrich's. But that is *Nazi* ancestry, and it clears the way for Jäger and his group to claim the money for their own cause."

Vera nodded. "Not legally, but…"

"But with the Pale Boy on his moral mission, a generous

helping of death will be beneficial for everyone. Starting with Katerina, which is why she's in hiding. So the next best target … is Estelle or Marco."

Vera stood, and looked at Marco. She gestured for us both to stand and we did.

She said, "Mr. Park, you must go. We have much to prepare."

With the threat of murder hanging over the camp, I departed with a million theories competing for prominence, the most outlandish of which I wanted to put to Jess. It seemed ridiculous to me, but no less so than the facts I'd been considering of late: the notion of a spirit guiding the investigation, or a supernatural entity occupying the body of an ageless empty creature that served as an assassin, or even the notion this could ever have been a simple matter.

I parked at my hotel and, ensuring I wasn't followed, walked through a grey drizzle-soaked night to where Jess was staying, a significantly more upmarket venue than my own. It was a four-star establishment from a famous chain made to resemble an independent, and when I asked the receptionist to call up to her room, Jess agreed to meet me in the bar, which was an attempt at an upscale piano lounge, permanently absent a pianist. The barstools were comfortable, and I ordered two generous measures of an ancient scotch whiskey I had never heard of, but was priced appropriately. It didn't taste like a complete fake.

Jess showed up behind me, and said, "Adam?"

"Hey," I replied without turning. "What's a nice girl like you doing in a place like this?"

Terrible line, but I had a lot on my mind.

"She's with me," replied a gruff male voice.

I turned on my stool, and found myself face-to-face with Jess and, beside her, a sixty-five year-old man with a beard that could have nested a family of pigeons.

"Harry," I said. "What are you doing here?"

"What am I ever doing when I have to fly out and see you?" he said. "I'm here to give you a bollocking."

CHAPTER TWENTY-SIX

"It was my idea," Jess said.

"I guessed," I replied, holding out her whiskey.

She left it hanging there, but Harry snatched it, sniffed it, and took a sip. We had adjourned to a booth in the corner, where a speaker tinkled annoying Muzak designed to sound like a piano.

Jess said, "I'm sorry, Adam, but I'm more worried about you now than I've ever been."

"You do realize I'm an adult?" I said. "I know what I'm doing here."

"But you don't. All this talk of ghosts and demons, and always killing or fighting. The Adam I know is a guy who tracks down missing persons, might get into a dustup occasionally, but doesn't run around like a teenage boy's fantasy of a computer game hero."

"That's not what I'm doing. It's … the world isn't the way we thought it was. We have other fights to win, and sometimes it takes a bit more than we would like to give."

Harry made a satisfied noise, the sigh of a man slipping

into a warm bath after a hard day's work. He said, "I take it calling the police was out of the question."

"Yes, Harry, I considered that."

"So walk me through your process."

Harry. Ever the pragmatist.

I said, "I go to the police, they start asking questions about local hard nuts who disappeared recently."

"I don't mean now. I mean before a' this all kicked off. As soon as yer kidnapped, and escaped, you coulda' reported it, then stepped back from the case. Any investigation into those people would've revealed everything yer trying to find here today."

"Not true. If I'd reported it, these people have influence. The Israelis would've disavowed them, and Judge Kravitz could nix any other investigation into the family's history, and I'm not working for him. I'm working for Estelle."

Harry sipped the whisky again, and placed it carefully on the table. "Son, the girl is what concerns me the most."

"Don't lecture me. She concerns me the most too."

"That's why you've had her kidnapped by a pair of certifiable killers?"

"That's why I'm protecting her."

Jess placed a hand on mine. I had clenched them into fists without noticing. I eased them flat to the surface.

"That was the final straw," Jess said. "Think about it, Adam. You're a private detective. A citizen. You have no power, no influence with the police or any politicians, not unless you get that psycho Fanuco involved. Please tell me you haven't done that yet."

"I haven't."

"But you're tempted. Aren't you?"

"No," I lied. My whiskey lay untouched.

Harry finished his with a flourish. "Yer not stupid.

Impetuous, don't think things through, but you make the sort of deductions I could only dream of when I was your age. And you get there far quicker than I ever did. So you must accept, if a kid is hallucinating her great-grandfather inside her head, she's bloody deranged, and needs professional help."

Jess bit her lip but said nothing.

"Because she witnessed it," Harry said, "it's your duty to report it to the authorities. If someone's forcing it on her, then she's in even more danger, and your responsibility is doubled. And if the same maniac made of mud or clay or whatever is lookin' to take her out … Jesus, what the hell are you thinking doing this yerself?"

My old mentor had a way of making me feel stupid, even when I was right. It was one of his more annoying qualities.

"I'm not by myself," I said. "I have two employees who are highly skilled in areas we lack. I've got Jess who won't quit now she knows Estelle is in trouble. *Bigger* trouble than we thought. And now I have you."

"And what makes you reckon I'm gonna join this stupid mission of yours?"

"Two reasons. First, even though I'm sure you genuinely believe I could have gone to the authorities before it got so out of hand, you know me well enough to be sure if I *can* quit, I *would*. But if Jess has filled you in with everything, you understand there are too many lives at risk to not handle this head-on."

"And two?"

"Because you're here."

He held onto me for longer than I was comfortable with, and when I shifted, and downed my whiskey in one, his teeth flashed beneath his beard in a satisfied grin. "Fer Jayne's sake I'm gonna keep you alive. You don't go killin' people on purpose, maybe this Pale Twat excepted, and you use your head."

"Since I learned a bunch of new stuff this evening, that's all I've been doing."

"Good. Like Jess said, you investigate missin' persons. Seems to me someone is missin', and you need to find her. Time to go to work, son." He waved the whiskey tumbler at me. "Now get another round of these bad boys."

I recounted the story as told to me by Vera and Marco, as well as their theories about why Katerina was in Austria immediately after Petr's death. We spitballed ideas regarding why the Pale Boy wanted me, and any trace of the investigation, dead. Harry pointed out—having given no firm indication of interest in the LaPortes or specifically Estelle—the only definite target was me. But when we added the intelligence reports confirmed by Clara and Abba, we agreed the Pale Boy's mission was probably more widespread.

All the questions hung over what really happened to Katerina during her period of captivity on the farm. I did not want to reveal to Jess and Harry my latest, and most unrealistic, theory. Not yet. The best working hypothesis we had was that, traumatized by the murder of her grandmother and mother, Katerina was unwilling to fight a sexual predator who appeared asexual in public, and when she fell pregnant to him, he used that child to control her further. But to survive, she numbed all feeling for the child, and sent it away. When the shock of her husband killing himself jolted those emotions to life, she went in search of him or her, but was unsuccessful in reuniting. That failure would have spurred her on to the degree that she could, conceivably, build a multi-million deutschmark business from scratch, but that seemed unlikely.

She would have needed seed money. She didn't sell the farm until after she set up her Parisian gallery, so the finance that bought her way into the art world clearly came from elsewhere.

After three of those large drinks, Harry and I were light-headed enough to start segueing into places I hadn't been for years. We joshed and joked, sending insults back and forth like old mates always do, and it took Jess to keep us on track. We deferred to her for a while, and she brought up several old pieces of research. Most involved Professor Jäger and his march to prominence in the world of Nazi war criminals, and the ethics of prosecuting them in their twilight years.

She also pulled out of her digital bag the latest version of DDS.

At no point can our penetrative software act alone. It needs input. Without that, it cannot trace credit cards, bank accounts, license plates, or property. Usually, when a wealthy person goes on the run, they use cash to get around. It is only out of desperation they will use a credit card, because unless they are some inbred weirdo who inherited their money, the wealthy are usually smart. And Katerina was most certainly not some inbred weirdo; she had *earned* all she possessed.

Jess was able to talk Herman the lawyer into giving us Katerina's bank details, but not her passwords or numbered accounts in other countries. That was privileged information, whereas the other numbers could be found around the house.

Jess had worked with less in the past.

Money had, indeed, been moved around. First, twenty-four hours before she fled, Katerina transferred a million euros from her "everyday" account to a bank in Switzerland. This was not an institution the Deep Detect System could penetrate. However, there are other steps to take when investigating a missing person.

Every transaction has three points at which it can be detected: the originator, the person who holds the card; the bank that processes the transaction, in this case one invisible to our software; and the recipient, such as a shop, transport firm, or third-party. And then we combine that with something unpredictable, something that cannot be programmed or anticipated: our imaginations, our instinct. Cops call it "gut feeling." What we end up with usually pans out.

By the time we switched out our drinks to soft sugary ones, we had a working theory. Harry urged caution, and Jess wanted another hour to corroborate the findings, but I was certain.

We knew where Katerina was hiding. We just didn't understand why.

Her trail appeared to end around the time she transferred funds to the Swiss account, then paid cash for a cab to a town several miles from Hamburg. From there, I imagined, she would have caught a second cab to an airport either in Hamburg or another major hub. With the family Cessna grounded for use in Estelle's investigation, a commercial flight was her only option, my reasoning being that a woman of her age, even one so well-minted, could not easily disappear in her own country. With the cash moving out of Germany, it made sense she was running, and running far.

So, our guestimates put her destination between Austria, where she allegedly stashed her ill-gotten gains after the war, and Paris, where she still held an upmarket apartment and two galleries kept on as philanthropic ventures. Since it was near-impossible for civilians to hack flight manifests or customs security, we had to rely on ancillary services.

We picked a selection of flights leaving Hamburg and

other local airports that might land in the target cities, and Jess trawled things like pay-as-you-go phones (or "burner" phones) bought shortly after those flights touched down, covering Paris and Geneva.

No hits.

Perhaps the experienced great-grandmother knew how easy it was to trace her, or maybe she simply wasn't as attached to her phone as most.

There were other areas that needed ID. Too many banks to check for cash transfers, and without the account numbers we had no chance of a trace. That left other services requiring valid documents, and, from some deep corner of my mind, of information gleaned days earlier—right after I escaped from the farmhouse, in fact—I made a suggestion to Jess.

And we got a hit.

Not a phone or financial trail, but a hotel. She paid cash, but had to use her real name as they insisted upon such things for criminal checks and insurance. Since the insurance company was underwritten by one of the banks in which DDS was anchored, we found her.

AUSTRIA

SALTZBURG

CHAPTER TWENTY-SEVEN

SALZBURG IS NOT ONLY the birthplace of Mozart and the setting for one of the most magical films of all time—*The Sound of Music*—but the composer and movie are its most famous drains on the tourist euro. Nestled at the north edge of the Alps, the fourth largest city in Austria is home to around 150,000 people, popular for its baroque architecture, the world-class Salzburg Festival, and its general all-round prettiness. It is shaped by a number of hills, and the imagery folk are most familiar with is its mediaeval town center, itself epitomized by the wealth that sprang up here in the seventeenth century, largely thanks to its gold mining history, and in recent years a less famous repository for people's illicit financial gains.

We crossed the border in Hugo's hire car, which he was forced to legalize by purchasing additional insurance that spanned the whole of the EU. The expense didn't bother him, but the red tape of administering it did. Only when I pointed out the possibility of us entering official databases that the Fist of God may be monitoring—such as being stopped by the cops in an uninsured vehicle—did he relent. When I first suggested driving, Harry floated an accusation of me being crazy, assuming it would take at least a day and a half, maybe more. But the mapping software I pulled up revealed a seven-and-a-half-hour journey, if we didn't stop.

It actually took eight-and-a-half hours, setting off at three a.m., with Jess taking the first shift at the wheel, while Harry and I waited our turn, sleeping as the alcohol left our systems. At dawn, we were driving through mountainous terrain, and the sun spiked through the peaks, waking me up as efficiently as any cup of coffee could hope to. After one driving shift each, and much coffee and sugary pastries, we arrived at Lake Wolfgangsee by two p.m. local time.

Approximately thirteen square kilometers, the glacial lake lies around 1,700 feet above sea level, is divided into two parts by a peninsula, and surrounded on all sides by green mountains. Dotted around its diameter are several settlements. On the outskirts of one such settlement, called Grunshause, a certain Professor Jäger's house overlooked the water from its southern end, and was far enough out of town to be considered private, but not so far as to label him a hermit. Because Salzburg isn't only home to singing families and way too many Mozart memorials; it was also home to the Paris London University of Salzburg, which just happened to be Professor Jäger's stomping ground for the past eight years.

And now Katerina was here. Somewhere in the region.

A cynic might suggest she came to Salzburg to definitively end Professor Jäger's campaign against her family, but even the most spry of ninety-five-year-olds would struggle to take out a man who ran a group like the Fist of God. She would surely hire someone, as would most multimillionaire matriarchs I know.

The real reason for her being in the same town Jäger called home didn't matter all that much. For now. But of all the cities she could have chosen, this one was far too coincidental to have no bearing on the present, or the past.

Had Hugo or Emiliana been with me, we would no doubt have pulled guns and approached the property from several angles, shooting dead any thugs or troops handed the misfortune of guarding the place. With Jess and Harry, it required a lighter touch. It required parking up in Grunshause, and finding an English-speaking waitress at what looked like a popular cafe.

"You know Professor Jäger?" I asked her after she took our orders. "We're from Oxford, and met him when he taught there. Hoping to surprise him."

She assessed us for a moment. Our dress sense was not what people would associate with Oxford dons, but our clothes were clean and pressed, and although I displayed a couple of bruises to my face, my smart beard probably helped me pass as an academic. She nodded. It was a small town not far outside Salzburg rather than a metropolis, so she likely knew most of the patrons on some level.

She said, "He comes twice a week sometimes. I have not seen him this week. You say you are friends?"

"Colleagues," I corrected. "How is the Voltrasse Hotel? I hear good things."

"Expensive. But very good. Very nice. I think Michael Jackson once stayed there. Before…" She trailed off before having to articulate what may have been a slander on the late King of Pop.

But the Voltrasse was Katerina's destination, not accommodation in central Salzburg. She journeyed here specifically, close to where Jäger's home looked out onto a lake, where he taught, where he would eventually return. If he hadn't already.

We left a generous tip and marched up one of the several hills on which Grunshause was build, to the Voltrasse, a grey stone obelisk amid boutiques and upmarket restaurants with a small drop-off point rather than the manicured gardens I'd been expecting. The air was biting and fresh, the sun smoothing the edge off, but stood in the hotel's twenty-foot arch we could see over the rooftops of the lower buildings all the way to Lake Wolfgangsee, where the surface rippled and fierce white light bounced off the water.

Inside, the lobby opened into a cavern of marble and oak, low leather seating and a reception desk stretching the whole wall and boasting six check-in points, ready to receive all those coach parties paying through the nose for a quiet town-based holiday. Only one person served today, though; with no new customers at the time, why have more than necessary?

"I've got this," I said, leading them toward the pristine young chap with the yellow piping on his blazer.

"You speak German now?" Jess said.

"I get by."

"What grade you get again?" Harry asked.

"It's not about grades. It's about finesse." At the desk, the receptionist greeted us with a smile and hands clasped before him. I said, "Sprichst du Englisch?"

"Wow," Harry groaned. "Am I listening to a native?"

Jess giggled and punched Harry's shoulder.

"Of course," the receptionist replied, his smile not wavering an inch. Static, in fact. "You would like a room, perhaps?"

Sometimes, there is gut instinct, taking a stab in the dark when all logical avenues are exhausted, such as how we located Katerina. That's guesswork based on available but incomplete data, later verified by facts. Reading people is whole different skill. I'd booked in to enough high class hotels, conversed with dozens of employees like the robot before me, and never once had any of them asked if I would *like a room.* They always asked if I *had a reservation.* Okay, I had to consider the possibility that all guests with a reservation had checked in already, leaving the only possibility of three tourists walking in off the street being to want a room. And yet...

That still didn't ring true because this wasn't the sort of place where people just walked in. The Voltrasse was a *destination.* It wasn't a whim or improvised accommodation the way a youth hostel or motel may be.

You would like a room, perhaps?

This kid was half-expecting us, and our presence made him nervous, so he fluffed his usual lines.

It sounds like a lot to take in, but I barely missed a beat when I asked, "So, was it a substantial tip that's going to make it difficult for us, or a threat of some sort?"

"Sorry?" the receptionist said.

"Adam?" Jess tugged at my arm.

I said, "Either Katerina Caine has asked for serious discretion through serious tipping, or serious individuals have made serious threats that if these people speak to an English detective about Katerina's whereabouts, serious things will happen."

I glanced at Harry, who was stifling a grin. He nodded at Jess. "The lad's back on form."

To the receptionist, I said, "We don't want trouble for you."

The kid picked up a pen, gripping it so hard the end of his finger turned white. "I can't say anything."

"Threat or bribe?" I asked.

He shook his head.

I breathed out pointedly and my shoulders dropped.

Harry said, "Stay with us, son."

I hadn't noticed my jaw tighten, but as I relaxed, it drove away an urge to pull the receptionist over the desk. I tried a new tactic. "She might be in trouble. Even if she doesn't want to be found, we've learned things that she didn't know before."

The lad fiddled with the pen. Didn't speak.

I said, "If you talk to us, we won't reveal where we got the information. It will not come back on you. But if you don't tell us why you're so nervous, why you 'can't say anything,' an old lady might be hurt, or worse. You want that on your conscience?"

He shook his head again, more rapidly than before.

I went in for the kill, with a deliberate word choice. "What did they say to you?" Emphasis on "*they*".

And he didn't correct me.

"They came here two days ago. She went with them. She already checked in and promised the staff big tips if we kept her visit secret. If a British man asked for her, we should say she checked out. I did not see her after that first day."

Two days ago.

"Who did she leave with?" I asked.

"A man with a grey beard and a funny hat. And a woman."

"Did she appear under duress?"

"Under ... what? Sorry, I do not—"

"Did she seem scared?" Harry asked.

"No. They had tea and cakes in the Philpott Room. Then they left, and Mrs. Caine gave these instructions." His face bloomed red and he tapped the pen, his gaze following it to the desk. "Will they hurt her?"

Jess stepped forward and placed her hand over his, waited until he looked at her, and gave him her best wide-eyed reassurance: "If they haven't already, we'll help her."

And then we left, heading out to Professor Jäger's home, with no plan, and no clue what awaited us.

CHAPTER TWENTY-EIGHT

HIS ADDRESS WASN'T hard to find, although the images on Google Earth had been scrubbed, a privilege that takes an almighty amount of influence, usually reserved for high-end criminals who could influence the courts in any number of countries, and politicians who cited security fears. Not that we needed it. After a mild winter brought spring early to most of Europe, the nearby hills were so thick with foliage, even around the roads, we were able to drive up to a vantage above the property, park, and venture into the woodland for a near bird's eye view.

Three sets of binoculars bought in town revealed to us a sprawling wooden structure on the edge of the water, with a jetty and two rowboats to one side, protected by a ten-foot fence and an electrified gate set twenty yards back from the road. Driving past, we probably would have missed it. From my position, I estimated five bedrooms over the single story, and an airy living space. The main windows were clearly reserved for the glacial lake, as I could see little glass this side.

The first armed guard appeared, walking a German Shepherd on a thick chain, his other hand on the butt of an MP5K submachine-gun strapped across his chest. He wore loose police-like clothes and a baseball cap featuring a star-shaped badge which, again, resembled garments the police might wear.

An illusion of authority.

I lowered my glasses and waited for Harry and Jess to do the same.

"What do you think?" I asked.

"Not much," Harry said. "If she's in there, I can't see her."

"Him either," Jess added.

"No," I said. "But the guard is there for a reason. And that one."

A second member of the security team strolled by, visible without the binoculars. No dog this time.

"So, it'll be freezing," I said. "But I can get around the outside—"

"Adam." Jess tilted her head pointedly.

"I know, I know, but it's the easiest way. Trust me."

"That's not what I mean."

"Then what *do* you mean?"

"Your first instinct is to sneak around, put yourself at risk. Why?"

I pointed and held my voice in check. "Because they're there to deter visitors. We can't simply knock and ask Katerina to come out and verify my theory."

"Which one?" Harry asked.

"The theory that's stupid, but makes perfect sense. I'm just missing one piece. If she gives it to me, I'll have it all. In the meantime, I have to get in there."

Jess said, "Adam—"

I gave her my best "I'm serious" expression. "We have to do it like this. Once they know we're here, they'll shut us down, or leave again. If Katerina is in there, she's either in trouble, or … something else."

"Fine." Jess turned away, and leaned against a tree in a sulk, fiddling with her phone.

I said, "Right, we go a half-mile down the road. I'll skirt the property, then go swimming when I get close to the fence. I can stay underwater for three minutes on a good day, probably two now since I'm out of practice, but it should be enough to get me under the jetty. When I'm there—"

"Well, look at that," Jess said.

I raised the binoculars to the house. More movement. Professor Jäger emerged from an awning that must have hidden a door, and as he approached the gate, the two guards we spotted earlier rushed to him. He dismissed them with a flick of his hand, and continued to his destination. He halted by the gate, hit some numbers and touched the bars. The code must have disengaged the electrical current. He stared straight at me, and waved.

I snatched the binoculars away as if it was they who gave me away. But it wasn't them.

I glared at Jess. "What did you do?"

Jess waved her phone, grinning. "Sent him a text."

Harry stepped back as I rounded on her. She stood her ground.

I said, "Why would you do that?"

"Better than your alternative, Rambo."

"So you had his number all this time? Why didn't you track it?"

"It's with a Middle Eastern carrier. We don't have a Trojan horse in their system. But this number is listed on the account with his website host, so I saved it. Just in case. Seems like he wants to talk."

Sure enough, Professor Jäger was beckoning us down.

I faced Professor Jäger through the barred gate, having asked Harry and Jess to wait a ways behind me. His head was bowed, his funky new fedora blocking his face as he leaned on his eagle-headed cane. I said nothing. Once he deigned fit to focus on me, he didn't seem to know what to do with his hands.

"That business in Kraków," he said. "Unfortunate. But you understand … it had to be done."

"I'm sure you believe that. It doesn't excuse it, though." I flashed to the moment when I was sure I would die in the chair, unable to breath, gagging. "You're holding Katerina? Did you do the same to her? Because I'm not sure she'd survive it."

"I'm not holding her. She contacted me of her own accord. I must admit, I was surprised she showed here. It is very dangerous for her."

"So what's this about?" I gestured between me and the gate. "Going to warn me off?"

"No. I am going to let you in. As soon as you assure me my staff will not be required to do anything I would find distasteful."

The dog growled from the wings. A yank of its chain silenced it.

I said, "I'll behave."

I looked back to where Jess and Harry waited and signaled them to follow me.

Jäger opened the barrier and the three of us walked through, watched by the guards as we followed the professor to his front door. The dog woofed at me this time, deep and throaty, then at Harry. Not at Jess, though.

"Those guys at the farm," I said. "Locals?"

"Yes," he replied. "We thought we solved our detective problem, so had to move quickly when they engaged you. Do not worry. Small time gangsters are no great loss to world."

"So it *was* you who sent Tony Luca on his way."

"Others commanded it. But please believe me, my daughter played no part. A certain other interested party had the final say."

"Katerina."

He led us into his hallway, and to an open-plan living area, which looked exactly as I expected an affluent home on a lake-side to look: wood panel walls, polished floor, thick rugs, and comfortable furniture. Floor-to-ceiling French doors gaped and windows filled the lakeside wall, bestowing maximum natural light inside.

On one high-backed chair, her walking stick leaning close by, Katerina stared out at the water, untroubled by the harsh light dappling across the surface. Her head turned slowly and she said, "Hello again. I hear you know my secret."

"A version of it," I said.

"A version? I have only lived one life."

"Feels like a lot of versions flying around. One minute, there's no way anyone could lay claim to the farm, then Estelle starts having these episodes, and—"

Jess held my arm, and Harry made his presence known by stepping toward me and holding still. Both had their own way of hinting when I was going down the wrong track.

"Why are you here?" I asked softly.

"To appeal," Katerina replied, facing the lake again. "To tell Professor Jäger the truth, in the hope he will call off his golem."

"And…?"

"And," Jäger said, "morally, her money should be split

between her family and the gypsies. Legally, it is different, perhaps, but I do not believe Katerina is a traitor. A victim of rape, a woman trying to raise her children, this is not someone we should be pursuing. And with her husband risen to right the wrong she committed, she is keen to resolve things. And I applaud that."

"So the Pale Boy goes back in his box?" I said.

Jäger removed his hat and held it before him. "Sadly, no. I have done much wrong too. Made mistakes. Like what we did to you … but this is why I sent Clara away. I disagree with my superiors, and they say I made a mess of this case, so they seek to tidy things up. Which means a clean break."

"Meaning you can't call him off."

"I cannot call off the Pale Boy, because I did not send him. He will destroy everything he has been assigned, no matter what." Jäger stood beside Katerina. "After what she endured under the reign of empty men following orders from on high, I hope this woman can forgive me. I can, after all, forgive her mistakes."

Katerina patted his hand. "The professor sent word home to appeal, to explain. It may be too late. But Estelle is safe with your friends, Adam. And I am safe here. Things will play out as they will."

I wandered to the window and stared at the lake. The dog barked outside yet again, and then was silenced. The gentle lapping of water gusted through the open door.

I considered keeping my mouth shut, not saying what I had to. But that wasn't something I could do.

"Professor Jäger is clearly more trusting than me, Katerina. Because I don't believe a word you've said since we met." I faced her, noticing the frowns on both Jess and Harry. "You're a liar, Katerina. And everything hinges on those lies. So how about you come clean, and we can finish this once and for all?"

"Finish it how?"

"You're a stone cold sociopath," I said. "You've hidden your true nature for years, and now it's finally caught up with you."

CHAPTER TWENTY-NINE

A SOCIOPATH IS someone who feels nothing, unless it is an internal, self-focused emotion, more commonly linked to desire. What they *want* is the same as what they *need*, and nothing will stand in their way of attaining it. They will lie, cheat, steal, set up a friend, physically hurt someone. A true, pure sociopath can even kill. Unlike a psychopath who might take pleasure in inflicting pain or torment or death, a sociopath cares nothing for those things. It is the *goal* that drives them. Their *want*.

"Don't you think 'sociopath' is a little harsh?" Jess asked.

"One of the things that makes me good at what I do is spotting patterns," I said. "And when I get little snippets, facts, counter-facts, when I glue it all together, I have an outstanding pattern."

She glanced at Harry, who gave a tiny nod and said, "Let's see where he's going with it."

"You saw your mother executed," I said. "And your grandmother beaten to death. Those men, following orders. Empty of feeling, but brimming with power. You saw that too, didn't you? How no one opposed them, because of their sheer strength."

She watched the lake, as if not hearing me. When Jäger uttered a vowel as if to speak, she squeezed his hand tighter and his mouth closed.

"You learned you must do whatever. Heck, if the stories are true, the Angel of Kraków issued the instruction herself. She practically ordered you to lie and cheat. If it meant staying alive."

"This is ridiculous," Katerina muttered.

"Patterns, remember? When I work your life backwards, there are too many coincidences, too many convenient deaths. You rebuilt your house on the land stolen from your grandparents, but you needed money. Influence. From Paris, you got to the top awfully fast. I checked. You had an artist who was considered wonderful but not great. Until he died in a mysterious accident."

Katerina's fingers nipped her top lip, but other than that, she remained focused on the harsh light. Not once had her eyes flickered.

"There isn't much on the artist, but word has it he over-dosed on opium. A fine way for an artist to go. It could only have been better if it was absinthe. But the timing was perfect. Were your backers about to pull out? Your money from Geneva running low? No, a dead artist inflated the price of his work, and others flocked to you as you expanded. Used more of your stash as seed money, purchasing your own artists' works as you flogged the real art—that looted from Jews and Roma, and stashed in Geneva by your lover, Friedrich Goetz."

"Lover?" Jäger said.

The breeze blew in through the open French door, ruffling Katerina's clothes and thin head of hair. The dog barked as the guards made another pass close by.

I said, "Which takes us to Geneva. The Nazis were really just militarized thugs and gangsters. They looted and pillaged, and hid the jewelry and money, and—yes—artwork, in vaults in Switzerland and Austria, and even shipped it overseas for them to monetize when things settled down. Once the Third Reich spanned the globe. And your Captain Goetz was one of them. With him gone, and your husband too, you had access to the vaults and to the accounts."

"That's insane," Jess said. "Adam, how the hell did you come up with this?"

"It's all that makes sense. The reason this has escalated so much. And her sudden jumps in wealth. The access. The discrepancies in stories. Everyone thinks Petr died cleaning his gun, a euphemism for suicide. But that wasn't it, was it? Katerina, you made your statement to the police, that you were in the building at the time, along with Beatrice. A man like that doesn't kill himself with his wife and child *in the house*. He waits until they're out, or he takes himself to the woods. No, *you* killed Petr, Katerina."

Again, no reaction, except a tiny twist of her fingers.

"When he discovered your secret, or when you told him about the fortune waiting for you, and suggested to him you use it to improve your lot. Because a farm was never going to be enough for you, not really. Not when you remembered that big house in Hamburg, taken by the government. What you were *entitled* to. But Petr didn't share your goals, and when he realized the extent of your collaboration with Goetz, he wanted to turn you in. You epitomized everything he fought against. You had to act so you'd be free to reap your rewards."

I stood at the open frontage, absorbing the cool afternoon air.

"And going back further. To Goetz's death. I don't know how much you felt for him, but those stories don't add up either. On the surface, sure, you could be a victim of a controlling scumbag, but I don't think he was quite as empty inside as his friends. He wanted the farm for the same reason he built the tunnels under that rickety old house; a staging point. He controlled the flow of artwork and other valuable items; antiques, furniture, bearer bonds, whatever. The tunnels were to hide his cut from his paymasters as he creamed a bit off the top. A nest egg, for him and the woman he fell in love with."

I paused, looking for anything in the woman's face. She used her cane to hobble through the door onto the deck. I joined her, while Jäger, Harry, and Jess eavesdropped from the frame. The shift in the wood, some minute creak, must have alerted that damn dog, as its woofs echoed across the lake, and his master admonished it in German.

I said, "He fell in love with you. And you with him?"

She swallowed.

"Perhaps not completely without feeling after all. If it really *was* love. Sociopaths rarely experience true love. They find someone who can service their desires in life, and give affection in return. Having a baby with a man would help cement that relationship. It would not have been hard for you to run, not with your grandmother's reputation and the resources that remained throughout the war. So you stayed voluntarily, and when word got back to you that the tides were turning against Germany, you went into preservation mode. You killed the man who was feathering your nest, and convinced the help you were a victim too, and they helped you cover up the whole thing."

Merciful silence descended. Only water lapped beneath us. At the edge, a fish darted from my movement as I glanced over.

"You stuck to your part so well, Katerina. But when you play it forwards, which version of events is more likely? A woman, raped and controlled, had a baby, murdered the father as liberation was around the corner, gave away the baby, but … her long-dead husband comes back from the dead, and after siring a daughter, he kills himself; you swan off, first to Austria, Geneva to be precise, and then Paris, where—before selling your farm—you established an art gallery, and a massive stroke of luck lands you traction in an art world dominated by men, and make enough money to rebuild Kochany Dom. Or…"

I caught Jess's expression, her mouth turned down so far it could have slipped from her face.

"Or," I said, "a young woman, with a high-ranking officer in her home, under her thumb, spies an opportunity: hiding her Jewish roots, she seduces him, does his books, and during the liquidation of the ghetto, the murder of thousands, she realizes an opportunity to step things up a notch; she knows the local terrain, the secret routes, so why not a farm? She runs the business side while the Army captain conducts himself impeccably, until he is no longer useful to her, and she disposes of him. Along with all evidence of her collusion. Yet, why not *kill* the baby along with Goetz? Because it's *hers*. She was *entitled* to it. Instead of killing a child she had little affection for, she concealed its existence until she could risk claiming it. Then a complication in her husband appears, and she has to start the charade all over again. Until she can dispose of him too. No pigs needed this time, though."

Katerina pulled her cardigan tighter. Stepped to the edge. She still hadn't looked at me. I stood directly behind her, and spoke to the back of her head.

"This woman, she knows all about the accounts and vaults, because she set them up. We can verify it through the professor's unit. And I hear the Austrians are more cooperative these days. So since you're not denying it, let's play it forward again.

You can't monetize the stolen antiques and art, so you decide to set up in a city full of culture, but chaotic after the occupation. Paris. You make contacts, dark ones who want the works you've hidden away, but you need to launder the money. You stage your star artist's overdose, elevating his value, and attract more to your stable. The fencing of stolen goods, plus the fortunate uptake in business, you make enough to fight for the return of your land, and to rebuild the house. You've come full circle. You've won."

"Mr. Park," she said. "That's…" Her chin dropped to her chest, mouth working, but she closed it tight.

Silence descended like an anvil. Even the water ceased lapping and the breeze died. No dog. No nothing.

"Now we know," I said, "we will look at that trail more carefully. But I'm still not sure how you've managed to do what you did to Estelle. Want to fill me in?"

Katerina gasped. She hunched over, hands to her stomach.

Suddenly, I was deeply aware the dog hadn't barked for some time.

Katerina turned to me, her face crumpled into a mask of terror. Blood oozed between her fingers. She collapsed into my arms.

And revealed before me, the Pale Boy crawled from the lake, a bloodied knife in one hand. His grey suit was plastered to him, his hair flat to his head, water cascading from him to splash to the deck as he straightened himself like a scorpion tail readying to strike.

Jess screamed first. I tried to move Katerina aside, but Jäger made it in front of me before I could act.

"No matter what the truth of her life is," Jäger said to the Pale Boy, "the money will go where it belongs. To the coffers of the victims of the Devouring, and the ancestors of—"

The next sound he uttered was a wet gurgle, as the Pale

Boy drew the knife across the old man's throat, from one side to the other, slicing the trachea and one of his jugular veins. Blood gushed, Jäger's eyes rolled back, and he was dead in seconds.

"No matter the truth," the Pale Boy said. "Only justice matters. The Nazi line will not profit from the Holocaust, or the Devouring."

Then he closed in on me, aimed a bulky handgun my way, and as soon as it made a "phut" noise, a barb stung my neck, and my world turned black.

CHAPTER THIRTY

TWO SPIKES SPEARED the inside of my nose and I awoke to an overwhelming scent of aniseed. The Pale Boy moved the smelling salts from under my nostrils, and I blinked away the fog and stars. He sat before me on a stool, his feet perched on a bar around its base, watching me without moving a muscle.

The room was largely metallic, and I hung from the ceiling, topless, my arms above my head, toes touching the ground so my shoulders didn't gradually dislocate. It was cold. To my left, a walk-in refrigerator hung open, like you may find in a butchers, with empty meat hooks arranged on a rail. On the floor, amid the cold mist, lay a black bag, of the sort used to transport the recently deceased, holding a mass too small to be Katerina, but large enough to be either Jess, Harry, or Professor Jäger. To my right, an open door showed a staircase leading up, and I recognized furniture in the professor's living room, although I could not recall a door leading down here. A secret compartment, or perhaps a panic room of sorts. The walls sweated, situated as it was under a lake bed. I wondered how many years a construction like this would last.

"Is that long enough?" the Pale Boy asked.

"Long enough for what?"

"To understand."

"You killed the professor."

"That is a deeply boring response. Yes, I killed the professor. But do you *understand*?"

I couldn't see where he was going with this, as if he was tenderizing me before ripping me apart and consuming the meat.

I said, "I'm under Professor Jäger's house, you killed him. The dog shut up a few moments before you climbed out of the water, and there are no guards firing weapons, so I guess nobody is coming."

"Indeed. But that is not what I am asking."

I found the body bag again. "The professor?"

The Pale Boy's clothes were now dry, so either I had been unconscious for a while or he had time to change. He pulled a second body bag from behind a cabinet on top of which he had laid out the dart gun he used to incapacitate me alongside a number of sharp and twisted metallic objects, which I suspected were either there to intimidate, or for ease of access.

Since I wasn't dead yet, he needed something.

The Pale Boy unzipped the second bag and angled the opening to show me Professor Jäger lying within.

"Who's in the other?" I said.

He straightened and returned to his perch, and resumed his surveillance of me. "Isn't it better if you don't know?"

I closed my eyes. Willed myself to stop imagining who lay in there. Or tried to. And failed.

With Katerina dead, floating in the lake, Professor Jäger with his throat cut, and me unconscious through what I assumed was a tranq dart, it would have left Jess and Harry to face him alone. I could only assume one of them held off the ghoul who crawled from the freezing water, giving the other an opportunity to escape.

One of them, either of them, no longer in my life, left a void nothing could fill.

Had I come here alone, I would have found a way to force my way in, to commit an act of violence, or more than one, if it meant I could subdue the professor, and drag the truth kicking and screaming out of Katerina's past. They had pulled me back from the brink, but I had to consider: was that the right thing to do?

If I had sent Estelle away with Harry instead, and brought Hugo and Emiliana with me, the guards would still be dead, although I would likely have insisted on preserving Rover's life. Their very presence may have deterred the Pale Boy from acting, and allowed Katerina to say whatever she was about to before the blade entered her.

Was she ready to confess? Or deny my allegations?

"Where's Katerina's body?" I asked.

"Floating," he said. "Somewhere."

I tried my bindings, rattling the rope that tied my hands. It fed through a metal loop, secured to the ceiling constructed from cement. I wondered what size wall plug it would take to screw something like this in there, what its true purpose might be. I doubted it was designed for hanging people up by their wrists.

I opened my eyes. Blinked again, this time holding back the grief I would surely feel if I knew who he had killed. Because it must only be one of them, or there would be two bags, two mounds of formerly-human flesh and blood. Either the man who had acted as much like a father as my real dad, or the girl—the *woman*—I met when she was a teenager, a brilliant seventeen-year-old who demonstrated genius with computers even then, who I sponsored through university, and gave a job when she graduated, who I have never seen as a romantic option in all the time I had known her, but who had, I realized recently, harbored a crush on me from the day we met until the day I abandoned her following my disagreement with Roger Gorman. Only in the past year had I started viewing her as a grown woman, someone with whom I might involve myself, and so nearly made the first move in that Kraków coffee shop.

If it was Jess in this bag, I would never learn what could have been.

If it was Harry, it would be like losing another parent, and I would have to face Jayne, his wife, who had looked after me through some of my darkest moments.

Unless it was an elaborate psychological trick.

"Who is in the bag?" I asked again.

"Someone."

"What do I have to do?"

"Finally, a real question."

The Pale Boy strode to the cabinet and rearranged some of his pieces, including a long, curled implement that tapered into two points, which he raised to his face, and I swear he almost broke into a smile. He placed it down with the others, and handled a pouch, allowing the zip to clack slowly before he opened it.

"Your enquiries," he said. "I need to know how advanced they are."

"Which ones? I've been busy."

"Do not be funny. You broke quickly with the water. That is interesting. But information you knew they could find without your cooperation." He selected something from the pouch. I could not see what. "Torture is a strange thing. If a subject does not wish to give up what I wish to learn, he holds out for longer. With water, the trick is to persuade the brain you are drowning. Those with real secrets, like protecting a girl whose knowledge of the afterlife could dent the plans of God's chosen people, he will rather die than reveal that girl's whereabouts. So if I threaten you with death, it is pointless."

He turned, inserting a syringe into a medical phial, and withdrew as much fluid as the plastic could hold.

"But ongoing pain, the notion that such agony will never end until you talk, this is a different kind of torture altogether. And begging me for mercy will do no good, because your pain is nothing to me, nothing more than a means to an end."

"You want the money so badly?"

"It is not that I want the money, nor that my facilitators want it. But Katerina committed such sins. She bred with the Nazi, and modern laws dictate this line will profit. If I take away that line, it ends with the girl. But that girl is tainted too. She holds the genes of a great betrayer, so nobody will now benefit from such crimes."

"Why wait this long? Why wait until an investigator comes to uncover it?"

"Jäger wanted to do it thoroughly. His was a small corner of the operation that finds the criminals of the Holocaust and the Devouring, and punishes them. It went unnoticed until you, Mr. Park, drew us to it."

"I didn't ask to come. I was trying to help a girl."

"Once your predecessor was dealt with, the professor assured us the matter would fade, and that no crime had been committed. But unlike you, he does not get involved in matters such as these unless there is more at work. When the professor and his agents lost you, we noticed, and came to the same conclusions. You just have to fill in the details."

He flicked the needle the way I've seen countless doctors and nurses do in both real-life and on TV. "And now you will tell me where I can find Estelle, the Romani heir, and the lawyer who holds Katerina's accounts in secret."

I could not look away from the needle. "What is that?"

The Pale Boy held up a pen torch in the same hand as the syringe, and a remote control in his other darkened the halogen strips overhead, so I was left staring at the dot of bright white.

"Watch the light," the Pale Boy said.

I had little choice. In the pitch black, there was nothing else to see, and when a prick flared in my neck, I could not have guessed what this man was about to do.

CHAPTER THIRTY-ONE

YOU ARE AN ANGEL. Not a figurative thing, but a real angel, soaring through the sky. The air rushes over your skin, and your wings are an extension of your body, as natural as your arms or your legs. You swoop beneath a flock of eagles, and they regard you with curiosity, not fear. And you meet their curiosity, because you did not know eagles gathered in flocks, or flew in this way. Because eagles stick to family units, at least now their numbers are so small.

You dive. Your stomach whooshes backwards. The G-force pins your brain to the top of your skull, and flattens your arms to your side, and your toes are pointed at the sun.

You are an angel.

Sent by God.

You will protect the innocent, and the weak.

Until the ground rushes up to meet you, and—

BANG!

You are broken. Crushed under the weight of your own mission. Your wings are snapped. Someone—something—has ripped them from your body, tearing through the ligaments and muscle that once attached these appendages. You cannot see this beast. But it is there.

You try to stand, but the beast's claw gouges into your back, its thick muscles pushing you into the earth. Earth that cracks under the sheer strength of this creature, and what lies beneath glows red.

Your ribs crack.

Your face burns.

Smoke fills your nose, your mouth, your lungs.

But, somehow, your heart continues to beat.

You will your hand to form a fist. Your knuckles wedge into one of those glowing cracks beneath which you feel the magma flowing. Your shoulders and triceps strain to push back the beast, but it digs deep. It pierces your lower back, its middle, your lungs, and its breath heaves across your soul.

But you do not give in.

Your arms scream for mercy. Your knuckles flayed and raw. And you push. You push until you think you can bear it no more, and then you push some more.

There is air between your stomach and the ground.

The beast howls, and its other claw anchors itself into the dirt, for better leverage on the one concentrated on you. But every sinew, every ounce of strength, flows upwards, and nothing the beast can do will hold you down. You are winning.

The beast's howls become a scream, and the louder it screams, the easier it is for you to stand.

Its claws retract, and you are upright. The creature crashes to the floor, spraying magma from the cracked earth. But you do not flinch. You roll your shoulders and stretch your back, accepting of the wounds inflicted, and drawing strength from them.

Then you turn.

And you face your beast.

Its name was Vila Fanuco. He was a man. We were stood in a meadow, surrounded by long grass and wild flowers. He dressed as he did when I first met him, in the suit of a banker, impeccably-coiffed dark hair, and plasticky skin that screamed "Botox." His mouth always seemed to contain too many teeth, displayed in a lizard like grin. But that was not all.

He tempted me. He engineered a situation in which I had to kill for the first time, an act that drew no nightmares or guilt, and showed me what I was capable of. It was not an act of kindness, though; he did it to amuse himself. But still, it helped me arrive in good stead for the lives I needed to take down the line.

Then he helped me.

He sent Hugo and Emiliana, and had them watch over me. Not out of altruism or friendship, but because he was afraid I might damage his business. Yet they were helpful. And this man allowed them to assist me, and without them I would not have survived. I would not have been living my boring life on a Greek island, learning about guns, and hoping for someone to present an opportunity to return to the ways I had sworn to avoid.

I wanted this.

I knew that now.

My inner self, my *beast*, craved the challenge. And somewhere deep inside, I knew there were not many people like me.

My skills were needed.

Fanuco waved, and his head split down the middle, shedding his skin like a snake, leaving Harry underneath.

"You're a monster, son," Harry said.

"I'm not," I replied. "I *slay* monsters. Without me, the bad men go free."

With Jess's voice, Harry said, "You don't have the right to

make those decisions. We showed you that today. We showed you that you don't have to confront these people alone. There's a better way."

In his own voice, Harry continued, "Use your brain. Use the brain you were given. That's your true gift."

Then the world spun, only Harry and me in its center, the sky turning black, until it slowed, and I was in Bangkok. Harry was no longer with me, replaced instead by Roger Gorman, the ex-chairman of Park Avenue Investigations, and the man suing me for its destruction.

Bangkok was a city in which I got hurt. I was already investigating missing persons, lost on the road. A job that paid moderately well, putting people's minds at ease back home, checking on their newly adult children, especially when they had not been in touch for a longer period than had been agreed upon. It was my introduction into this game, and where I honed my instincts. But at this time, in Bangkok, I was only in my early twenties, and nowhere near as skilled as I am now.

I had been taken by men to a secluded location to be warned off looking into the latest woman to go missing. That place, where we stood, was a derelict house, where men could do what they liked to me. A short man in a tan suit told me the woman I sought was dead, and that the man who assigned me to find her—her husband—knew this already, but was using me as cover to deflect blame. He had gambled her life and lost, and the Man in Tan collected in spades.

I agreed to stop, but they did not believe me. And rightly so.

To persuade me more strongly, the Man in Tan gave an order, and his men beat me, an act I now watched, shoulder to shoulder with Roger Gorman inside a stuffy damp room with only a dirty mattress for furniture.

I had never witnessed this before, and it was impossible that I could be here.

They ripped off my clothes, and did far worse than beat me: they forced themselves upon me. In my mouth, in from behind, and I vowed to never allow anyone to hurt me like that again. I vowed I would not allow anyone to hurt another person in that way.

When they'd had their fun, they beat me some more, and the room spun, until it morphed into a beach, where my broken body was dumped in a cloud of sand.

Gorman pointed at me, lying there, unable to move. He laughed. He started small, growing into a huge belly laugh which he barely contained.

I yelled at him to stop. Told him it wasn't funny, that it really happened, that it was why I trained so hard, in martial arts, in my athletics, in the gym; so I could fight, so I could last the distance, so I could grow the strength to take my vengeance.

But this man, Gorman, in many ways he defined me even more than this attack. After Harry tamed me, and brought me back to myself, Gorman shaped me into a corporate entity, who moved fluidly between the boardroom and the drugs den in which a girl or a guy might be lying having run from their home for one perceived reason or another. But it wasn't Gorman laughing; it was Harry.

Harry, who might be dead in the real world, and who I was beyond helping.

"Who's in the bag?" I asked.

Everything around me froze, including Roger Gorman, mid-laugh.

Night descended.

Then all was black.

You are no longer broken. But your beast holds you back. Your beast, the thing that allowed you to rebuild yourself, now resists all your attempts to make the pain stop.

The broken earth beneath your feet glows once again, and your friend Harry melts into a pool of blood and bone. That pool coalesces into a shape, and rises, revealing your childhood image of a demon: a coal-black creature on two legs, with the head of the human morphed with that of many animals; the horns of a goat, the snout of a pig, the teeth of a wolf, yet the eyes are always that of a human.

They are your *eyes.*

This beast will never let you go. The beast will be with you forever. If you wish to rid yourself of this burden, and be fully human once again, you can. You can feel the way you did before those men in Bangkok defiled you, when you were free.

Because that's what this is all about, isn't it? You yearn to be free.

When your father died, and your mother took up with a rich man whom you hated, you left, ran as far as possible, and found you enjoyed the run, enjoyed the life of zero commitments, of pure, unadulterated freedom. Alcohol, sex, drugs, rock 'n' roll. Life out there in the world is not something you can return to with a creature pulling you back, weighing you down.

Say goodbye to that beast.

And as you see "emeth" materializing as a brand upon the beast's forehead—the Hebrew word for "truth" that breathes life into the golem—you understand what you must do.

Throughout it all I remained standing in the room beneath Professor Jäger's house. My tiptoes firm, my thighs tensed, holding me up so my shoulders and arms did not seize.

"The truth," the Pale Boy said. "Take the 'E' from the

beast. Tell him he is dead. Be free of him. Give me the truth. Give me what I need, and he will be gone."

"Thank you," I said.

"You are welcome. I am setting you free. All you have to do is reveal what you know, and the beast will die."

"You misunderstand me." Drool spilled down my chin. "I'm not thanking you for setting me free."

The Pale Boy, so impassive, so calm, allowed his forehead to furrow, and he took a step back.

"You revealed the beast to me. And that is how I'm going to destroy you."

His voice was as calm as ever, but I sensed it took real effort. "And how is that possible?"

"Like this," I said.

CHAPTER THIRTY-TWO

A BEAST inside someone can be a destructive force for that person, as it clamors to get out. It needs to be set free, and is often let out temporarily in the form of violence, addiction, or perversion. I did not know what the beast inside me wanted, but it was not for me to give up. Perhaps it was born in the hovel in Bangkok, or when I pulled the trigger and blew the back of a man's head out at the behest of Vila Fanuco; whatever, it was there. But it did not rule me.

The fact my head remained relatively clear probably helped subdue it. That my youth had been spent experiencing the occasional chemical haze, embracing cultural traditions, from South America, Asia, across Africa (it would be rude not to engage with the locals after all), enjoying the freedom of mind and of body. And it is perhaps that experience that saved me.

The Pale Boy's concoction was at least partly LSD, and with my body's muscle memory I coped with it better than most. So whenever I drifted into the worst of the hallucinations, I pulled back and remembered the corpse of one of my closest friends lying hidden in a freezer beneath an Austrian lake. I would take my revenge upon the person who killed either Harry or Jess. It didn't matter which one; both were too precious to pass without holding someone to account.

Another benefit to a partially-clear head was my ability to concentrate on my surroundings; although the ring by which I was held was cemented into the ceiling, manufactured as solidly as any material you could hope for, and not even a three-hundred- pound gorilla could rip it apart, cement in a damp environment does not retain its solidity well.

But cement in a damp environment does not retain its solidity well.

It becomes brittle, and whatever you use to hold it in place can loosen. So while your tormentor is concentrating on the application of drugs, and the judicial use of a pen light, with the smallest, incremental movements, the screw fitting with which it is fixed, can be used to your advantage.

"And how is that possible?" the Pale Boy asked.

"Like this," I said.

I grasped the iron loop with both hands, leapt up, my knees to my shoulders, and thrust both feet into the Pale Boy's sternum. He flew backwards. I jerked with all my weight, and the fitting above me sprayed dust, but did not give. I twisted the left, then the right, and as the killer regained his feet, I heaved my legs up, kicked all my bodyweight downwards, and yanked harder than ever before.

The corkscrew end exploded out of the ceiling, showering me in a mist of stone and plaster, and the huge plastic wall plug-type implement had split. Although my hands were still bound by rope, fed through the metal hoop, I had time to glance once into the freezer, at the body bag lying there, before lunging to turn on the lights. I had only seconds before the Pale Boy rushed towards me.

When we last clashed, the onus was on me to start the fight, which allowed him to use my momentum and body weight against me and toss me around like I was made of plastic. This time, despite his grave-like expression, he appeared to be unravelling.

I swung him to the side, thinking I had gained the upper hand. He simply dropped his shoulder, dug his heel into the floor, and heaved me over the top. I slammed onto the ground, but energy surged through me. I barely sensed the impact. In fact, I had instinctively bent my knees and flattened my feet so they took the brunt of the shock.

Because of their position I was able to bounce back with ease, lock my ankles around the seemingly-supernatural assassin's neck, and drag him forward. I twisted and contracted the hold, and his rock hard fists pummeled my legs, and grappled for my arms and genitals. Whenever he came close to the Crown Jewels, I smacked him with the iron ring, and on the third time I felt his wrist break.

It did not take long for him to realize his predicament.

He tried a new tactic, and formed his one good hand into a spear and jabbed it between my ankles, twisted his body, and broke free.

I rolled away, leapt to my feet, and faced him once more.

His hair was messed up, his suit covered in dust, which matched his complexion. But now his eyes were bloodshot, the only sign of color in his entire getup.

It could be said I should have run. While he was physically impaired, and my body was flooded with adrenaline, it gave me a primitive advantage. Yet, if I were to flee now, I would not know the fate of the deceased friend within the freezer until I encountered the survivor. And that survivor, no doubt, would be crippled with guilt at the other who gave their life to facilitate an escape.

But not as crippled as me.

Not as crippled as the Pale Boy would soon be.

We circled one another, neither willing to yield an inch or show a moment of weakness. With both my hands tied, perhaps he smelled a way to even up the disability of a busted wrist.

I was right next to his cabinet of mediaeval devices. He glanced once at the surface, and it was enough for me.

I picked up the double pronged implement, pulled it back to my shoulder, and threw it as I imagined a dagger should be hurled during a circus act. Instantly, I followed it in, rightly predicting the Pale Boy's reactions would be fast and decisive. He gripped it, wielded it like a weapon, but I was already upon him.

Ignoring the object, I threw myself through the air, and slammed both heels into his knees. One of them cracked and he crashed to the floor beside me. His weapon skittled away. He did not cry out, but could not hold back a grimace of pain.

He turned over, and I dropped on him feet first; one in the gut, one to the chin. He spat blood. I heaved the ring around, and cracked it off his skull. He glazed over, but he did not lose consciousness. That meant he could still recover, and retaliate.

I gripped the ring. Pictured that word—*emeth*— emblazoned upon his forehead. Then I drove the loop's screw fitting through the first "E" into his brain.

"You are dead," I said.

It took some force to remove the corkscrew spike from the bone making up his cranium. I had to kneel on the side of his head, and pull. Bone, blood, and brain matter, sluiced out of the hole, and all I felt was relief. I used the knife that gutted Katerina and slit Jäger's throat to cut myself free, and walked slowly to the freezer.

I crouched beside the bag.

Gripped it.

Found the zip, and held it between thumb and forefinger.

Harry.

Jess.

One died so the other could live.

How typical of both.

I pulled the zip down, placed fingers from both hands inside, and prepared to open it.

CHAPTER THIRTY-THREE

I MET Jess and Harry in very different ways.

Harry, I knew from a young age, probably since I was a baby, although only in passing. He was my dad's friend, a drinking buddy, who sometimes accompanied us to Elland Road to watch Leeds United play every couple of months, because that's how often we could afford to go. When my father died, we pretty much lost touch, except the occasional nod if we passed in the street or at the stadium. Then after I returned from Bangkok, and strengthened my body and trained hard in Krav Maga, I was finally ready. So, with a head full of vengeance and fury, I was about to board a plane to track them down, when during one goodbye, a friend seemed distraught at his daughter having run away to London. I knew my dad's old friend was a private detective, and although I never really promoted myself as such during my time out in the world, I thought of missing persons as a particular specialty. Needing guidance within the UK, I asked Harry for tips, and he helped me locate the girl, and was shocked at the violence I meted out upon the gang who took advantage of her innocence. He saved me, and caged my beast, but that same beast enabled me to defeat the Pale Boy.

When I convinced Harry I could be a civilized person again, we went into business together, a small-scale operation that eventually grew into Park Avenue Investigations, and the big business entity that allowed Roger Gorman to corrupt it into a corporate security venture, and ultimately drive me away.

It was in those early years I met Jess. Her mother called me, under the opinion the police were not doing enough to track down Jess's runaway brother, and when I explained about GPS tracking on mobile phones, it didn't quite work with the equipment I had. But Jess, a seventeen-year-old who had shown an affinity for such technology since the age of fourteen, twigged onto my explanation, and expanded on it. She used my equipment, and hacked into a phone company's servers, and in a world before the worst terrorism and cyber-attacks forced superhuman levels of security on all major businesses, she tapped into that company's satellite data, and tracked her brother to five miles from their home, where he had set up a little base on the banks of the River Aire.

We retrieved him, having suffered only mild hypothermia, but so impressed was I with the girl with such incredible intelligence and swiftness of thought, that when our business started making proper money, our first steps into the corporate world, I used the money to get in touch with Jess and her parents, and invented a scholarship for which Jess might qualify, and funded her education. As soon as she left university with the highest honors possible, I snatched her up and put her to work at Park Avenue Investigations, where she not only developed impressive technology, she created the Deep Detect System. It became the cornerstone of the business in which we tracked corporate fraud as well as runaways and spouses who had absconded with children to which they were not entitled.

On top of that, both Jess and Harry had shaped me as a man; one who helped me rediscover my old self, the other who might allow me to understand what lay in my future.

And now, people who once did noble work, who once hunted the most vile men in history, had taken someone dear from me, simply because they did not agree with who was entitled to €100 million.

€100 million was nothing compared to what I had lost this afternoon.

Jess.

Harry.

I wondered if those issuing kill orders were to come before the Israeli government, all the victims they claim to represent, or even their God, could they explain their actions? I had to separate the Pale Boy and his ilk from the Fist of God, made up of Professor Jaeger, his daughter Clara, her counterpart Abba, and whatever ancillary staff they employed; and also from Mossad, although I expected elements within their secret service would be aware of these actions.

But now their pet psychopath was dead, their primary weapon nullified. I had proven Katerina's account of her time in the war was false, and that—bizarrely—the supposed ghost inside Estelle was correct. All that remained of this case was to report back, to rubber-stamp the historical trail that no doubt cemented Katerina's wrongdoing in her use of looted wealth, and for Gottfried to negotiate a settlement with the Roma.

And all that remained for me was to know which of my friends I had lost.

I parted my hands.

The bag opened.

Frost crusted the face, staring at nothing.

It was not Jess.

It was not Harry.

Although I had only seen pictures of the man, my predecessor on this case, Tony Luca, stared up at me.

CHAPTER THIRTY-FOUR

I STORMED into the hospital whose name was the fascinating *Unfallkrankenhaus,* but I did not waste time trying to pronounce it. Having already made several desperate phone calls, I established the so-called "English gentleman and his daughter" had been spotted here hours earlier. They were carting with them an elderly lady with a severe laceration, and suffering from hypothermia.

It took longer than I expected to find an English-speaking staff member, but when I did they brought me straight to the relatives' room. The young nurse in a striped uniform asked if I was also a family member, as the other two had claimed to be. I said the injured woman was my great aunt, but I did not know what happened. The nurse had virtually no details, only that my dear elderly relative was still in surgery, and seemed eager to add that my friends' clothes would be returned shortly, as soon as they dried. They had been swimming to retrieve Katerina, and the cold lake had helped slow her blood flow enough to keep her alive. For now.

As soon as the door opened, Jess rushed into my arms, and hugged me so tight I thought my head might pop off. Harry beamed beneath his ungainly beard, and perhaps a tear troubled his eye for a second, but a manly cough soon drove it away. Both wore hospital scrubs.

"What took you?" came Harry's affectionate response to my appearance.

With Jess still buried in my chest, I replied, "Got a little messy. But no one is coming after us."

Jess pulled away from me, but kept her arms locked behind me. She checked me over, as if searching for wounds I hadn't yet declared.

"Did you kill him?" she asked.

With the nurse out of earshot, I told her the truth. "Yes. Please don't tell me it was wrong—"

"No. You absolutely did the right thing. That … thing … whatever it was, it deserved whatever you did to him. I'm just so…"

Harry sniffed. Jess and I looked his way, and found him studying the German language pamphlets with conspicuously deep concentration.

I leaned in, kissed Jess, and she tightened her grip. She pressed her lips harder. I cupped the back of her head. Her tongue flicked against mine, and her hand slipped up my back. She pushed against my groin, and I felt the shape of her against me.

A cough sounded.

We broke away, and turned from each other, embarrassed at being so caught up in a place like this. Had we been in a hotel room, no doubt things would've gone differently, but the cough came from a doctor, not Harry, who had maintained his position reading what looked like a flyer for an Austrian heart disease charity.

The doctor, who had been told both Jess and I were related to the woman she and Harry delivered, behaved with remarkable neutrality. He said, "Your … grandmother is stable." His English was heavily accented, but far better than any of us could hope to offer in German. "She is strong for a lady of such advanced years. She will need to rest. Then more surgery. I am sorry, but I am unable to offer a prognosis at this time."

When he departed, I paced and told them exactly how I spent my afternoon.

"The Fist of God bribed Tony Luca," I said. "He must have come here to receive the final payoff, but the Pale Boy was waiting for him. Whoever sent the Pale Boy forced Jäger to return to Kraków and gather the evidence himself. They didn't want this getting out into the public domain."

"Aye," Harry said. "If it got out, they'd have to abide by the legal results, or risk exposin' 'emselves."

Jess stood in front of me, forcing me to stop pacing. She held both my hands in hers. Looked up at me. "If Katerina did all those things, if she really is a sociopath, then why has she been manipulating everything from behind the scenes? She hired a lawyer, she encouraged Estelle to follow what Petr told her. Is it possible Katerina seriously believes it's her husband's ghost? Does she think she can make things right without revealing herself?"

"That's what I'm thinking," I said. "She's spooked by the supernatural, but she's still afraid of people like Professor Jäger and the Pale Boy finding out. So she wanted someone to expose the true heir."

"That's where you came in," Harry said. "But none of you, not even she, could've known they'd send such demented killer to wrap it up."

I pulled Jess close, and wrapped my arms around her, resting her head on my chest. Harry gave me a hard stare.

He said, "It's not over for you, is it?"

"If Katerina was truly spooked," I said. "Why would anyone find out about the investigation?"

"She wasn't on the radar," Jess said.

"The Fist of God had no idea. She's the granddaughter of the Angel of Kraków, so how can she be under such suspicion? The Roma wouldn't have the resources."

"The journal."

"No, that came later, after Estelle returned to Hamburg, but before Tony Luca disappeared. Jäger was already involved. Someone else tipped them off."

Harry nodded. "Someone who stood to lose even more than her."

"There's nothing more we can do for Katerina here. It's time to go back to Germany."

GERMANY

CHAPTER THIRTY-FIVE

WE SET off as soon as their clothes were returned, but there were other stops to make along the way. I needed Jess to work the research engine that powered this investigation, while I used Harry as a sounding board. He complained about his back and how the traveling was playing havoc with his sciatica, and although he agreed with me that it would be worth it in the end, he continued to complain until a couple of Ibuprofen kicked in. Later, his frustration at my not revealing everything at once shook him into a near-frenzy as we breakfasted in a cafe in Germany's capital city, Berlin.

"Bloody hell, this isn't an Agatha Christie story. Just tell me."

"If I pitched my theory on Katerina's past before laying it on her, you'd have stopped me. Told me it was going too far."

"But this is different. We don't know the full story."

"I don't want to prejudice your view. If I tell you, you might go looking for it. When you see the link, if it's there, you'll agree. And I need a bit of help getting there."

We'd slept on the road, a motel in the south of Germany, having left our details with the doctor without yet revealing

Katerina's true identity. The local police had been informed of the incident, and we gave statements detailing how an intruder had killed Professor Jäger and his guards, then stabbed Katerina, before he was chased off the premises by a dashing Englishman and his trusty sidekicks.

That last bit didn't go down well, and I agreed to edit the term "sidekicks" before the cops arrived.

Prior to leaving Jäger's house for my dash to the hospital, I dragged the Pale Boy's body into the freezer, then heaved Jäger up to the deck where his blood had sprayed the surface. I had bled a little during the fight, and so dabbed some on my fingers and shook it around the place. Once suitably staged, I returned below with bleach and scrubbed the place with a mop, dumping the bucket's contents three times in the lake. I locked the freezer containing both Tony Luca and the Pale Boy, and backed out, cleansing my path as I went, thus erasing all trace of my presence. One final wipe—of the mop handle —and I closed the panic room, ascended to the living quarters, and closed the hatch, replacing the finger hole hidden in a notch in the wood. Because the beams were split at irregular intervals it looked like any other part of the floor, so I had faith the police would not discover it immediately, even if they moved the rug that lay over the join. Unless its presence was registered with them, as panic rooms often are. Or they had official plans to hand.

I had to take that chance.

If all went according to plan, by the time anyone discovered the bodies, both would be too frozen to accurately assess which month they died in, let alone which day or hour. It didn't matter if the cops did not believe our story; they would attain no proof to refute it.

As we left Austria, with notice from the local constabulary that we may be required to attend for more questioning, Jess and I found chatting difficult. The initial high of releasing every drop of pent-up emotion in that one kiss now waned, like adrenaline after a fright. It was Harry I felt sorry for. After his initial "I told you so" he was stuck between two people on the verge of something we could not vocalize. We even slept in separate rooms at the motel, a wordless agreement we'd untangle our personal lives once we ended the case.

It also gave me the opportunity to report Katerina's current condition to Gottfried, which he met with a catch in his throat followed by upper-class stoicism. I did the same with Emiliana, and asked her to pass on the news to Estelle once she woke.

In the center of Berlin, the post-rush-hour city bustled with cars and trams, and the grumbling of a sixty-something Yorkshireman jonesing for a fried breakfast in a place that served pastries and what he called "sandwich meat" but most locals referred to as "quality cuts" or whatever the German translation was. I drank strong coffee while the grumbler relieved himself. Jess had not yet joined us, as she needed to tend to business back home; she was still the co-owner of a company, so treated this morning as an e-commute from a global coffee shop with fast Wi-Fi two streets away from our café. She didn't want us nearby, and I suspected her conversation with Phyllis, her partner, would be rather tense. She'd been racing around with me for nearly a week, and Phyllis didn't like me at the best of times. I instructed her to invoice the Kravitzes for her time rather than write it off as a favor, which would probably soften the blow.

I called Emiliana again, having only wished to talk about Katerina before, and when she put me on the cellphone's hands-free mode, I spoke in a code I made up on the spot. "I meant to mention earlier, our ill-looking friend won't be joining you after all."

She paused before replying, "And you helped … um … cure him?"

"Let's call it that, yeah."

She laughed. "Wow, good on you, hun. Get a load a' you, takin' out a professional assass—"

"Yer on a mobile," Hugo said in the background.

"Sorry, just really pleased for the lad. *Curing* a professional virus in a professional … guy like that. I'm proud of you, Adam."

"Err, thanks?" I said, picturing the incredulous look of some GCHQ eavesdropper detailing the devious code words. "I'm in Berlin. It's a three-hour drive, so I'll be in Hamburg by four this afternoon. How's Estelle? Can she travel?"

"Her episodes have calmed a lot. No more full-on visits from her great-grandpappy."

"Okay," I said. "If you think it's safe, let's get her home. Same safety protocols as before, though. Motion cameras, full equipment inventory. That Clara is still out there, and her bosses might send someone else too."

"Equipment inventory?"

"Guns," Hugo said. "He's dancin' around the word 'guns', you daft bint."

"Oh, now who's invitin' wiretap evidence? Call me a bint again, I dare ya."

"Bint. Binty McBintFace. All bow before the Queen of the Bints!"

A slap sounded.

"Now," Emiliana said, "where were we?"

"What's a bint?" Estelle asked, far away from the speaker. She came across as lucid, but hesitant, like any kid in the middle of a squabble.

"Just a bad word, sweetie."

"How are you?" I asked.

"Mr. Park? Adam?" Estelle said. "These two, they fight so much. It's extremely annoying."

"Yeah, I feel your pain."

"Are you coming back? I haven't heard from Petr for a long time. I think this means you will tell my father the truth?"

"This afternoon, Estelle. Stay safe, and I'll be back with everything you need. I promise."

I rarely make promises, but this was one I was confident I could deliver.

As with most first-world countries, Germany holds the records of registered businesses online, which lists the owners, their history with other companies they run or have run, and obtaining credit records is not hard. Once those details are picked up, DDS is able to dig deep into those people's personal banking archives, and since most business owners generally take a salary, business and personal accounts are almost always linked in some way. Those personal accounts can reveal much about an individual: their travel, their tastes, and how much they earn versus how much they declare.

But DDS also collates intel from different sources, and reveals when others cross financial paths with that person more than once.

For example, if I pay for a hotel room with my Visa card, and Harry pays with his MasterCard, there is no trail. But then, if that same week I purchase a plane ticket flying from Berlin on my American Express, and Harry buys one on the same day with a Visa, those two transactions count as a crossed path.

Neither applications of the software would stand up in court, partly because DDS was an illegal Trojan horse, but also because it wasn't proof of anything. It was groundwork, somewhere to point the camera or deeper digital investigations.

So when someone stood to lose out upon the completion of a transaction awarding a huge chunk of the Kravitz/Caine fortune to the Roma, checking that person out is a must. As well as that person's associates. And when a dead end crops up, there's no one better than Jess at bringing those barriers crashing down.

We needed access to a physical records office, and once a small "donation" facilitated a sped-up session of form-filling and other red-tape, we were able to access files that would ordinarily take days to view.

When Harry saw it, and Jess confirmed it was real, he slapped me on the shoulder and said, "Yep. You were right. I'd have thought you were crazy."

"You both agree, then?" I said. "This is the final piece."

"If it ain't, it'll lead to it."

They both agreed, and we returned to Hugo's hire car, and set off up the A24 autobahn for Hamburg.

"You know what?" I said to Harry. "The stately home, the rich-nob grounds, and a collection of suspicious types. This kind of *is* like an Agatha Christie denouement."

At my request, the family was gathered on the deck with the fountain full of koi. Staff had set out a low table and comfortable chairs. Francis watched the grounds from the roof along with two new guys with sniper rifles, while Jess set up her laptop, and Harry and I hung back, watching the gathering in silence, having colluded to look as menacing as possible. Hugo and Emiliana remained close to Estelle, the girl herself reclining on a sun lounger reading a paperback translation of *Yesterday's Gone* by Sean Platt and David

Wright. Gottfried and Herman sipped whiskey from heavy tumblers, while Stephan, Angela, and Konrad—Gottfried's brother, wife, and their son, newly returned from their skiing holiday—stared at their phones and occasionally moved their fingers.

To be honest, nobody seemed particularly menaced.

"Shall I begin?" I said.

"Someone should," Gottfried replied.

"Before we get to the juicy bits, let's recap. First, Estelle found herself occupied by the spirit of her great-grandfather, a scenario accepted by the majority of the family. Not Gottfried, even though he believes the Angel of Kraków shares space here."

"That is because we have all seen her," Stephan said, a slimmer, marginally taller image of his brother. "We know her. She is one of us."

I knew my mouth turned up at the sides, but I could not convey my fake happiness at the lad's interruption to the rest of my face. "Thank you. But you see the disconnect. A man believes in ghosts. But when a spirit infects his daughter, he writes it off as nonsense. That's the first point. Second is, as soon as a detective makes ground on tracing the family tree, the detective disappears. Initial reports suggested he was bribed and living in a country with no extradition, but we now know—when he showed up to collect his fee, he was murdered."

That was new information to Stephan, Angela, and Konrad, as all three sat up straighter. Konrad looked away from his phone for a full three seconds, before resuming whatever urgent business he was conducting. Gottfried straightened himself too, while Herman raised his chin and angled his ear towards me.

"Someone wanted whatever he found to stay buried. And

when the next guy along—me—headed in the same direction, they had to use a different tactic."

"And what did he *supposedly* find?" Gottfried demanded.

"That the ghost was telling the truth. He found Katerina used jewelry, cash, and other valuables looted by the Nazis to launch her business." I intentionally omitted my suspicions of her murderous spree. I had no proof to present and, frankly, only her confession would confirm that. "She had a child to the officer on the farm, a son, whom she sent away after killing Goetz. But she didn't abandon him. She intended to retrieve him later. Once the heat died down, and the victors no longer suspected her of any wrongdoing."

"She never wanted to lose him," Estelle said, as if she now revered her great-grandmother even more. "She loved him all along."

"More than likely."

I kept the white lie within the realms of possibility, but a true sociopath wouldn't *love* the child; she would feel *entitled* to him, and need to *own* him.

I said, "But when she went through all she did—watching those she loved perish, the whole Nazi occupation, killing Goetz, losing her husband—then the refugees who were supposed to look after the boy were too afraid to shelter him, and passed him on."

"To the Roma," Estelle said.

"Petr tell you that?" Gottfried said.

"Worked it out myself, daddy."

Gottfried didn't seem sure if it was sarcasm or not. He said, "Is there a point? Or any evidence?"

"Always," I said.

Jess turned the laptop screen so Gottfried, Estelle, and Herman could see. The others would have to move if they wanted a view.

I resisted the urge to pace and twirl an imaginary mustache, *a la* Hercule Poirot. "The Roma, who his biological father helped slaughter ... they adopted him. For a fee perhaps, or maybe he was left at their door, and they took him in. Either way, he grew up with them, and learned of his roots, and was deeply ashamed. So ashamed he dedicated his life to helping prosecute those responsible for the atrocities of the past. He even became a lawyer."

All looked at Gottfried.

"Too young," I said, and turned to face Herman.

The lawyer—in his early seventies—placed his hands flat on the table.

"Did she seek you out?" I asked.

Herman nodded, evading the looks of even Gottfried's family. Everyone watched.

"I am not my father," he said. "I was Roma. I *am* Roma. And proud."

Estelle was on her feet. "So ... we are related?"

"Indeed." His face was stone. "Katerina found me many years ago. We talked. She offered me money to stay away, because ... she had built a life. I rejected her offer, but I did not blackmail her. Nothing like that, no. I just wanted to meet her."

"Why the deception?" I asked. "If you knew all this, why the detectives, the Fist of God ... whatever you did to Estelle?"

"I wanted none of this. I wanted to do nothing. But Katerina was more eager to send money to my line of children even though we did not need it."

"You're related to the LaPortes?"

"To Vera by marriage to her aunt, not blood, although Marco is my grandson. He is the true heir."

Gottfried scoffed. "You could prove everything?"

"The paper trail is dead. Hence..." He gestured to me.

"When Petr made his presence known in Estelle, we could not hide any longer. Katerina insisted on making it right, to save the girl, to cleanse her own conscience. I was happy just being her son. But she wanted more for my descendants."

"Petr isn't as strong," Estelle said. "He doesn't come to me as often."

"Because Mr. Park has driven away those who wanted the money for themselves."

"Professor Jäger," I said. "He concluded the same as us, and was happy for the Roma and Estelle to split the money. But since the state of Israel disbanded them years ago, the group funding his activities activated the Pale Boy, so they could seize it all for themselves."

"Why?" Herman asked. "The detective would have delivered proof, Katerina would have faced her accusers, and Professor Jäger would be satisfied."

"Because they didn't know. The professor, Clara, Abba, the remnants of a previously-sponsored freelance outfit. They didn't know that the organization funding them were nothing more than profiteers, and even the Pale Boy believed he was acting for a cause. That the offspring of a Nazi should not profit from the Devouring, even if it went back to the people it was stolen from in the first place. The paymasters used him, and Jäger's group, and warped their conviction into a tool for their use."

"Who are they?" Gottfried asked.

"We don't know," Harry said. "I doubt we ever will. I sure as hell won't be lookin' fer 'em."

"But to make sure they don't come for you," I said, "for any of you … you have to officially agree the rightful lineage. And sign over what the Roma should have had all along."

"So, wait," Konrad said, his phone now in his lap. "We lose … house? Lose … all this?"

"If you want to live. They'll send others, unless it is ratified in law."

"That will stop them?" Angela said.

"Make it public, and they do not risk exposing themselves. The concentration camp guard in Italy, the case Gottfried was working on, that was something they were interested in until it made the press. Then they backed off. We need to get the process started as quickly as possible."

"How?" Gottfried said. "We don't even know where—"

"They're five miles from here," I said. "I called Vera LaPorte yesterday. They're waiting for us."

CHAPTER THIRTY-SIX

WE ENTERED the Roma camp in two Range Rovers. Hugo and Emiliana accompanied Estelle and Herman, while I travelled with Jess, Francis, and Gottfried. The extended family chose not to witness the relinquishing of the inheritance no longer heading their way. Angela, Stephan's wife, gave a long monologue in German, which Herman summarized after she stormed inside as calling Gottfried a coward for not fighting harder. Harry also opted to stay behind, and plan his flight back home. No point in watching a bunch of people signing papers.

Herman already possessed a draft agreement, the first step, not the final one, to file with the courts to get commencement of the process on the record. Once established, anyone moving on either the Kravitz family or the LaPortes would draw serious attention to themselves. And, it was hoped, putting pen to paper would see Petr depart for good.

I doubted he'd be attending any court hearings.

Jess and I took the back seat. She crossed her legs and looked out the window. I did the same. As we left Kochany

Dom, we passed by the gardens Katerina showed me, and the scent of coriander and other fragrances revisited my nasal memory. A sharp sense of recall probed my thoughts, one much older than a few days, but it evaporated as soon as I reached for it. Something about that garden…

Once on the road, I focused on the task at hand as the sat-nav commented we were fifteen minutes from our destination.

"Francis," I said. "Does this work like a limo?"

"Privacy?" he said.

"That obvious?"

He raised a finger and plunged it toward a button on the dashboard. A glass screen whirred up between us.

I turned my body to Jess. "It's nearly done."

"Right," she said. "Almost."

"So."

"So." Her face came to within inches of mine.

"Wanna be my girlfriend?"

"Sure. Wanna be my boyfriend?"

"Yeah, alright."

We broke out in odd snorting laughs, but still didn't touch each other.

"Weird, right?" she said.

"Gonna be weirder when you tell Phyllis."

She made a "yeah, shit" face and said, "You know, I said a lot of bad things about you to her."

"I probably deserved it."

"You did really well, you know. In Austria. I know you had to … kill that guy. But it wasn't like back at the farm. You went into that planning to take them out. But you tried to get back to yourself in Salzburg. We actually investigated something."

"Like the old days."

"What's next? Coming back to England?"

"I have a canal barge costing me a fortune in mooring fees. It's summer. I can sail it down south if you fancy a holiday."

She pretended to consider it. "Well, I'm the boss, so as long as the business isn't going under, I suppose I can manage a few days off here and there."

I reached for her hand. She clasped mine.

"You're really back?" she said.

I was about to reply when the car slowed much sooner than I expected as it approached a turn-off. The sat-nav lied.

The camp was smaller than the one in Kraków, with vehicles that appeared more temporary than many of those I'd encountered before. No picturesque gypsy cabin here. 4x4s were hooked up to double-berth aluminum caravans, RVs, half a dozen static units; probably thirty homes in total, arranged in passages that could constitute streets. We were losing the light, and generator-powered spots illuminated the place already, while toward the middle of the makeshift town a bonfire raged ten feet into the air. Someone waved our mini-convoy that way, and we followed the instruction.

As we parked, Vera LaPorte waited alongside Marco and the Beefcake Brothers, all bathed in the orange flickering glow. She had dressed once again in the stereotypical gold-trimmed skirt, flouncy shirt, and headscarf. Marco and the Beefcakes wore jeans, T-shirts, and work boots as they always seemed to.

"Hey," I said as the engine died. "Does 'Marco and the Beefcakes' sound like a good name for a band?"

"What?" Jess said.

"Nothing."

A pause. Then, "A striptease troupe, maybe."

I grinned her way, and our doors opened simultaneously. The Beefcakes. How nice.

We climbed out and gathered at a long wooden table set

up close to the fire but not scalding us. Gottfried stood at the head, waiting. Vera coughed. He looked at her. Marco gestured for him to move. He got the message, and stepped around to one of the longer sides, so Vera could step into the position of power.

Silly games, but they were important in some situations.

No one used the chairs.

They agreed to continue in English. I thought at first it was for our benefit, but Herman pointed out only *he* spoke both German and Polish, and since both parties were good English-speakers it made sense to continue.

"Adam," Hugo said.

He and Emiliana helped Estelle along, but she wasn't coping well with being upright.

"What's wrong?" I said, rushing to help.

"Let's get on with it," Gottfried insisted.

"What? You think *paperwork* will exorcise this … whatever it is in her?"

"He works in fuckin' Brussels," Hugo said. "He thinks paperwork's the answer tae every-bloody-thing."

Estelle's face was pale, her eyes rimmed with red. She clutched her stomach.

"Started as soon as we pulled in," Emiliana said.

I placed my hands on her face, cradling her, trying to see beyond her blank stare. She was hot. She muttered words in German, her gaze beyond me. I made out only the word "Petr."

"Marco," Vera said. "Bring the medic."

"You have a doctor on-site?" Jess said.

"Not an official one," Marco said as he departed.

One Beefcake brought a lawn chair for Estelle, and we lowered her into it. Gottfried appeared to lose patience, as his usually overly-sanguine demeanor dissolved into anger.

"You people did this," he said. "*You* brought Petr's spirit back. *That's* why Katerina is finally coming clean. It's why her being *here* is making her ill."

Vera calmly folded her hands before her. "If it was us who disturbed this war hero's spirit, do you really believe we will let you go easily?"

"I'll sign over half of everything right now. If you free her."

"Half?" Her smile was one of amusement. "You will sign it all over. Immediately. Herman, make the notations."

Herman did not make a notation. But he did prep the papers. "That may be premature."

"Please," Gottfried said.

Estelle coughed roughly and moaned. Emiliana hugged her. Gottfried rushed over and pulled her from Emiliana's arms, embracing her himself. Tears streamed down his face.

"This is the worst so far?" I said.

Herman nodded. "She has been agitated, confused, and even violent in short bursts. But never like this. Never … hurting."

I circled the father and daughter, Gottfried cupping her head, stroking her hair, saying soothing things in her own language, but she just sobbed.

"Petr … Petr … please…"

Gottfried turned on Vera, but the older woman stood firm.

"I cannot leave her with nothing," Gottfried said. "Leave *something* for her."

"I would have been kinder," Vera replied, "if you had listened to your soldier's soul earlier. Now you pay. Think, Judge Kravitz. How will it look for you to have married into Nazi gold? How will it affect you?"

"I will quit. I do not care for my career, or my ambition. I will not leave Estelle with nothing. Be reasonable. Seventy-five percent."

"Ninety," Vera said. "Sign now. Or I return to one hundred percent."

"And you'll take the spirit back out?"

Vera smoothed her skirt. "It does not mean we admit witchcraft. But I give my word, we will do all we can."

Gottfried glared at her over his daughter's shoulder.

"Vera," Herman said. "That is too much."

She spat on the fire, emitting a sizzle. "Do not address me this way, lawyer."

"I am part of this. My profession isn't *Romanipen*, but it has brought you more than you deserve. I wanted what was right, what was just. But you are taking advantage of a desperate man—"

"You are nothing more than *the help*," Vera said. "And your employer commanded you to give us ninety percent of everything he owns."

Herman's pen hovered over the pre-contract. The idea was that the hastily drawn up document had been left with gaps to fill in details during any negotiation. Herman anticipated the back-and-forth to go on for hours, if not days, but Estelle's decline caused Gottfried to panic to the point where he could only make the most cursory of gestures toward negotiation. The document was a precursor to the final decision and would be handled through the courts. It would carry significant weight unless coercion could be proved. I doubted the Germans' legal system would take into account the notion the Roma may have summoned the spirit of a World War II veteran to hold Estelle hostage. If they went to trial, and Gottfried told the judge the LaPorte's "haunted" his daughter in order to force his hand, would any judge believe him?

"Now, please," Vera LaPorte said.

Marco returned with an elderly gentleman wearing a coat over pajamas. He looked somewhat confused, but it was clear who his patient would be. The man rushed to Estelle and knelt before her, out of breath and bearing a frown that refused to depart. From his black leather satchel, he selected a stethoscope and listened to her heart, then a thermometer which he tried to insert in her mouth. She spat it out, gagging the foreign object. He spoke in German to Emiliana, who nodded, fiddled with Estelle's T-shirt, wound it up over her shoulder, and accepted the thermometer from the doctor—if that is what he was—and gently held her still as the thermometer took a temperature from her armpit. It was a momentary pause in which the group held its collective breath. Even Vera stopped haranguing Herman for a few minutes until the doctor took back his thermometer and shook it, then read the results.

He announced his findings, and Emiliana translated: "She's burnin' up. Needs a hospital."

"Please stop it," Gottfried said. "How can you do this to her?"

"We are doing nothing," Vera replied. "Now sign document. Is owed to us, and all Roma. This money will give us new start. We buy land all over the continent, and make those patches secure for Travelers, to keep out thugs who blindly hate us even now." Her eyes took on the mien of hot coals in the glow of the fire as she appeared to be talking directly to me. "You think our persecution ends in 1945? You think Jews and Muslims and blacks are only victims of hatred in modern world? The people who took up the Nazi banner and follow their leaders' propaganda are still alive today. And more than willing to obey without looking inside themselves for goodness that all humans should possess. My husband was murdered by such people, because they thought we took a child. The child

… simply hiding. But because of our presence, people's first suspicion was us. Money buys security we need in countries where Hitler's hate still reigns. We will hire people to lobby government for greater protection, to include us in their legislation for inclusion of society. Our new wealth brings humanity back to Roma, after it was taken from us long ago. We think Professor Jäger is a friend. One who will help us, not summon the golem to destroy us."

Marco stood beside Estelle. The doctor doused a flannel in water from a bottle, and laid it on the girl's forehead.

"We did not do this to her," Marco said. "But if it is Petr's will the Roma are paid, perhaps signing papers will help."

Gottfried shook his finger at the papers. "Herr Prinz, you work for Estelle. Katerina would tell you to do it."

"Ninety percent is too much," Herman said. "It is not what Katerina planned."

"The estimate is one hundred million euros," Vera said. "Ten million is plenty for a girl like this."

"Do it." Gottfried's voice was a low growl. "If Estelle is not cured, I will fight them forever." He released Estelle into Emiliana's care, and leaned on the table with his fists, angling his shoulders at Vera. The flames to his left flickered, casting a shadow over the Romani matriarch. "The only reason I am signing this is for her."

"Once it is in the system, we all start to heal."

Everyone cast their attention on Herman. He sighed, leaned over the table, and with the shadows dancing behind him, while both parties stood motionless, awaiting his acquiescence. His pen touched the paper and rode a couple of loops, before the shadows behind him changed.

From the undulating black, the shadows cast by the large fire, first a hand reached for the lawyer. It landed on his head, and tilted it to the side. Then a blade sliced across Herman's throat, spraying blood to the front and the side, drenching all within a 5 foot radius. The fingers released him, and the corpse flopped onto the table, more blood flooding over the top.

Then the Pale Boy morphed out of the shadows, and stood before us.

CHAPTER THIRTY-SEVEN

IT WASN'T the blood that shocked me the most. It was the impassive expression upon the Pale Boy's face, like returning from the dead, fully intact, with not even a scar where I impaled him, was simply something he did.

The two Beefcakes rushed him, and he flung one to the side hurling the would-be hero onto his back, where he rolled and sprung up. By the time he regained his feet, the Pale Boy had thrust his knife through the other Beefcake's chest, and as the first charged again, the Pale Boy simply shook the corpse off his blade, shifted to the side, and sliced open his assailant's stomach as he passed. The Beefcake stuttered to a halt and turned, hands to his gut. The Pale Boy stepped towards him and kicked the wound. The Beefcake's innards showed, and several feet of organic piping slipped out, before the man folded at the knees and fell flat on his face.

This all took approximately five seconds.

Within those five seconds, Francis, Hugo, and Emiliana pulled their weapons, I put my arms around Jess and ushered her aside, while Marco did the same with Vera, and Gottfried scrambled to return to his daughter.

Francis was the first to speak, as his was one of three guns trained at the Pale Boy.

Yet, if driving a spike through his skull, and locking him in a freezer set into the bed of a glacial lake did not stop him, I did not hold out much hope for bullets, no matter the expertise with which they were fired.

The fire created a circle of light and heat, and the effect of this creature returning from the dead forced us all to seek the safety of the flames. We drew closer, all except Gottfried.

As soon as he wrapped his arms around Estelle, he froze, and would not move. He sat on the floor, at the edge of the circle, cradling his daughter in his arms, tears streaming down his face as he pleaded with them not to take her. Or perhaps he was pleading with a higher power. But there he was, frozen now, as powerful handguns pulled a bead on the assassin.

I have never seen Emiliana or Hugo hesitate, so all I could put it down to was shock, and since Francis had recently lost his principal, he may well have been wondering about his career options after this. With Jess safely behind Hugo, the flames to her back giving no avenue to sneak up on her, I was the first to act.

With a log from the fire in my hand, I leapt the table, and when I was mere feet from the Pale Boy, I threw it. A distraction that worked. My foot connected with his knife hand, which slammed it back against his midriff. He released it before he could stab himself and I followed up with an elbow uppercut to the jaw.

One-on-one would not work against such an expert fighter. Distraction, misdirection … being sneaky. That was the only way to go.

While he was stunned, I moved aside, and shouted, "*Shoot him!*"

"Yeah, sorry," Hugo said. "Wigged out there for a moment."

But nobody moved.

The Pale Boy regained his composure, a bloody trail forging a path down his chin. He grinned.

In that moment I realized two things: first, this man facing me was two or three inches taller than the one who tried to make me talk in Salzburg, and who I most definitely killed before fleeing; and second, somebody was pointing one gun at Gottfried, and one at Estelle.

Gottfried was on his feet, Estelle murmuring, lying floppy in his arms like a baby.

From behind him, Clara showed herself, dressed all in black, including a trench coat, so she looked like a character out of *The Matrix* movies. She held both guns, while Abba showed himself from between two caravans, aiming at Marco and Vera.

Hugo and Emiliana chose their targets: Hugo remained with the Pale Boy, while Emiliana drew down on Clara without a clear shot. Francis aimed in Abba's general direction, but again there was no line of sight, except through a hostage.

"This is unacceptable," Vera said.

"Quiet," Abba said.

Clara jabbed one gun into the back of Gottfried's head. She said, "We are taking the girl, and you are donating your estate and liquid assets."

"Who *is* this?" Gottfried said.

"Consider us a charity," Clara replied. "Dedicated to hunting down war criminals, and recovering what was stolen during that time."

"It is ours!" Vera insisted.

"That…" Clara flicked a gun toward Marco. "Is a product of an unholy alliance between an invading genocidal race, and a conspirator who plundered that genocide. Nobody here deserves one cent."

Jess stood firmly in front of Gottfried and Estelle, blocking their path as Clara tried to march them forward.

She said, "No one except you?"

Clara shifted one barrel from Estelle to Jess. "We will do good with it."

"Jess, stand back," I said.

"No," Jess replied. "This has always been about the truth, and the truth is … no one can choose their parents, or their grandparents. Katerina did wrong, and Marco's granddad sure as hell did too. But that is no reason to punish Marco or Estelle."

"Not your decision," Clara said.

Emiliana shuffled to her left, gaining a better angle on Clara. "Jess, sweetie, back off. They don't care about you."

"Seriously, Jess," I said. "Please. You *have* to listen."

She turned only her head towards me. "If you learned one thing this year, it's that you can't handle everything without losing a piece of yourself along the way. And *I've* learned sometimes you have to make a stand, whatever the cost. Even when they clearly have power we can't possibly understand." She hadn't twigged the way I had to the Pale Boy's subtle change in appearance. She landed her attention back on Clara. "What kind of person keeps working with a … thing that killed her father? You must be so damaged—"

"My *father*…" The woman's arms slackened momentarily, the guns shifting a fraction of an inch before she steeled herself.

"You didn't know," I said. "You didn't know they killed him."

"A traitor, then." She swallowed. "Shielding an enemy of our people—"

"He believed Katerina," I said. "It doesn't make him a traitor."

"Adam." Jess lost all expression, her chin up, blinking away tears. "Someone has to break this deadlock. I hope Emiliana is as good as you think."

"No, wait!"

Jess thrust her hand inside her jacket as if reaching for a gun. The weapon in Clara's hand bucked and roared, and Jess dropped to the floor.

It was enough movement for Clara to reveal herself.

Emiliana fired, and Clara jerked sideways, shifting the gun from Gottfried's head. Emiliana fired again, catching Clara's chest dead center, dropping her where she stood.

Hugo also fired, but the Pale Boy already ducked behind the table, and threw it upwards and at Hugo, forcing him back towards the fire.

Francis shot Abba square in the head, and dashed towards Marco and Vera. He ushered them aside, and shouts and cries from around the camp rose, and yelling commenced. Marco waved madly, directing people to stay back as he shouted words I did not understand.

But understanding did not matter, because I was already screaming Jess's name as I sprinted to where she fell.

Hugo had lost his gun, and took on the Pale Boy in a manner that suggested he had never encountered such a creature before. The Pale Boy tossed him aside, while Emiliana checked on Estelle and Gottfried, before turning her gun towards the Pale Boy.

And all the while I cradled Jess in my arms, pressing down on the wound high on her chest as blood oozed around my fingers.

She sputtered. Managed to say, "Thought she'd … be quicker…"

The Romani doctor was still here, and he knelt beside me, issuing orders I couldn't hope to comprehend. He gestured I should let him inspect her back, I found myself pleading with fate, pleading that such a thing as fate exists, that if fate exists then so too must that higher power in which all the Kravitzes appeared to believe. I could see from the doctor's inspection an exit wound also threatened to drain Jess of life.

Her eyes were wide, her breaths shallow. She tried to speak. I hushed her.

"I'm not going to lose you," I said. "I can't."

Again she tried to speak. Again I hushed her.

"No," she managed. "Get … him."

I looked over my shoulder, where the Pale Boy held Hugo in the air with what looked like superhuman strength.

Hugo was beaten, bloodied, and almost broken, his hands slack to his side. The Pale Boy had laid into him so hard and efficiently, I knew for certain it was not the man I killed; that man enjoyed toying with his prey, while this one just wanted to win. And he was smart. Every time Emiliana shifted for a new angle, the Pale Boy swung her husband and used him as a shield, then struck again.

I eased Jess into a position as directed by the doctor's sign language. And while he applied pressure to both entry and exit wounds, I prepared to embrace the beast inside once more, and made my move on this latest incarnation of the Pale Boy.

CHAPTER THIRTY-EIGHT

Hugo was a professional. I cannot emphasize that enough. Imagine, if you will, a photographer, earning his living taking snaps of movie stars, royalty, their properties, and making them look glorious. Let's say he's been doing this since before the advent of digital SLRs, and understands composition, white balance, and even what an F-stop is. He has understood those things for decades, to the point that it is simply instinct as to where he angles the reflector to achieve the desired effect. Now take some guy who kinda, sorta, fancies himself as a photographer, and scours websites for the cheapest digital camera he can find. He spends as much as he dares on new lenses and takes a few classes, even ventures out into the countryside and snaps off a few images. Then he persuades his mate to let him document his wedding.

There is a difference between an enthusiastic amateur and a professional with years of experience.

In terms of violence, Hugo is an artist in comparison to my own level. I am perhaps ahead of the chap running around the wedding trying to herd bridesmaids and crossing his fingers that the sun doesn't bleach their skin. But to see someone such as Hugo reduced to a bloodied rag doll in the hands of a sadist, it should have been enough to give even the most seasoned professional pause for thought.

Luckily, I did not have the experience to know an impossible situation when I saw one.

I hurled myself at Pale Boy with both feet, crashing into his side, and releasing Hugo.

Emiliana yelled at Gottfried to carry Estelle to safety, to follow Francis, Marco, and Vera, but the judge could not move. He held Estelle so tightly she might have had trouble breathing if she wasn't already overheating and trembling uncontrollably from whatever lurked within. And Emiliana still could not get a clear shot.

Which was at least partly my fault.

As with his counterpart in the graveyard, he knew exactly how to combat my fighting style, but I was ready for most of the counter-attacks he could throw at me. And he wasn't quite as adept.

In that room under the lake, a combination of drugs and —despite what I learned from Dr. Rostov—what I can only describe as a hypnotic technique, plunged me into my subconscious where I faced my own demon. At the time, I absolutely believed the creature to be real, and that revealing what the Pale Boy was trying to extract would have slain the beast, ridding myself of that side of me. It was, in that moment, an absolute certainty that this thing physically existed. But resisting that knowledge whilst under the influence of his technique left it simmering near the surface, ready to break out as soon as I opened the door. And seeing Jess dying in the arms of the Romani doctor left that door gaping.

I let the Pale Boy swing me onto my back. Where most people would be bracing for the impact, I wound up a counter of my own in the form of a kick. Because that was the key here. I could not prevent him from damaging me, but if I struck back instantly as he attacked, no room for maneuver, I could survive this.

Brains synchronized with brawn.

At the same moment as my shoulder blade hit the mud, my heel crashed through his knee. My body splashed into wet dirt, drops hitting the inside of my mouth. The gritty slop was tinged with copper, and I realized the ground was doused in blood.

I spat it out.

As my opponent reeled, I rolled and sprung up, and moved in sideways, to land a second kick in his face, but it only landed in his hand, and he yanked me over yet again. Like before, my brain clicked into gear and my standing leg bent at the knee, then launched so I used his own body as a pivot, and thrust my foot around into his head.

It cracked.

Although I landed again on the blood-soaked ground, my mind was sharp and clear, and I tangled my legs up in his, and applied pressure to his ankles, which brought him crashing down. As with my preplanned counter, I already knew what I would do once I had him in range. He toppled like a demolished chimney. I shifted my body, pointed my elbow towards him and he could do little as he flopped my way. Sure, he swept his arms up to block, but with his momentum and my arm flying backwards, I smashed my elbow into his face, crushing the cartilage within his nose.

His predecessor did not say more than he had to, and this iteration was no different. This one no doubt hauled from a cell, brought out of training too early, to complete a mission his paymasters saw as essential to their continued existence. How many others like him were training? How many killers drawn from their justice system and given a purpose?

How many others lurked out there, waiting for the command to strike?

Side-by-side, rolling on the increasingly muddy ground, I punched him in the side of the neck. His eyes rolled sideways. My knee connected with his groin. My head crunched into his already-broken nose. I pushed him aside, and straddled him.

A year ago, I nearly lost control, hitting a man in virtually the same position, and it needed a villain to make me realize I was going too far.

Today, as I pummeled this creature, punch after punch after punch, his head, his throat, his soft middle, his head again, I do not believe my heart rate rose more than a dozen beats per minute. As I detected his jaw breaking, my vision crystallized, and a sense of accomplishment bloomed within my chest as his left eye bulged, and his right swelled closed.

The body beneath me slackened.

I ceased hitting him.

He did not seem dead, but I suspected he was not far from it.

I took stock of the scene: Gottfried cradling his daughter, too afraid to move; Emiliana checking her husband with one hand, unwilling to relinquish the SIG in her other; Jess, conscious, mouthing something as her body drained, despite the best efforts of the doctor.

Soaking wet, with mud formed of other people's blood dripping from me, I crawled over to Jess. I did not want to touch her, and yet stroking her face was the one thing that would make me feel human.

Her lips trembled. "Adam…"

"Hush." My fingers hovered over her blanched skin. "Hear that?"

Sirens wailed in the distance.

"That's help coming. They won't take you from me. I promise they won't."

She mouthed words, trying to hack them up from her throat.

I said, "No, don't speak."

"B—" Her eyes widened. "Behind you."

I spun, to find the Pale Boy on his knees.

Emiliana noticed at the same time as me, and raised her gun.

I said, "No," and marched over. I stood to the side. Looked at Emiliana. I said, "Okay, now do it."

She pulled the trigger. The gunshot rang out. The assassin's chest spat blood.

Then he tipped over, stiff with shock, a tree felled by an expert woodsman, crashing into the filth with so little fanfare I almost felt disappointed.

Everyone stared at the body in silence. Were they as disappointed as me that he didn't explode or die screaming an ancient curse?

I bent down, hefted him over my shoulders in a fireman's lift, and stood. I tramped over to the fire, all my hate, all my rage, focused on the thing on my back.

Jess shook her head minutely.

I stared for a moment.

She closed her eyes.

And I tossed the body onto the fire.

The corpse lay there on top of the flaming debris accumulated by the Roma, and was motionless for at least five seconds.

Jess had moved enough, much to the doctor's annoyance, to view what I had done.

The Pale Boy twitched and writhed, before emitting a howl so loud and full of pain that, had it been an animal, I would have been filled with revulsion and pity. Here, though, I stared as if watching some effigy on Guy Fawkes night, and felt an equal amount of remorse as I would for a bundle of old clothes stuffed with newspaper.

Jess's stare drilled not into the improvised funeral pyre, but into me. It looked scared—of me, of death, it was not clear. I could not read her mind, after all. I just knew it was over. In more ways than one.

But it was not over. Because although the Roma now gathered around us, Marco and Francis leading what should have been a cavalry charge, they stood back from me. I was caked in mud infused with the blood of one of their elders in Herman Prinz.

They had brought towels, first aid kits, and weapons no longer required. The newcomers examined Jess and Hugo, stemming the bleeding, helping the injured.

Some, though, stared past me, and slowly others joined them. I followed their gaze, to Gottfried and Estelle, who were now on their feet again, and Clara had recovered and returned the guns to their heads.

CHAPTER THIRTY-NINE

"GOTTFRIED WILL SIGN OVER THE ESTATE," Clara said.

A vest of Kevlar body armor hung loose from her chest, although the bloody hole in her right shoulder inhibited her movements. The pain in holding the second gun on her injured side made her grit her teeth with every gesture.

"You think you can win?" I said.

"There is a trust in Israel. A compromise. I negotiated it ... before my ... *father* betrayed us, and took Katerina to safety. He has influence, and his death would have sealed the fate of the people who control the Pale Boy. So I think this is why they agreed. Give them the estate, and they will decide how much should be used to continue our hunt, and how much is owed to yours." She was speaking directly to Vera. "It is a fair result. We both want what is ours, and as long as it doesn't go to those our great betrayer intended, that is a win for all."

I said, "You don't get to win."

Clara nudged Estelle, and pressed the gun harder in Gottfried's back. "Tell him you will cooperate."

"The contract is soaked in blood. It's not legible. There is nothing to sign."

The sirens wailed louder now, and Marco glanced around as if searching for them. Others in the crowd did likewise, an electric current of tension falling over everyone.

Clara said, "I am taking the girl until the money arrives."

"No!" Gottfried answered. "Shoot Estelle and you are as evil as the people you track. Shoot me, you get nothing." Tears soaked his face, his mouth an open black hole in the night, contorted into the snarl of a predator protecting its young. "You murdered innocents tonight, those two big men, the lawyer, I didn't know them. But I am a witness, and I will see you prosecuted."

Clara cocked the gun aimed at Estelle.

"But if you can cure her," Gottfried continued, "I will sign anything. If I have to live in a tent for the rest of my life, I will do that. But please, whoever has infected my daughter with this violent spirit, this soldier needs his revenge, or justice, or for the simple truth to come out. Please expel him from her soul, and you can have my money. All of it. You have my word."

I had not left Jess's side, but I had to tear myself away and stand before Clara.

"The problem is," I said, "I don't think anyone here can do that."

Emiliana shifted behind me, aiming at Clara, but Clara had learned her lesson, and made Gottfried a more efficient shield.

"Estelle wasn't drugged," I said. "Not according to the blood tests. But who was present for those? Who ensured they were pure? Untainted?"

"Katerina," Gottfried said.

"When the Pale Boy interrogated me, it was part hypnosis, partly drugs. And what he did to me, I completely believed was real. I can't imagine the effect it would have on a child."

"Impossible."

"When I was in South America, I enjoyed a lot of new things. Probably ingested a few too many chemicals. But the most eye-opening session was called an 'Ayahuasca' ceremony. Mostly smoke based, like really powerful weed, but hallucinogenic on top. Its origins are in Native American folklore, where people go into a trance, a metaphysical journey, and get in touch with the Earth, mother nature, meet spirit animals, all that stuff. I've got to admit, I tripped my head off, a really special event. A bunch of us tried to replicate it, got the ingredients together, but it didn't work. It's more than a case of mixing it all together. But one of those ingredients … I knew it rang a bell when I saw it in your garden. Leaving the grounds today, it finally came to me."

Clara readjusted her weakening grip.

The sirens were so close I had to raise my voice over them.

"Mimosa hostilis. A plant from South America. Grind its root, mix it with a bunch of other stuff, and you end up with the base compound for the herb that drives the Ayahuasca ceremony. I'm sure it wouldn't take much effort to work it into something that could be ingested with food, or injected, then add some suggestion, perhaps full-blown hypnosis. Must have been fairly simple from there to warp the mind of a girl who lives in a house where the Angel of Kraków is considered absolutely real."

Gottfried nodded. Perhaps it made sense to him, or else he was simply desperate.

I looked at Jess. "There is no ghost involved here."

She seemed unable to focus, and although there were two people pressing on her wounds, the doctor held his mouth in a grim line.

I said, "Gottfried will give the courts power of attorney, until the system here in Germany decides how to allocate it.

He won't move it anywhere, and if any part of this process suggests you are entitled to any of it, it'll be yours. If not, you walk away with nothing."

"I can accept that," Gottfried said.

"I cannot," Clara said.

I held my ground. "Is this what you hoped for? When you started on this path? Murdering people for cash? Didn't you, didn't your father, hope for something noble? Something good?"

Blue flashing lights filled the camp, sirens screaming now.

"Time for you to go," I said. "Unless you want to hang around and plead your case to the local cops."

Clara again firmed up a grip. Watched everything, searching, searching.

"You're well-trained," I said. "And I'm guessing you have a way out of here, a backup plan on top of a backup plan. So continue this stand-off, and it will end in you dying, either when Emiliana shoots you dead or when the German police refuse to let you run."

Another glance at Jess. The sirens were right on top of us.

"She might not have long," I said. "And if Jess dies, I will dedicate every last resource, *including* embracing the darkness Vila Fanuco sees in me, to hunting you down. Because I see it now too. It's part of me, and always will be, probably always was on some level. Providing I have an anchor, though," I took a subconsciously-led step toward Jess, "it won't rule me. But if I lose the things most dear to me, I will not even *try* to control it."

On the floor, Hugo coughed, spat blood. "That include me?"

"No, it does not include you," I said, facing him. "But I wouldn't rule out supporting your wife in whatever plans she has."

"Oh, I dunno," Emiliana said. "We've got pretty comprehensive life insurance, you know—"

"You're ruining my menacing speech."

"Sorry," Hugo said. "Carry on."

Emiliana waved a hand. "Sure, sweetie, you menace away."

When I turned back, Clara was gone, and Gottfried and Estelle were free.

Then the German police descended upon the camp, swarming from three angles, and those involved in the fight here today knelt on the ground, our hands on our heads, and gave ourselves up without a fuss.

CHAPTER FORTY

DON'T you hate rich bastards who can afford the best lawyers to dig them out of pretty much any situation? Well, I'm not quite that rich.

When I made tens of millions through the sale of my company, shortly prior to its unexpected but ultimately essential liquidation, I used most of it on salving my conscience through paying out to all the employees who lost their jobs, and through hunting for men who escaped my first foray into the world of real violence. I retained enough to live the rest of my life in relative comfort if I chose never to work again. As it turned out, not working isn't something I can do, but the type of work doesn't necessarily need to involve violence.

Or ghouls who won't stay dead for that matter.

Wealth-wise I was destitute compared to the Kravitzes. For now anyway. For now, they had access to the best lawyers money could buy, and through his duties Gottfried knew plenty of sleazy but incredibly competent defense specialists, and leveraged his position to ensure the authorities took things easy with me.

Despite all the rumors and allegations of the past, all they knew for certain about me, Hugo, and Emiliana was that we were attacked by people known to have facilitated the assassination of a well-respected professor in Salzburg along with an attempt on his female companion, a German national and relative to a folk hero whose derring-do extended to schoolchildren's storybooks.

From here, the lawyers concocted a version of events that would be difficult to prove false, starting with our visit to Katerina's son at the home of his adoptive Romani family. We were there to convey the news of her injuries when said assassins showed up to finish him off too. Because Herman was sired by a Nazi, he was—as far as this psychotic splinter group was concerned—a legitimate target. They murdered him, and tried to violently extort Gottfried by threatening his daughter. Francis was a licensed bodyguard, while Hugo and Emiliana—ex-military and ex-secret service—managed to wrestle firearms from the criminals who killed our friend.

They questioned exactly who we were, what our relationship was with the Kravitzes, an interrogation met with an accusation of victim-blaming, and attempting to politically smear a good judge who simply wanted justice to prevail. I was happy to drop in a long soliloquy concerning me being a detective looking into land registry and history, the details of which caused the cop in charge of questioning me to nod off for five minutes.

Almost.

The fact I tossed the dying body of one of the bad guys onto a fire was probably the biggest sticking point, and the reason I was last to be released. Hugo was technically under arrest, but his busted ribs, an internal bleed in his kidney, and a fractured cheek bone rendered him unstable for extensive questioning, yet the impression given was that it would all be a formality.

I did not wish to return to Kochany Dom, no matter how nice the scotch. It wasn't that I was frightened, but something hung over that house, the pallor of death, of corruption. Nothing was as it seemed, and I still didn't fully comprehend Katerina's motives. Frankly, if she'd come clean with her knowledge of what transpired all that time ago, it would have been solved without involving myself or the late Tony Luca. That she was willing to drug and hypnotize her own great-granddaughter to push people in the right direction meant motivations so much darker, so much more corrupt and evil, were at play. Not for the first time, I hoped I was wrong.

At least I would not have to fight to ensure I found the truth this time.

When I met Gottfried at the least impressive cafe I could locate in central Hamburg, Estelle was not with him. He ordered a large espresso but only held it, not deigning to allow it near his mouth.

"She is recovering," he said. "The information you provided helped, and a second blood test confirmed a course of sedatives is the best plan."

"Flush it out naturally," I replied.

"She is unlikely to remember much about that night. Herman gave her a dose before we left for the camp. A pill, we think, which he passed off as paracetamol. He was alone with her in the back of the Range Rover too, and he whispered things to her, all to push me in the negotiation. Vera ordered him to keep it up. But it was Katerina all along, wasn't it?"

I nodded over my coffee. "She thought she could get by on people accepting the spirit world theory. Or at least use it to obscure the truth."

We were alone. Emiliana persevered at Hugo's bedside, and Jess underwent further surgery, so Harry agreed to wait with her. He did not want me to tie up this final loose end with her life in the balance, but I hoped she would understand.

A deeper explanation for my actions would hit the nerve within me that did not allow for passivity; I had to *do* something, even if it did not directly involve assisting the surgeon.

"I do not know what to do about Katerina," Gottfried said. "She … betrayed us all. Estelle too."

"In all honesty, I don't think it will be an issue. She's in her nineties. Stable at the moment, but there's no coming back from that wound. If she's ever able to travel, it'll be to die in her home."

"I'm not even sure I should grant her that wish."

"Have you asked the Angel of Kraków her opinion?"

"No need for sarcasm, Mr. Park. We feel her presence, some have seen her wandering. It is not common for mortals to interact with the spirits."

He lifted the thimble-sized cup, about to consume the contents when he glanced around and thought better of it.

"Why did you want to see me?" I asked.

He presented me with a leather binder containing several forms headed with court crests and a number of banks' branding.

"Sign in the notarized sections," he said. "The Kravitz estate is now in your hands."

I blinked. Twice. "*My* hands?"

"Who else have I met recently that I can trust to do the right thing?"

I stared for a moment, then slipped the heavy pen out of the loop inside the binder's spine. It was as fat as my thumb, a brushed aluminum piece with Gottfried's initials engraved.

"You're giving me all your money," I said. "That's a little above the fee we agreed. Which was zero, by the way, and I didn't rack up that many expenses."

"I'm holding back ten percent of the liquid assets, plus Kochany Dom. It's for Estelle, and I will fight anyone to the death if they object. The rest is to go into a trust of your choosing, until a qualified neutral party can mediate."

"Why me?"

"Because you only cared for the truth. You turned on the people who employed you—Katerina and Herman—at the expense of the 'win' if it can be called that."

"The truth, Judge. That's what I was hired to find."

"Even though Katerina already knew it all? I do not understand why she did that."

As I signed the papers, I said, "I'll hold your cash, and I'll abide by whatever is decided. But yeah, I don't understand either. And I've got other questions for her too."

"Is that what you will do next?"

I thought of Jess, hemorrhaging pint after pint in my arms. I hadn't fully cleansed the blood and mud from my hair —hers and others'.

"It's the final thing I need to know. I hope I'm wrong."

AUSTRIA

SALTZBURG

CHAPTER FORTY-ONE

KATERINA WAS as frail as a sparrow starving in the snow. I sat beside her in a private room of the Salzburg hospital, and she seemed almost pleased to see me. She could speak, move her mouth, her head, and her right arm; the doctor said her mind was lucid, but she would tire quickly. She flexed her hand enough to wrap her fingers around mine. Her wrinkled skin was dry, and hard upon my own.

I explained what was happening with the money. Forensic accountants would wade through the past, I told her, and although it would not be easy, they would prove all we now knew. The Nazis expected to *win* the war, so did not hide their allocations very well. The only obfuscation would come from institutions whose history dated back that far from trying to hide their complicity, but that would not hinder the investigators, not with the fate of a European judge at stake.

While I drove back to Austria, they tested Estelle's blood again, and compared it with the original samples from when "Petr" first showed up, and confirmed the first ones closely resembled Katerina's, although DNA evidence would take a few days. It was low priority, with the events at the Roma camp taking up most of the police efforts, not to mention headlines.

Luckily for me, Gottfried's scummy lawyers cited privacy laws and human rights legislation to keep my name, and those of my friends, out of the papers. With a little nudge from Vila Fanuco, I did not believe the editors who learned our names dared risk exposing such sensitive information.

Within Estelle, the effects of the Ayahuasca were easing, and she would make a full recovery.

At that news, Katerina simply nodded as a normal person might receive the news of a train having arrived on time.

"You *are* a sociopath," I said. "You have no feelings, no emotions. You have urges, and desires, but you don't care about Estelle. Not one bit."

Again, she simply took my assertion with neither excitement or insult.

"Why would you do this?" I asked. "You must have known it would come out."

"I did not expect you to succeed," she replied, speech only moderately slurred from the painkillers. "I did not expect the Fist of God to interfere to this degree. They were to bribe Mr. Luca, but we started down a path. We had to stay the distance."

"Wait, you *didn't* want it to come out?"

"I wanted the money to go to the people who deserved it. I did not want anyone to discover all of it. My other child, yes, but I could not admit to that. After all, who would trust me when I lied for so long?"

"So you brought back your dead husband. Made an innocent girl think he was haunting her. You can't hypnotize someone that way, but combined with the Ayahuasca it really did alter her mind. Why couldn't you pretend he was with you?"

"Again, who would believe me? I am just a … *potty* old lady."

"Still doesn't explain why."

"It is simple. I was going to tell you on the dock. I am too tired to go on hiding, and you appeared to know it all. You know why, do you not?"

She paused, as if waiting for me to get it. I drew a blank, and let the silence hang.

She said, "My *soul*, Mr. Park. I feared … for my *soul.*"

She made a sound like a dry gurgle. I passed her a glass of water and she sipped through a purple straw.

"Thank you."

"What do you mean?" I said. "Your soul?"

"I have done a great many things I wish were not seen as evil. When I look at them, I think my grandmother would disapprove."

"Betraying the people she tried to protect? I reckon you're right, yeah, the Angel of Kraków might have a thing or two to say about you taking their money and valuables for your own use."

She managed to make a tiny gesture of her hand look like a dismissive wave. "Things. Objects. Jewelry. Bearer bonds, artwork, antiquities. Just things. No use to the dead. And with no descendants to trace … why not build a life for myself?"

"Because it's wrong?"

"Do play a different tune, Mr. Park, this one is getting boring."

"You did this because your soul pricked your conscience?"

"As you say, I do not have such a thing as a conscience. No. But I am old. And I believe in ghosts. Which means I believe in the afterlife. And if an afterlife exists, perhaps judgment exists too. I had to make things right before I passed."

My stomach was empty already, but now a chill swept through it too.

I said, "You did all this to bribe your way into heaven?"

"Crude, Mr. Park. But if you see fit to put it in those terms, go ahead. I wanted someone to detail the exact route of the money, because I did not know how. And I preferred not to conclude this matter by explaining myself to Estelle."

"The increasing frequency of your infections," I said. "You expected to die. Part of your collusion with Professor Jäger."

She moved her head in a tired nod. "Now you're here to finish it?"

"One more thing." I could not keep holding that hand. "You tried to justify your actions before, didn't you?"

"I did."

"Your daughter, Beatrice, she knew about the wealth, about how you made your money?"

"Yes."

"But her husband was a bigwig in finance, and he tried to learn more. The world didn't pay much attention to you succeeding and rising from the ashes of the war, especially with your family's history, but your son-in-law wanted everything clean. Something like that? Is that how he found out?"

It had never sat right with me, all that death in one family. In isolation, each was a tragedy—an accident, fate, call it what you will. Coincidences exist, but when secrets are rife, and someone involved is as deeply disturbed as Katerina Caine, it's worth exploring how big a part chance played in such sadness, and how much was engineered.

She said, "And Beatrice promised to back him up."

"So after she left you an heir, you stopped the investigation dead. Literally dead. Somehow faked birthing complications in Beatrice, then later manufactured an accident for her husband."

"Money has many advantages."

"What about Beatrice's daughter? Helena. She did the same?"

Katerina's eyelids hung heavy, then closed, and when she opened them she spoke more slowly than before. "When Gottfried became involved in the prosecution of Nazi soldiers, Helena looked into our own past without telling me. She wanted to pass things on to Estelle. Give her a sense of where she was from."

She licked her lips and asked for more water. I gave it to her and she resumed.

"She found discrepancies … like you, she suspected. Back to Paris, to Austria. She found Friedrich."

"Your jailer?"

"The only man I ever truly loved."

"Loved?"

She smiled sadly. "I felt he was the best fit of any man I've met."

"And you murdered your granddaughter to protect his reputation, and yours? Sabotaged her motorbike?"

Her face darkened. "It was necessary. You do not understand. Your brainwashed schoolteachers, brainwashing the next generation, and the next, and the next. Speak out and you are branded a racist or anti-Semite. Question the official story and you are jailed in some countries." Spittle flecked her chin. "A simple equation: too many harmful people in society means a poor society; erase the harm and you give your world a chance. Same with family. Same in business. If an accident, a death, a disappearance makes life better for all who remain, it is the duty of those with the power to do so to make it happen."

Her concentration roamed over me. I gave her nothing.

"Friedrich gave me this perspective. Jews, gypsies, homosexuals, negroes—all these make a society poorer. The Jews' greed and manipulation, the gypsies' awful ways, men performing unnatural acts with other men, and negroes —*monkeys* who failed to evolve properly. If the Fuhrer were alive today, he would deal with Europe's Islam problem the same way."

The old woman tried to sit up. If she were well, and able bodied, I predicted she would be pointing at me, wide-eyed and waving her arms around and jutting out her jaw in the manner that all demagogical speech-givers do. That "swivel-eyed loon" insult dished out to various ranting groups was well-earned some days.

I said, "You sent your son away with Friedrich, not the Roma. He escaped."

"Yes."

"You shot one of your farm workers in the face, and fed him to the pigs. What did you do? Free a bunch of them first, send them in different directions, so when another didn't show—"

"You really know how to get into someone's mind, Mr. Park."

"I'm told I have an affinity for this."

"I fed another to our pigs, and Friedrich went on to Austria. I planned to sell the farm and meet with him."

"Then Petr returned…"

"And I had to maintain my cover. Beatrice was a mistake, but I thought—"

"You thought Friedrich would forgive you. And when he learned the truth about you, that you were of Jewish stock, and now had a child to an enemy of his people, he rejected you."

She closed her eyes in the approximation of grief. Or what she thought it should look like. They fluttered open gently. "As I confessed to him, he rejected Herman too. Four years of doting on the boy, but because of my corrupt parentage, my lies, it was like his son died right there. And to punish me, he promised I would never, ever find him."

"He passed Herman to the Roma. To both your enemies. Somewhere you would not dream of looking. And the money? Blackmail."

"Really, you should go into mind reading. Yes, he paid me off with a portion of our acquired wealth, the key to a vault, and I never saw him again. But he was sloppy. Sloppy enough to leave a trail. His financial gift to me, had you worked on it longer … you would have seen it. Helena found it."

"And you killed her. Why did you suddenly grow a conscience?"

"Why do you think?"

I had already worked it out, but wanted *her* to say it. She waited. I twisted my neck to ease the tightness crawling up it. Flexed my fingers. She won. Again.

I said, "The man in Italy, he volunteered intelligence, didn't he? And Friedrich Goetz's name came up."

"No, Mr. Park. The man in Italy, as soon as I saw his face, I knew. That man *is* Friedrich Goetz." She allowed another smile. "He was living in Belize all these years, stolen the identity of another soldier, a guard. In the early days those hunting our heroes only wanted the officers. He thought he was safe. But Belize is where we sent Tony Luca. Because there are accounts we can access, property that can be transferred to his name."

"And when those memories came flooding back, with Goetz resurrected through Judge Kravitz, you started to worry for your soul, and used Estelle to redeem it."

"Friedrich did not know of that coincidence, of the connection to me. So I would keep it that way until I could right all our wrongs. To draw out the Fist of God, it left a clear path to the fortune, and would mean I pay for my sins. An old lady, dead from what would surely appear natural causes, is not looked into too closely. Estelle would never know the truth."

"And you care about that?"

"It feels … cruel to put her through more."

I stood and turned my back on what, under other circumstances, might be deemed a serial killer. A racist, anti-Semite, and murderer, unrepentant in her zeal.

"Don't put her through more," she said. "End it now. Please."

I looked back at her, eyebrows raised. "You want that?"

"Yes."

I placed my hand over her face and pinched her nose. She sighed and closed her eyes. I prepared to clamp down on her mouth.

But all the scenarios cascading through my head involved looking out from within a cell. An elderly lady passing in the night should not usually draw an autopsy, but she was stabbed recently, an attempted murder, so although any death would be attributed to that, an autopsy would be required. Since suffocation frequently causes blood vessels in the eye to burst, and any number of other telltale signs, as the only person to visit, I would immediately fall under suspicion.

Her final revenge on me for exposing her fully.

I let go.

"Sorry," I said. "You'll have to wait a little longer to burn in hell."

Outside, I sat on a wall beneath a stone lion that looked out over a car park and, beyond, a green field rolled into the middle distance where a mountain swelled and pulled to a point. It was the most beautiful hospital car park I ever saw.

A message from Harry said Jess was out of surgery and resting in stable condition. I said I'd be there in less than five hours. After, I scrolled through my contacts, and found a number labeled "Mike's Carpet Cleaning", a number Emiliana gave me before I set out to Austria.

I would like to say I debated a while longer, but halfway through my interaction with Katerina I made up my mind. She did not deserve the life she led; the entitlement, the privilege, the joy of a family. Not that she felt any joy. Likewise, Estelle did not deserve the pain of knowing her great-grand-mother drugged and hypnotized her. She did not deserve the stress of learning Katerina manipulated her into passing on her fortune for the sake of her murderous soul, and to commit suicide by rogue psychopaths, and be remembered fondly.

I dialed. He answered.

"Hello, Adam," Vila Fanuco said.

"No violence," I said.

"He deserves it."

"No one deserves it. Not even Roger Gorman. Can you do it without hurting him?"

"Yes."

"I'll owe you *one* favor. In return, I will not do anything violent for you, and I won't cause harm to come to innocents. Clear?"

"Absolutely, Adam. We should have a drink when it's all over."

"If you come calling for a drink, that'll count as the favor I owe."

A pause.

He said, "You have taken the first step, but still resist. Very well. Baby steps. I will take care of you."

I hung up without saying thank you, placed the phone in my pocket, and returned to the car. Not nervous, not guilty, just fearful of what that first step may lead to.

Nothing, I vowed. It would not lead to me becoming like Fanuco or Katerina, or even Hugo and Emiliana Hunter.

I know what lurks within me, and I will control it, no matter what.

UNITED KINGDOM

LEEDS

EPILOGUE

"THERE WERE NEVER ANY GHOSTS," I told Harry over a post-dinner brandy. "Just some perverted but clever bastards."

"Except the Angel," Harry said.

It had been four weeks since Jess's surgery, and Harry had been cool with me, unsure if my actions had yet again brought this violence down upon us. It had not. I thought it over when I accompanied Gottfried et al to the Roma camp, and Jess backed me. She also told him I had no choice, that throwing the Pale Boy on the bonfire was an accident—the same story we told the police: after murdering several people at a peaceful mediation, he ran at me with the knife, and I was able to turn him away at the same time Emiliana fired, but he crashed into the fire, and could not get out. That I convinced Jess I genuinely believed him dead when I did it was enough for her to affirm my white lie to Harry, but I did not believe she accepted that fully.

"Except the Angel," I agreed. "She was obviously real."

"Why the sarcasm?" Jess asked.

We were in Harry's back garden, a patch of well-tended

grass thirty feet by ten, surrounded by flowers and tipped with a small vegetable plot. Not quite the grandeur of Kochany Dom, but immaculate nonetheless. Jayne would have it no other way.

Shop talk was banned over dinner, which I agreed to as long as the subject of Jess and I was equally taboo. Following a spread of roast beef and all the trimmings, plus an apple crumble and custard pudding—my favorite food since childhood—we were allowed a brief respite, and ventured out into the garden. Jess still used a wheelchair to get around the streets, but she could maneuver through a house on foot if she was careful. She hobbled using a crutch, and sat on Harry's rattan swing, nursing a glass of milk, careful not to sway too much. Harry and I remained standing and swilled our brandy like big shots. No cigars, though.

"Just being me," I replied.

"Everyone was pretty certain about her," Jess said. "And we still aren't sure what happened with Estelle."

Harry glanced my way and shot me an eyebrow raise. I'd explained the hallucinogens to him but not Jess. I don't know why. Perhaps I like having someone in my life who sees an unresolved mystery and can accept the situation on face value.

I said, "No, but I'm sure the police will work it out."

She might look into it more, follow up with the cops, but I doubted it. She had barely spoken of the case since regained consciousness.

"The money?" Harry asked.

"Gottfried kept his ten percent and the property, and without the so-called possession to their advantage, the LaPortes agreed to a more moderate fifty percent of the cash, plus the jet."

"They wanted the jet?" Jess said.

"Who doesn't want a jet?"

"Fair enough."

"The mediators awarded a quarter more back to Estelle and Gottfried, the judge having added to the total quite significantly."

"It's been a while since I did fractions," Harry said, "but by my reckonin' that leaves one more quarter."

"A trust, in Israel. Kept away from the Fist of God, but something Professor Jäger started. It'll do the same work, but mainly investigating corporations that have hidden their involvement in the original pilfering of loot."

Jess finished her milk. "How did it end up there?"

"To convince the Israeli government to place the other recipients under their protection from the Fist of God. If they have more Pale Boys lined up, whoever was pulling his strings, they'll have Mossad to contend with if they step out of line."

"And you?" Harry said.

"I'm on my own."

I sniffed the brandy, decided it was the right temperature, and sampled it. Not bad, considering it was probably second-cheapest bottle on the supermarket shelf.

"What're your plans?" Harry asked.

"Not sure. I still have some things to work through." I looked at Jess, who evaded eye-contact. "I'm going to load up the van, drive down towards Greece. I have a lease there to sort out."

"How long?" Jess asked.

"A few weeks."

Harry downed his brandy. "I'd better help with the washing up."

"Leave it for me. I'll be there in a minute."

Jess tutted. "Adam, they have a dishwasher now."

Harry grinned, slapped my shoulder. "I'll help her load, or I'll never hear the bleedin' end of it."

He left us alone. We hadn't been alone since she woke in the hospital. Once she returned to the UK ten days ago, she had mostly been cared for by her mother and two brothers. I was stuck with a number of legal loose ends to tie up back in Germany and one in Austria—namely the discovery of the secret room beneath Professor Jäger's place, thanks to my "anonymous" tip. It made things more difficult for me, but I wanted Tony Luca's family to know what happened to him, that his personal journal showed he intended to refuse the bribe he was supposed to collect, and travelled there personally to throw it back in the professor's face.

"Gorman went away?" Jess said.

"Yeah."

"Any idea why?"

"None."

"You sure?"

I finished my drink, placed the glass down. "I had one of Gottfried's lawyers reply to the letters."

"Which one?"

"Sorry?"

"Which lawyer?"

I stuffed my hands in my pockets and took four paces, then stopped and weighed up the notion of lying to her again. It wasn't the same as letting her believe in the possibility of Petr being the real motivator behind Katerina's decision to mess with the family's finances.

"Nobody got hurt," I said.

"But you owe him."

I lowered myself to the seat beside her. "By the time I get back, you'll be up and about. Maybe if I give it a few more weeks, you can tag along."

"Where?"

"Out there." I held an open hand in front of me. "The world."

She gave a solitary, "Ha!" and followed it with, "I have a business, Adam. I'm a grownup."

"Where does it say grownups automatically become boring past a certain age? Sell your half of the business. Phyllis hates you now. She'll jump at the chance."

She threw a weak punch in my arm and winced at the impact. "She doesn't hate me. She hates *you*, and hates the fact I was helping you when I got hurt."

"So? Come on, do it!"

"And, what? Drive around the world in your van solving mysteries? Hey, we could get a talking dog and a really nervous guy to join us."

"Why do we have to be boring? Why stick to a proscribed life? You always said you envied my old world, of travel and just living instead of hanging around making money."

"Because … because…"

"If you can't think of a reason before I come home, then maybe make that offer to Phyllis."

"Give it all up?"

"Start again. Take a chance, Jess."

She said she'd think about it.

Another two days later, word reached us that Katerina Caine died in hospital, with only doctors and nurses present to mark her passing. In an odd coincidence, the very next day, the elderly man in Italy, who had been revealed as Friedrich Goetz thanks to my anonymous tip, managed to climb up onto the third-floor balcony railing of the apartment in which he remained under house arrest, and hurled himself off.

Harry, Jayne, and Jess came to my apartment block to see me off. My VW camper was packed, my ferry ticket booked, and my gear loaded in the back, ready for several stops between here and Paramatra. My route would see me chug through France to the south coast, and make my way east, camping anywhere that looked interesting, or when exhaustion threatened to drag me from the road. Harry and Jayne had accepted I was back to my old self, and I gave them no reason to suggest this was not the case. Jess was out of the wheelchair most of the day, but had to be careful when lifting or any physical exertion.

I hugged Jayne and shook Harry's hand.

Jess hugged me.

We had spent a few nice evenings wrapped on my couch, my arm around her, the sort of kissing reserved for teenagers fumbling their way through their first blooming of infatuation, not yet ready to take it to the next level. Not for any emotional reason, though; she was simply not physically able, and wanted to do things properly.

Despite all that, we still hadn't fully discussed the big subject: "us."

And now, out of earshot of Harry and Jayne, I said, "Come with me. We'll simply drive. It'll be special."

"Promise me one thing."

"What?"

"You won't go after them. The people who sent the Pale Boy, this 'Fist of God,' whoever they really are."

"Why would I do that?"

"Because you think you're the only person who can."

"I won't go near them unless they come for me." Our foreheads touched. "Now how about you get in the van and—"

"I thought of a reason," she whispered.

I didn't want the hug to end. If I let go, it would force her to finish that thought, and the possibility of doing things, as she phrased it, "properly."

She kissed me firmly and pulled away. "You've still got some sorting out to do. In here." She tapped my head. "I can't keep lying for you. Even if they're good lies. You made me part of your thing with Fanuco."

"I don't have a thing with—"

"Except now you do. You need to fix that. When you're ready, come home. I'll be waiting. Might even take you up on your offer. But I can't be involved right now."

"You'll wait?"

"Not forever, Adam. Don't think I'll be sat at my window in a chastity belt … *sewing*, or spinning a loom, or—"

"I get the imagery."

"Then you get what I'm telling you?"

"We can't be together until I'm completely free."

She kissed me again, softly this time. "Gold star to you."

What choice did I have but to accept that? It wasn't a "yes" but it wasn't a "no" either. While it would have been my first choice for her to jump in and commence our first big adventure as a couple, she was right. I had things to sort out first. She did not deserve to share my life in its current form.

And as I drove away from my friends, with them waving in the rear view mirror, I felt something new, something I hadn't sensed in many years.

Hope.

For the first time in a long while I wasn't only existing. I was *living* for something, for the future. My life wasn't where I hoped it to be, but I had goals, and I knew what I wanted from that life. I had beaten the darkness inside, or at least tamed it, and I would no longer feel guilty for who I was or what I have done.

For me, finally, the ghosts are fading. And I do not intend to make any more.

Adam Park returns in:

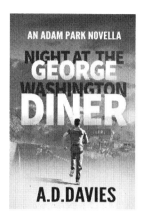

As Adam journeys home from Greece, he pulls in at an American-themed diner in the far north of Croatia where he cannot resist stepping in to defuse a seemingly simple domestic confrontation.

Unfortunately, the man instigating the violence has friends. Violent friends.

When they return to deliver punishment upon Adam, they do not expect their prey to fight back, a man for whom the last year has been a nightmare, and Adam is no longer the sort of man who is ill-equipped for such a situation.

About a third the length of a regular Adam Park thriller, this novella serves as a neat bridge between *Shadows of Empty Men* and the next full novel, *Master the Flame*, out NOW.

NEWSLETTER

If you are not already signed up, please copy the below link into your browser :

addavies.com/newsletter

And if you would like other readers to discover these novels, please take a moment to leave a review on the retailer where you bought this. Reviews from real people like you really do help authors find new readers, and keep these series going for as long as possible.

NOVELS BY A. D. DAVIES

Adam Park Thrillers:
The Dead and the Missing
A Desperate Paradise
The Shadows of Empty men
Night at the George Washington Diner
Master the Flame

Alicia Friend Investigations:
His First His Second
In Black In White
With Courage With Fear
A Friend in Spirit

Standalone:
Three Years Dead
Rite to Justice
The Sublime Freedom

Co-Authored:
Project Return Fire – with Joe Dinicola

Writing as Antony Davies

The ancient world is not what we thought...

Tomb of Aradia

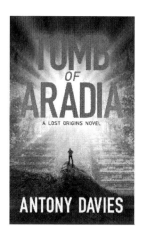

Freelance treasure hunter Jules has finally located the bangle
stolen from his dying mother, an artifact that may unravel a
centuries-old secret: the location of the Tomb of Aradia. But
when a reclusive billionaire beats him to the artifact, Jules has
no choice but to join forces with an institute of unconven-
tional archaeologists who reveal to him clues penned two
thousand years ago, and who claim the bangle holds properties
that science cannot explain. And Jules appears to be the only
person who can activate them. As both parties race to decipher
the bangle's origins, they uncover a trail meant only for the
holiest of men, leading to an apostle's manuscript, the hunt for
a tomb alleged to conceal great power, and a breathless, globe-
trotting adventure that threatens to destroy them all.

Three Years Dead

When a good man ... becomes a bad cop ... but can't remember why...

Following an attempt on his life, Detective Sergeant Martin Money wakes from a week-long coma with no memory of the previous three years. He quickly learns that corrupt practices got him demoted, violence caused his wife to divorce him, and his vices and anger drove his friends away one by one. On top of this, the West Yorkshire Police do not seem to care who tried to kill him, and he is offered a generous pay-out to retire.

But with a final lifeline offered by a former student of his, Martin takes up the case of a missing male prostitute, an investigation that skirts both their worlds, forcing him back into the run-down estates awash with narcotics, violence, and sex, temptations he must resist if he is to resume his life as the good man he remembers himself to be.

To stay out of jail, to punish whoever tried to kill him, and to earn his redemption, Martin attempts to unravel the circumstances of his assault, and—more importantly—establish why everyone from his past appears to be lying at every turn.

His First His Second

An Alicia Friend Investigation

Meet Detective Sergeant Alicia Friend. She's nice. Too nice to be a police officer, if she's honest.

Yet, despite a perky personality that irritates the most professional of detectives, she is also one of the most respected criminal analysts in the country.

Now assigned to DI Donald Murphy's team, she finds herself in the grip of a northern British winter, investigating the kidnap-murders of two young women - both strikingly similar in appearance. When a third is taken, they have less than a week to chip away the secrets of a high-society family, and uncover the killer's objective.

But Richard - the father of the latest victim - believes the police are not moving quickly enough, so launches a parallel investigation, utilising skills honed in a dark past that is about to catch up with him.

As Richard's secret actions hinder the police, Alicia remains in contact with him, and even starts to fall for his charms, forcing her into choices that will impact the rest of her life.

TIER Unit 3-1: Days 1-5 - By Lincoln James

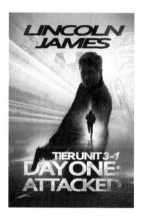

A terror cell spread far and wide…
A series of random targets…
Five days to take them down.

When a series of jihad-inspired "lone wolf" style attacks hits Los Angeles, tracking down the seemingly unconnected terror cells appears impossible. However, recently returned from a suspension that casts doubt on his ability to lead, Jack Miller rallies his *Terror Incident Emergency Response Unit* – TIER Unit 3-1 – and takes over from an overstretched LAPD.

But as Jack's elite squad battles to hunt the people responsible, a man of great intelligence - driven by a hatred that he cannot control - prepares his soldiers for war.

TIER Unit 3-1 sees Jack Miller attempt to first win over his team and his superiors, then bring in a terrorist mastermind whose endgame cannot yet be seen.

Day One: Attacked is the **first of five novellas** pursuing this story over the course of a thrilling action-adventure series.

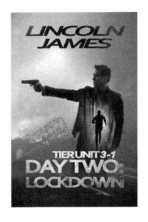

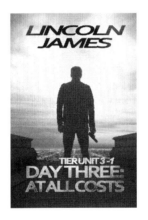

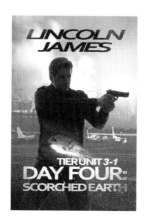

Printed in Poland
by Amazon Fulfillment
Poland Sp. z o.o., Wrocław